We hope you enjoy this book. Please return or renew it by the due date.

You can renew it at ww by using our free library

Otherwise you can phor please have your library

You can sign up for ema......................... too.

CW00346223

NORFOLK ITEM

30129 090 945 909

NORFOLK COUNTY COUNCIL
LIBRARY AND INFORMATION SERVICE

B
Boldwood

JUST DO IT

MAXINE MORREY

First published in Great Britain in 2024 by Boldwood Books Ltd.

Copyright © Maxine Morrey, 2024

Cover Design by Leah Jacobs-Gordon

Cover Photography: Shutterstock

A CIP catalogue record for this book is available from the British Library.

Paperback ISBN 978-1-83751-120-4

Large Print ISBN 978-1-83751-116-7

Hardback ISBN 978-1-83751-115-0

Ebook ISBN 978-1-83751-113-6

Kindle ISBN 978-1-83751-114-3

Audio CD ISBN 978-1-83751-121-1

MP3 CD ISBN 978-1-83751-118-1

Digital audio download ISBN 978-1-83751-112-9

Boldwood Books Ltd
23 Bowerdean Street
London SW6 3TN
www.boldwoodbooks.com

1

I stared at my boss, her words echoing around my brain. I had been so sure this time.

'I'm so sorry,' she repeated. 'I was positive they'd choose you. You're still the best candidate as far as I'm concerned.'

I opened my mouth to ask a question but instead of words, a hoarse raspy noise emerged.

'Would you like some water?' Inis asked, her tone soft and soothing as she poured me a plastic cupful without waiting for an answer and placed it on the desk in front of me. The only sound was the glug of bubbles from the dispenser as the level settled.

I took a few gulps of the icy cold drink, cleared my throat, then tried again with my question.

'Do you know who they went with instead?'

She gave a shrug and busied herself topping up the cup. Something smelled fishy.

'Inis?'

My boss returned to her seat and met my eyes for the briefest moment before looking away again and unnecessarily tidying her already highly organised desk. My desk was not tidy. My desk was never tidy. I liked the aesthetic of tidy, the thought of it. It was just that I could never quite manage the actual task. Or if I did, the result would last less than a day before it looked like a bunch of tomb raiders had upended everything in search of buried treasure. Not that they'd find any. At least not in my office. The London museum I worked in, however, had plenty, and those I was meticulous about cataloguing and storing carefully with the reverence the items deserved.

'But I've been instrumental in acquiring some of our most popular exhibits,' I said.

'I know.' Inis shook her head. 'And we're all incredibly grateful for the brilliant relationship and rapport we now have with the various museums and collectors in Egypt.'

'So who *do* the board think is the best person for overseeing what could be one of the most important digs for decades?'

Inis paused, then mumbled something as she turned to rummage in her Kate Spade handbag.

'Pardon? I didn't quite catch that.' I asked her to repeat as I raised my cup and attempted to wet my suddenly dry throat.

She faced me and spoke again, clearer this time but with a pained look on her elfin features. 'Friedrich Heckler.'

It was amazing how much water was actually in a sip. There was enough, certainly, to go down my throat but apparently that still left plenty to find a route down my nose. I swiped at my face with my cardigan before taking the tissue offered by a concerned Inis. 'I'm sorry,' she said as I took another and honked out an unladylike blow, causing my left ear to pop. 'I don't understand the decision at all. I mean, he's a good archaeologist but he doesn't have as much expertise in the subject as you, or your connections.'

'He has the names of a few people. I know that much. Stupidly I shared them with him before I realised he was a cheating...' I snapped my mouth shut, grabbed a pencil and drew a few quick hieroglyphs on a piece of paper.

'Inventive use of a dead language.'

'I like to keep my hand in.'

'Still. Even if he has those names, I can't think he has the relationship you do with any of them.'

'No, but he has things I don't have.'

'What's that?'

'Money and charm.'

'Aah.'

'Yes. Aah.'

Friedrich had grown up in a castle. A proper, honest-to-God, Disney-worthy castle. His parents still lived there amongst the gilded framed paintings of ancestors long deceased. There was a portrait of Friedrich too that I'd seen on my own visits. The painter had been rather kind I thought, and given my boyfriend-at-the-time definition in his pecs and biceps that wasn't necessarily a true representation of the sitter. Friedrich certainly wasn't complaining. I wasn't into all those muscled types anyway. People's intelligence was the most attractive thing to me. Friedrich had a nice face although I did wonder how he was going to get on in the desert with his insistence on wearing contacts.

'Glasses are so cliché,' he'd told me when I'd questioned him about it. 'They are too central to the classic image of the nerd. I refuse to be objectified and turned into the public's idea of what an archaeologist looks like.'

'I think most people think archaeologists either look like Indiana Jones or Lara Croft.'

Friedrich had given me a glare. Hollywood's interpretations of archaeologists over the years was one of his pet hates so I'd changed tack.

'I do think you're over reacting about insisting on contact lenses all the time. Lots of people – millions in fact – who aren't archaeologists wear glasses. It's not like we have dibs on them.'

'So, fine. You wear them!'

I'd frowned. 'I don't need them.'

'And now you're going to rub in the fact I have myopia?'

'No! I wasn't... You know I wouldn't do that. I just don't...'

'Just don't what?'

'Think it's as big a deal as you're making it out to be.'

'Then we will agree to disagree and move on with our evening.'

And we had. That time and all the others. It's kind of a thing with academics, whatever the field. Hardly anyone wants to agree with anyone else. I don't know why. I've always thought that we'd probably know a lot more about a lot more things if we all just tried to get along.

'Are you OK?' Inis brought me back to the present.

'Yes. Well, no. I'm disappointed, obviously.'

'Obviously. We all are. It would have been great for the museum as well as you personally. And off the record,' she gave a furtive look around, 'I think it's a shitty decision.'

Despite the crushing disappointment that had taken up residence in my chest, giving me severe indigestion pains, I felt the corners of my mouth tingle as they fought a smile. My boss never swore. She didn't like anyone else to. I'd smacked my shin against a stone sarcophagus lid one time whilst working with her. I'd cut my leg open and achieved a bruise from ankle to kneecap and the most I felt I could let out was 'Oh! Fudge!' It really had been most unsatisfying.

'Inis!' I said, the smile forcing its way through despite having just lost, quite literally, the opportunity of a lifetime.

'I know.' She blushed and the tips of her ears went pink. 'Extreme circumstances call for extreme language.'

This was not extreme for me and I could guarantee I'd be letting loose a whole string of expletives at the top of my voice the moment the opportunity arose. But for my boss, this was huge!

'Don't you tell a soul I said it.'

I drew a cross over my heart and made a zipping motion across my lips.

She put her hand across the desk and laid it over one of mine. 'And I really am sorry.'

I nodded, pushed the chair back and went back to my office.

* * *

'So? When are you going?' Bella, perched on a pile of books, whispered excitedly as I entered the room.

'I'm not.'

She straightened. 'What?'

'I'm not going.'

'I don't understand.'

'The board chose someone else to lead the dig.'

'Who?' she snapped. 'You're the best person for that job and everyone knows it.'

'Apparently not.'

'So who got it?' she asked again.

'Friedrich.' I replied without looking up.

'Son of a—'

'Bella?' Peter, our intern, knocked lightly on my open door. I would close it but there was too much stuff in front of the door so I pretended I liked it that way. Although right now I just wanted to be left alone.

'There's someone on the phone for you from Denmark.'

She jumped up. 'I have to take this but we'll talk, OK?'

'I'm fine. Really. There will be other opportunities.'

We both knew this was a big fat lie but the sentence sufficed to let my colleague know that while I appreciated her concern, I was done talking about it. At least for now. Bella and Peter walked away and I pulled out my phone.

Drinks. Tonight. A lot of them xx

Colette's reply came back quickly.

Time to celebrate, oui? Xx

Commiserate

The next moment my phone rang.

'*Quoi?*' Colette was French, spoke five languages fluently, worked as an in-demand translator all over the world and often dropped back into her native tongue in times of high emotion or extreme tiredness.

'They gave it to someone else.'

'That is out of the question! You are the only possible candidate.'

'So everyone keeps saying. But in the end they decided to go with Friedrich.'

Colette's intake of breath was so loud and, naturally dramatic, that it almost made me laugh. Except I was beyond laughing.

'Tonight. What time?'

'What time can you leave?' I asked.

'I've just finished a job so I'm already in town. I'll meet you here.'

'I'm going to try and leave as soon as possible. I'm sure Inis will be fine. She's as pissed off as me.' I dropped my voice to a whisper. 'She even swore.'

'She did not!'

'Uh huh. But I can't tell you what she said because I promised.'

'They are idiots, the whole lot of them. Get out as soon as you can.'

* * *

A quick trip home, a shower and a change of clothes later, I was on the Tube back into town to meet Colette. I didn't usually mind the ride. It gave me time to think. But right now I didn't want to think. I wanted to numb every single neuron I had. It was a short-term solution, admittedly. But it was still a solution.

'Cheers!' I clashed my glass a little too forcefully against Colette's and the barman swapped it for one that didn't have a fissure in it. 'Thanks,' I said as he handed it back.

'No problem. Happens all the time.'

'And on top of everything,' I said, my voice raised to be heard over the ebullient Friday evening crowd. 'I got an email just before I left. Apparently the project manager for the extension to the museum is going to be sharing my office.'

'Why?'

I shrugged and sloshed my drink over the rim. 'I dunno,' I said, then swiped my finger up the glass to catch the blood-red wine before sucking the excess off. Waste not want not. As I did, I locked eyes with a man from the large group near us who were clearly in a more celebratory mood than we were. He turned away but there was no mistaking the smile on his face.

'I think you have an admirer,' Colette said, her accent thicker now we were several hours into our commiseration.

'Pfft,' I said before downing a good proportion of the glass.

'He's good looking. Why don't you go talk to him? Take your mind off things.'

'Because he's probably married. Or gay. Or an arsehole. Or an archaeologist. Anyway, I don't want to talk to him. I want to talk to you.'

'OK.' She put her hand on mine. 'They won't all be arseholes, you know.'

'How come you can say any word and it sounds sexy? Even "arseholes" sounds sexy with your accent. It's an unfair advantage.'

'*Oui. C'est vrai*. But this world is cut throat. You have to use what you have. *Non*?'

'*Oui*,' I replied, unintentionally imitating her. 'I'm just not sure now that what I have is enough.' I twiddled with the stem of the glass now resting on the bar. 'I was perfect for this job, Col, and I still didn't get it. I don't know what else I can do.'

'Then perhaps you weren't supposed to have it.'

'What?'

She did one of those Gallic shrugs. 'Life is a strange thing. Sometimes what we think we want is not actually what we want at all.'

'I bloody well did want it!'

'OK. I'm just trying to help.' She didn't take offence. I didn't drink much and I wasn't a horrible drunk, but I was an emotional one. 'And I'm glad to see your French side is finally coming out.'

I didn't actually have a French side but my BFF joked that alcohol made me less English and more French. 'That means it's time to party.' She gave me a wink and glanced over to the group behind us. One of the other blokes smiled widely – men tended to do that when Colette was around – and headed towards us.

'Evening ladies. Could I buy you both a drink?'

'That would be lovely.' Colette did a little head tilt and the guy lapped it up. 'Two champagnes please.' He didn't even blink, merely caught the bartender's eye and placed the order.

'Are you waiting for someone?'

'No, it's just us.' She smiled back and his own smile widened.

'A bunch of us are here for a friend's birthday. Why don't you come and join us?'

'Oh, we wouldn't want to intrude.'

He waved his hand. 'The more the merrier. I'm Greg by the way.'

Colette placed a hand on her chest before indicating me. 'Colette and Elizabeth. *Enchanté.*'

'God, I love the French accent. It's so...' He waved his hands. 'You know?' he said, looking from Colette and then to me.

'*Oui.*' Colette said simply, before taking the drinks that the barman placed in front of us while her new friend paid. She gave a wink as she handed one to me and clinked my glass gently. 'To new opportunities.'

I let out a sigh. When Colette went into party mode I'd long ago learned that it was easier to go along with it and the group certainly looked like they were having a good time. Why the hell not? I'd put everything I had into that application and what had I got? Nada. I bloody well deserved some fun!

'To new opportunities,' I repeated and swigged at my glass, relishing the fizz on my tongue and the bubbles tickling my nose.

* * *

'He definitely likes you,' Colette slurred a little while later. Somehow her accent even made slurring sexy.

'He does not,' I replied before turning and frowning at her. 'Who?'

'Finn. The tall one who's hardly been able to keep his eyes off you all night.'

'Oh, pfft.'

'Why don't you talk to him?'

'I did.'

'I mean alone. Not as a group.' She made a swirling motion with her hands encompassing all of us in said group.

'If he's so keen, he'd have talked to me, wouldn't he?' I asked, fixing a slightly smug expression on my face, pleased with my razor-sharp reasoning.

'Can I get you a drink?' The deep voice close to my ear made me jump and I threw the remainder of my drink down my dress. 'Well, yes you can nowwwww...' My remonstration tailed off as I turned to find Finn's face unexpectedly close. He was even hotter this close up. 'Ummm...'

'Sorry, I didn't mean to startle you. It's just pretty loud in here. I definitely owe you a drink now.'

'Mmhmm. I mean, ummm, yes you do.'

Colette elbowed me sharply in the ribs whilst doing a brilliant impression of having turned to her companion and not listening in to our conversation at all.

'Oww! I mean, yes, that would be lovely, thank you.'

'Another champagne?'

'Oh, you don't have to. I can pick something else.'

Finn's brow crinkled, sinking into the faint lines that appeared to linger there all the time. 'Do you want something else?'

His eyes were the blue of Tutankhamun's eyeliner and they seemed to pierce straight into my thoughts.

'Not really.'

An amused smile replaced the frown. 'Then champagne is what you shall have. Back in a sec.'

'Excuse me just a moment.' I heard Colette put her conversation on hold. 'Oh my God! He's so into you! I knew it!' she whispered to me.

'You're over reacting. It's just a drink.'

'Did you see the way he looked at you?'

'Not really,' I replied honestly. 'The whole world seems to have gone kind of soft focus.' I looked around. 'It's actually quite nice.' Colette prodded me. 'Huh? OK, yes, he seems quite attentive.'

'And do you think that's good?'

A grin pushed its way onto my face. 'It's good.'

Colette winked then turned back to Greg who'd been hanging on her every word since we met. Before long, Finn returned.

'Here you go,' he said, waiting until I had a good grip of the glass before letting go. 'Sorry again about earlier.'

'Not a problem. This dress has had worse things than champagne spilled on it.'

'Oh...' The dark brows knitted once more. 'I'm not quite sure what to say to that.'

I took a massive gulp of the drink.

'That didn't come out like it was supposed to. I just meant...'

'Accidents happen?'

'Yes!' I said, pointing my glass at him and sloshing a plop of liquid on his pale blue shirt. 'Oh God, sorry,' I said, yanking my sleeve down over my hand and wiping at his chest manically.

Finn caught my hand and wrapped it within his own. 'It'll dry.'

'Oh. Right. Yes. And you've spilled worse things on it?' I attempted some witty repartee. And failed.

'Actually it's brand new.'

'Oh God,' I said, attempting to pull my hand back but Finn held on, gently but firmly.

'But give me time. I have a twin niece and nephew who I see a lot so I'm sure its time will come.'

I looked up from under the fake lashes Colette had, by message, insisted I wear for the occasion and met his eyes.

'Really. It's OK. Relax.'

'Oh, she's not very good at that.' Colette leant back, adding her thoughts to our conversation.

'I'm perfectly capable of relaxing,' I said, turning so that my back was to her.

'And what do you do to relax?' Finn asked.

'I... like to read.'

'About her job.' Colette poked her head over my shoulder.

'I love my job, so sue me.'

Finn and Greg exchanged a glance and apparently decided it was going to be easier to talk as a small group and moved accordingly.

'Finn, your lovely companion there is Elizabeth and this is Colette.'

'*Enchanté,*' Finn replied and my friend beamed.

'Maybe we should swap?' she said, throwing a glance at me but I'd seen the way she was looking at Greg and, even through my alcoholic haze, I knew she was teasing. His smile, however, faded for a moment.

'She's joking,' I reassured him. 'She's just the most enormous flirt.'

'Oh pah,' she said, 'I merely appreciate manners.'

'Finn's got all the smooth lines,' Greg replied, nodding at his mate. 'It's amazing any of the rest of us get a look in.'

'Very funny,' Finn replied. From the glance he shot his mate, there was definitely another layer of meaning in his reply but my brain was warmly, and quite happily, now dozing inside my skull and it was way too much effort to think about anything that deep.

Greg smiled, and grabbed his friend good naturedly around the shoulders, something he had to reach up to do, despite being taller than Colette who in turn was taller than me. Finn towered over all of us.

'You can call me Lizzie. Everyone does.'

Finn studied me for a moment. 'I think Elizabeth suits you better.'

I beamed to the point that it actually hurt. 'You do?'

'I do,' he replied, his own smile now showing.

'I prefer Elizabeth too! But you know how it goes.'

'I do. Handy having a name no one can shorten.'

I nodded, sagely. 'Very wise,' I replied, as if Finn himself had had something to do with choosing his own appellation.

'So what is it that you do?' he asked.

'Hmm?' I peered at him over the top of my glass.

'Colette said you enjoyed reading about your job.'

'Oh! I'm an archaeologist.'

His brows shot up. 'Really?'

'Mmhmm,' I said as I swigged the rest of my drink. This should probably be my last. I'd lost count of how many I had had which was never a good sign. And then the spectre of lost opportunity drifted past my mind's eye. If I could still remember that, it was likely a sign I hadn't had enough.

'So you go on digs and stuff?'

I nodded. *When they're not swiped from under my nose.* 'I have been, yes.'

'Wow. Interesting.'

Colette's hand found mine and she gave it a squeeze. Even plastered, she knew I didn't want to talk about work right now. 'But,' she announced to our small group. 'We are here to forget about work so, *allez*, impress us with your sparkling conversation.'

'Uh oh. Now we're really in trouble.' Finn grinned and disappeared behind his glass.

* * *

'Sorry if I brought up a sore subject earlier,' Finn said once Colette was finally satisfied I was capable of holding my own conversation and Finn had found us a corner table, pulling the chair out for me as he did so.

'It's fine. I just had a bit of a crappy day.'

'Hence hitting the bar.'

'Hence hitting the bar,' I agreed.

'I get the impression this isn't the way you generally like to enjoy a Friday night.'

I rested my chin in my hands. 'Uh oh. Busted.'

'I'm sorry you had a bad day, but I am happy you ended up here.'

I met his gaze. 'Me too.'

'Your friend seems happy about it as well.' He turned his head to where Colette and Greg were getting extremely cosy, her head resting on his chest, his head tilted down talking to her.

'So does yours.'

'True. Can I ask something?'

Finn received a shrug in reply.

'Does she do this a lot?'

My elbows had been sliding down the table but at this I sat up straight. 'What?'

Finn held up his hands. 'I don't mean any disrespect. I'm just... Greg seems really keen. He's not a one night stand kind of bloke. I just...'

'Wanted to know if Colette is a one night stand kind of girl? Maybe you should have swapped if that's what you think of her.'

'I don't think that,' he replied, his tone still calm. 'I don't think anything. I try not to judge people because more often than not, we get it wrong.'

'And you've got it wrong now. About this wrong!' I said, stretching my arms out as far as they would go to add what I felt was the required emphasis. 'She's not.' I studied the pair of them for a moment. 'Actually I haven't seen her look this interested in a long time.'

'He's a good bloke,' Finn replied before I'd even voiced the question.

I turned back to face him. 'And what about you?'

A mischievous smile hooked itself on the corners of the generous mouth and tugged them up. 'I'm pretty good too.'

* * *

Turned out he wasn't kidding. Finn kicked the door shut, his hands never leaving my body, as he backed me into the wall of his hallway. His mouth was on mine, my hands locked behind his neck as he bent to reach me. I'd worn my highest heels tonight as part of my armour against the world, but even those weren't enough to even up my five foot three frame to meet Finn's height of six foot five. His hands slid from my waist to under my bum and the next moment I was level with him, my legs automatically wrapping around his waist.

'Much better,' he murmured, his eyes dark with lust before his mouth once again claimed mine.

2

I forced one eye open and peered out at the unfamiliar surroundings. Light was flooding in to the modern, incredibly tidy apartment through large windows. An apartment I didn't recognise. Where was I? A noise behind me made me freeze and I held my breath. After a few moments, I steeled myself enough to turn my head, careful not to make too much movement. And there it was. Evidence of what happens when you make a very poor life decision on the back of someone else making a very poor work decision. I was looking straight at the incredibly hot, thankfully still sleeping, face of Finn... Oh my God! I had not only had a one night stand – which I never did. Like ever. But I didn't even know his last name. Shit. I needed to get out of here. Slowly I shifted again, careful to make as little movement as possible under the pure white cotton sheets. Wonderfully silky soft sheets that had a several hundred thread count start over my own. I slid one leg out, then one arm, following it with the other leg until I slithered silently to the floor like a knackered, exceedingly hungover snake. Moving as quietly as possible, I scrabbled around locating various bits of clothing until I had it all but my bra.

Where the hell is it? I rummaged back through the fuzzy memories of last night, trying to remember when that particular item of clothing had come off. Certain moments of the evening were pretty damn clear and something I did remember is that I'd already had one surprisingly quick and apparently satisfyingly loud orgasm if the grin on Finn's face was anything to go by, before half my clothes were off. That rather set the tone for the rest of the night. And the early hours of the morning. No wonder he was still sleeping. He'd had a pretty good workout. Muscles I'd forgotten about were already making themselves known but my sodding bra remained missing in action. Typically it was my favourite, most expensive one. Of course it was. Movement from the bed made me duck down beside it, holding my breath. A few moments later, the deep, even breathing of the man I'd left behind in the warm bed resumed and I decided I was going to have to abandon my search and head out. The thought of Finn waking up while I was still there filled me with mortification. Last night he'd seen everything and I didn't care. I'd wanted it all. I'd wanted him. But this morning, in the cold light of reality, I knew this was not me. I didn't do this. Relationships were long term, cerebral, with deep, meaningful conversations – usually about archaeology. At least the two I'd had had been. I didn't do frivolous, carefree, brain-exploding sex. Well, apart from last night. But that was a mistake. A huge, Great Pyramid-sized mistake and the sooner I put it behind me, the better.

I took one last glance. Even without champagne goggles on Finn was still immensely good looking. Far too gorgeous for his, and my own, good as last night had indisputably proved.

My phone rang almost the moment I grabbed it out of my bag, having unearthed said bag from under a cushion on the sofa, tiptoed from the freakishly tidy apartment and closed the door behind me as quietly as possible.

'Where are you?'

I wrapped my coat around me as I answered Colette's call. The truth was I had no idea where I was. Not ideal. I multi tasked, bringing up the maps app on my phone as I replied.

'Docklands.'

'Oh my God.'

'What?'

'You totally stayed with Finn last night.'

'So,' I said, dragging up as much nonchalance as I could muster which took far more effort than I had energy for.

'Don't give me that. So how was it?'

'How was what?'

'Lizzie.'

'It was... fine.'

'Oh dear.'

'What?'

'Fine is not great.'

'OK, it was more than fine.'

Now she was interested.

'How much more than fine?'

'Col, could we not do this right now? I'm about to go into the Tube station and my brain feels like it's mid-mummification.'

'You're not rich enough.'

'What?'

'You told me only the rich and people of note were mummified.'

'Now you choose to remember interesting facts I tell you.'

'I told you I listened.'

'Col, I really need to just get home.' I was the only one who was allowed to shorten my friend's name.

'OK, but call me later?'

'I will. Oh God! I didn't ask you how your evening went!'

Colette gave a melodic laugh. 'It was wonderful. Unlike you, I didn't fall into bed with him though, so he's taking me to dinner tonight.'

'Ha ha, but good. You seemed pretty interested.'

'I really like him.' Her voice was serious for a moment. 'We sat talking until half past three this morning. He's... well, I'm not going to count my chickens but yes, I like him.'

Colette had been burned badly once before which had ended the marriage she'd truly thought would last forever. It had taken a long time for her to put herself out there again and this was the first time I'd heard her take anyone remotely seriously. I remembered Finn's reassurance that Greg was a good bloke and hoped he was right. The thought of Finn's voice kicked off a whole bunch of other memories that liquified my stomach and sent flashes of heat to places they had no business being this early on a Saturday morning stood at the entrance to the Tube.

'Got to go, Col. I'll ring you later.'

'OK. Love you.'

'Love you too.'

* * *

'So?' It was Sunday afternoon and Colette and I were huddled in a coffee shop in Finsbury Park.

'So, what?'

'Are you seeing him again?'

'Who?'

She peered at me with a steady look over the rim of her swimming pool-sized hot chocolate.

'No. I'm not.'

'Why not? You obviously like him. And he *definitely* likes you.'

'It was a mistake. A *huge* mistake.'

'Huge, eh?' Colette grinned wickedly and I shot her a glare.

'Not like that.'

'Oh, really? Well, that's disappointing.'

'What?'

She made a gesture with her little finger.

'No!' I said, grabbing her hand and shoving it down out of sight whilst simultaneously subtly scanning the place to see if anyone had noticed. 'It was...' Colette raised her brows in anticipation of my reply. 'More than adequate.' She shook her head, laughed and returned to her cake. My friend had the ability to maintain her slim figure with apparently little effort. She swore by the French 'magic soup' method of detox. I tried this once and couldn't even get a cupful down. How anyone could claim it was delicious was a clear misrepresentation. I'd swallowed some of the 'soup' (also known as leek water), gagged and bunged the leeks in a pan with potatoes and cream and made something edible instead. Fair enough, it didn't have the same bloat reduction properties as the original claimed but it was bloody delicious. And I certainly didn't have to worry about calories this weekend. I must have burned about ten thousand on Friday night. *Oh God, what had I been thinking?*

'Ooh, it was obviously way more than adequate. You're blushing!'

'I am not blushing. Don't be so ridiculous. It's warm in here.' I made a point of pulling a book out of my bag and fanning myself with it.

She gave me a look that I knew of old. She wasn't going to argue with me but there would be no convincing her she was wrong, so I didn't bother. And, on this occasion, she was right.

'So why aren't you seeing him again?'

'Because I'm not looking for anyone and I'm certainly not looking for someone who picks up women in bars for one night stands.'

'He might think it was you who picked him up?'

'It wasn't! I don't do things like that. I'd had way too much to drink. Why didn't you stop me?'

'Because you looked like you were enjoying yourself for once.'

'I enjoy myself plenty.'

She gave a one-shouldered shrug. 'But this time you looked like you were really letting go, relaxing.' She did the shrug again. 'It was good to see.'

'He could have been an axe murderer and you let me go off with him!'

'I asked Greg. He promised he wasn't. So, he didn't suggest meeting up again?'

I topped up my tea and stirred in some milk.

'Lizzie?'

'Hmm?'

'What aren't you telling me?'

'Nothing. And no, he didn't.'

'And neither did you?'

'Nope.'

'Why not?'

'We've been over this. Can we change the subject now please?'

Reluctantly, Colette agreed and began to tell me about Greg. I smiled as I listened, trying to remember when I'd last seen her this happy. It was far longer than it should have been. She was totally and utterly smitten and Greg sounded great. If he broke her heart, I was going to give him a practical demonstration of what the Egyptians did to peoples' brains during the mummification process.

* * *

'Right. Well, I'd better get back. I need to go in earlier tomorrow and sort out my office.'

'Really?'

I pulled a face. 'It's not that bad.'

'Lizzie, Cleopatra's mummy could be in there under all that junk.'

'It's not junk and you're exaggerating.'

'If you say so.'

'I do.'

'How come you have to share your office anyway? I'd have thought they'd have been working from a PortaKabin outside?'

'That was the original plan but the council got a bit uppity about it. They're not the prettiest things to look at, even temporarily. But, understandably the board didn't want to make any more waves that might affect permission for the museum's extension so we were asked to find another solution.'

'Which is your office.'

'Apparently so.'

'Do you really mind? I know it didn't help getting that news after everything else on Friday.'

I peered into the teapot, checking that I'd drained it, before replacing the lid. 'Doesn't matter now, does it? It's happening anyway. Inis assured me that it would cause me minimum disruption.'

'Good.'

'I'd better get a move on. Are you coming?'

Colette looked momentarily shifty. I smiled.

'Greg's meeting you here, isn't he?'

Her own smile burst onto her face. 'Yes. Is it that obvious?'

'Who cares, if you're happy?'

'That is true.'

We did the two kiss thing, a habit Colette had never dropped and I headed out of the café and back up the road towards my mews house. Colette lived close by and had an income to match the area. I'd inherited my place from my much loved and much missed grandmother. A fact that hadn't surprised my mother even though it had floored me.

'You always were her favourite grandchild.'

'Mum, I was her only grandchild.'

'There you go then.'

'But it should go to you.'

Mum had touched my face and handed me a letter. I recognised the writing on the envelope. My name written in the loopy, yet elegant strokes of my grandmother.

My dearest Elizabeth,

Now you're reading this, my time has come. I'd tell you not to be sad, but of course you will be – and quite right too. I was, of course, remarkable.

Here she'd drawn a sketch of an elegant, older woman looking out from the paper and winking at the reader. I'd always envied Gran's artistic talents.

But in truth, my love, try not to be too sad for too long. I left you this house, which I know has probably surprised you, but I discussed it with your mother a long time ago. It's impossible to get on the property ladder nowadays and I had the opportunity to help with that. I have so many happy memories of you being here, and I hope you have the same. Decorate it how you like. It's yours now. Be free. And don't forget what I always told you. You are amazing. You can do anything you

*put your mind to. And if something's important to you, never
give up.*

I love you.

Gran xxxx

Ps – do try and keep it tidy, darling!

I'd cried for days but moving out of the noisy house share and
into Gran's house – my house – had helped me deal with my grief.
I knew she'd be happy about that. The last part of her letter was
the bit I had trouble with and I hoped her spirit was still turning
a blind eye to my mess five years later.

* * *

'Here's fine,' I said, putting my end of the desk down close to the
door and perpendicular to my own.

'Sure?' Kalif said, wiping his brow with his sleeve.

'It will have to do,' I said, pushing the chair I'd already
wheeled from storage behind it. 'Beggars can't be choosers.
Thanks for the help.'

'No problem. I'm going to get back to cataloguing that collection of Roman coins that came in last week. Shout if you need
any more help.'

'If they want anything else, they can damn well get it themselves. My back is not happy.'

'The request was a space for a desk, not to move the actual
furniture.' A deep voice came from the doorway.

Kalif straightened and I spun around. Inis was smiling at me
but I could tell she wasn't impressed. 'We wanted to make you
feel welcome, didn't we, Lizzie?'

'Umm...' I croaked then cleared my throat. 'Yes, of course.'

'So, as I said, you'll be sharing an office with Lizzie. She's our Curator of Collections and Egyptian Antiquities. Lizzie, this is Finn Bryson, the project manager for the extension of the museum.'

'Hi.' He held out a shovel-sized hand and I stuck out my own. 'Nice to meet you.' I focused on his eyes but there was nothing. No sense of recognition. Not even a flicker. He had absolutely no idea who I was. I was *such* an idiot.

'Yes. And you.'

'Lizzie has been rather busy lately so she's not had much of a chance to tidy up in here but I'm sure it's on her to-do list today, isn't it?' Inis gave me a pointed look and I fixed a smile.

'Mmhmm.' It was the only noise I could make with my teeth gritted. *Not had a chance?* I'd been in here since six o' bloody clock this morning getting the place tidied and that was the thanks I got. *Flippin charming.*

'I'd better get downstairs and on site.' Finn's deep tones jolted me out of my seething. 'Nice to meet you, Lizzie. Thanks, Inis.' With that he turned on his heel and walked off towards the lower floor where an underground extension was being carved out after years of planning and promises.

'Sorry about that,' I said, pointing at the desk.

Inis waved her hand. 'I don't care about the desk. He was right. You two could have hurt yourselves moving that.' She knocked the wood of the piece. 'This is about two hundred years old and weighs a tonne.'

'It felt more like two.'

'Is that the only one you could find?'

'Yes. Well, there was an incredibly ugly metal one but I've got to sit and look at it for months so we opted for that. I bribed Kalif with whatever he wants from the posh sandwich shop across the road to move it with me.'

'That sounds more like it. But I did ask you to tidy up this place,' Inis continued, looking around.

'I did!'

Her head turned sharply towards me. 'You did? When?'

'This morning!'

'Were we robbed between then and now?'

'Oh, ha ha.'

She touched my hand. 'I know it's not your thing but can I ask you to try a little harder. Maybe put some of those books on shelves? Clear the floor a bit more? If health and safety come in here, we're in trouble.'

'I'm using the books.'

Inis let out a sigh. 'You can still use them, just store them on the shelves when they're not on your desk.'

I eyed my desk.

'And by that I don't mean just move the pile to your desk.'

Damn.

'You're going to make a great mum,' I laughed. 'You already have the mindreading thing going on.'

She smiled back. 'I hope so. We've waited such a long time for this.' She placed her hand on her stomach.

'Everything's going to be fine.'

'Thanks, Lizzie.' She walked to the door, turning as she left. 'But you still have to tidy up.'

I plopped down on the ergonomic chair that didn't go at all with the carved walnut desk and thought about what just happened. Jumping up, I grabbed my phone, ran over and closed the door, pressing Colette's contact as I did so.

'Hi.'

'It's Finn,' I whispered. 'He's here.'

'What do you mean? He's visiting the museum?'

'I wish! He's the project manager for the build. The one I have to share an office with!'

'Ooh la la! Have you spoken to him?'

'Kind of.'

'What does that mean?'

'It means my boss introduced us and he told me it was nice to meet me.'

'Oh... maybe he wasn't sure how you wanted to play it?'

'He doesn't even recognise me, Col. I looked into his eyes. There was nothing. He has no idea who I am. Shit!'

'Lizzie.' Her voice was soft. 'I thought you were OK with that. I mean, not seeing him again.'

'I am. I mean, I was. But now the bloke I went home with doesn't even remember me! Personally I thought it was pretty memorable, but apparently not for him. I told you he was one of those men. And I bloody fell for it.'

'Memorable, eh?'

'Colette! You're focusing on entirely the wrong thing here!'

'Yes. Sorry. So what are you going to do?'

'What can I do? I'm stuck with him for the next however many months! But just because he's sharing an office with me doesn't mean I have to engage in conversation.'

'True. Although maybe a few little reminders might...'

'I don't want to remind him! If he can't remember by himself I'm sure as hell not going to beg him to cast his mind back and dredge up his drunken conquests!'

'Bit dramatic, *ma chérie*, but I get the point. Did you tidy up your office?'

'Yeah. And Inis just told me to tidy it. Again.'

'Ah... do you need some help?'

'No. It's fine.'

'Don't just make more piles. I've told you that before.'

'Stop ganging up on me. Right, I'm going to have to go and *tidy my office.*'

'Good luck and keep me posted.'

I hung up and got to work, ruing the day I set eyes on Finn Bryson! I then rued the board and the sponsors. And the decision-making committee for the Egypt dig. And Friedrich. It turned out there was quite a lot of ruing to do which at least passed the time as I once again tackled my office.

'Wow!' Finn stopped at the door.

I kept my head lowered, focused on my work.

'Thanks for clearing up in here. I hope it didn't put you out too much.'

I squeezed the last atom of life out of the stress ball on my lap. It was either that or Finn and the second involved too much paperwork.

'No problem. I'd been planning to anyway. I just hadn't got around to it.' I went back to work.

'Right.'

Silence hung heavy in the air between us, broken only by my somewhat furious typing.

'Showing no mercy, eh?'

I looked up and across at Finn, frowning.

'The keyboard.'

'I'm afraid if my typing is going to disturb you, you may have to make other arrangements for your work station.'

'No, I didn't mean...' He shook his head. 'I was just trying to make conversation.'

He has no recollection of me in his bed on Friday night but now he wants to make conversation?

'Oh, I see. Sorry, but I'm rather busy.'

'Yeah, Inis said you're arranging some big exhibition?'

'Yes, that's right.' I focused back on my screen.

'What's it about?'

Politeness forced me to squelch the enormous sigh I wanted to let out. "The Pharaohs of Egypt," I replied, not looking at him.

'Sounds interesting.'

'Yes, I think so.'

Silence thankfully returned.

'Sorry.'

I looked over at him.

'For disturbing you. I promised you wouldn't know I was here and now I'm rattling on.' He gave an apologetic half smile and I mentally yelled at my stomach to stop going all melty and squishy immediately. Been there, done that. And he didn't remember.

'It's fine. I'm just busy. I don't mean to be rude.'

He held up his hands. 'No, no, I get it. I only thought as we were going to be working together for several months, it might be nice to get to know each other a bit.'

Oh, you already know way more about me than I'd like. Or you would if I wasn't just another notch on your bedpost.

'We're not exactly working together.'

There was a pause. 'No, I suppose not.' He opened the laptop on his desk and I was left to get on with my work.

3

'How was it?' Colette asked without saying hello as I answered her call on my way to the station.

'He wanted to make conversation.'

'And did you?'

'Nope.'

'Why not?'

'Because I don't want to. What was I supposed to say anyway? Oh hi, how's the project going? By the way, I have to say I'm a bit miffed that you don't remember our wild night of monkey sex on Friday.'

'Oooh! Wild monkey sex? You didn't tell me that!'

'It's an expression.'

'One that I've never heard you use before. Friedrich's going to be pissed off there's someone better at something out there.'

'Funnily enough, that's not top of the list of things I'm bothered about.' I let out a sigh. 'Am I over reacting? Is this what happens with one night stands? I have no frame of reference. I just didn't think he was so drunk he'd completely forget me.'

'No, I agree. He didn't seem as drunk as you were.'

'Thanks for that.'

'You know what I mean. And no, you're not over reacting. If someone forgot me, I'd be livid!'

'They wouldn't forget you.'

'You're sweet but thank you.'

'I feel like an idiot.'

'Well don't. He's the idiot. He had a chance with you and he's ruined it.'

'Maybe he got everything he needed from me already.'

'I really want to give you a hug right now.'

'I'd take it.'

That was one of many things I loved about my friend. She didn't bullshit me. There was a good possibility that I'd spoken the truth and she didn't try and dress it up as something else. It was what it was and, whatever it was, she was there for me. 'I'm at the station now. I'll catch up with you later, OK?'

'Sure. Love you.'

'Love you too.'

* * *

Finn's bag was already beside his chair when I got to work the next day, his laptop open on a complicated-looking spreadsheet but he, thankfully was nowhere to be seen. I let out a breath I didn't realise I'd been holding and sat down at my desk, pulling open the top drawer to drop a snack bar in there for later. Inside was a small package folded in tissue paper that hadn't been there yesterday. I lifted it out and unwrapped it.

My eyebrows shot up my face and my mouth dropped open. Grabbing the package I hurriedly shoved it back in my drawer and slammed it shut, catching my finger in it as I did so.

'Fuuuuuu—' I looked up to see Finn's frame filling the doorway, his face creased in concern.

'Are you OK?'

I clamped my lips together. 'Mmhmm.' That was about all I could manage right now. That or a string of expletives a mile long.

Finn crossed the floor in a few strides. 'Let me see,' he said, bending to take my hand.

I shook my head. 'No,' I gritted out. 'Just throbbing a little. It'll go off in a minute.'

'If you grit your teeth any harder, they're going to explode. Let me see. I'm a trained first aider.'

I shook my head again and kept my hand rammed within the other one in my lap.

'Don't make me come and get it.'

My head snapped up and I saw the mischief in his eyes. And the recognition.

'You thought I didn't remember you?' His voice was softer now.

In my surprise, I'd relaxed my posture a little and he took advantage of the change to gently lift my hand and look at the finger I'd crunched. 'You did a good job there. We need to clean it up.' I looked down and saw the blood.

'Oh, balls.'

Finn grinned and pulled my chair out from behind the desk with me on it. 'Come on, let's get you to the kitchen.'

'No, I'll go and rinse it off in the loo. It'll be fine.' I moved and bumped my hand on the desk as I did so and the string of expletives I'd diverted earlier flowed out. Finn waited patiently until I'd finished.

'Creative.'

'Thanks.'

'Come on, let's get some ice on it. It'll help the swelling and the pain.'

'I don't think it's swollen, it's just sore.'

'Take another look.'

I did so and processed the fact my finger was now twice its normal size.

'Oh, double balls. You know this is all your fault.'

He waited for me to step through the door first, cradling my finger, before falling into step beside me. 'And how do you figure that?'

'Because I wasn't expecting to see... that... in my drawer.'

'You'd have preferred me to leave it on the desk?'

'No!'

He gave a shrug. 'One could argue that actually this is all your fault.'

'And how do you work that one out?'

'Had you not been in such a hurry to leave my place on Saturday morning, you wouldn't have left it behind.'

Annoyingly he was probably right.

'No argument to that, huh?'

'I'm thinking about it.'

He gave a low chuckle that brought back a lot of not unpleasant, but certainly not appropriate, memories. I stopped at the ladies' loos.

'You going to be OK?'

'Yep.'

'Because I can't come in there.'

'That was rather the point.'

He ignored it. 'So if it's split, you'll be OK?'

'What's split?'

'The finger, the fingernail, there's a range of possibilities. I can't see for the blood at the moment.'

'Stop being dramatic. I deal with dead bodies as part of my job.'

'Yes. Ones that have been dead over three thousand years. I'm guessing they don't tend to bleed all that much.'

'I will be fine. Go back to doing whatever it is that you do when you're not annoying me.'

'If you insist.'

I shoved the door open with my shoulder and headed to the sinks. Running the tap with one hand, I placed the other one underneath the gentle flow. 'Oh... Oh that's not good. That's...' I dived into a stall as my breakfast came back for an encore. Once my stomach was empty, I flushed and rinsed my hands, without looking at them. There was a knock at the door.

'You OK in there?'

I dried my hands and left the paper towel wrapped around one and tried not to notice it was gradually darkening with blood as I opened the door to find Finn casually leaning on the wall opposite.

'I thought I told you to go back to work. I imagine we're paying you a ridiculous amount to oversee our extension.'

'Enough. Not ridiculous. I'd go for ridiculous if you can swing it.'

'Ha! I have absolutely no authority in that area.'

'Shame. I guess I'll have to make do then. Besides, it comes with benefits I didn't expect.'

'Those "benefits" were a very drunken, one off lapse of judgement!' I whispered, prodding his chest once with my good hand for emphasis as I did so. He wrapped his own hand around mine and lowered it.

'That's not what I meant.' His face had lost its smile and his blue eyes were shuttered. 'Come on, we need to get you seen to.'

'It's not as bad as it looks,' Finn said confidently as he

cleaned my hand gently with a cotton wool ball and warm water. I turned my head back from where I'd been resolutely taking an interest in the street the kitchen window overlooked. Finn quickly placed his other hand over mine. 'That doesn't mean it's not still going to turn your stomach and I didn't bring a spare shirt with me.'

'Ha ha, I'm not going to throw up on you.' I turned back to my study of outside. The truth was there was every chance I might but he didn't need to know that.

'Better safe than sorry.' He faffed around a little more and apologised when I winced as he placed an ice pack on my hand. 'Sorry, but it's the best thing for it.'

'I've got stuff to do.' I looked down at the pack then back at him. 'I don't have time for this.'

He gave a shrug. 'I'm good but I can't perform miracles.'

From what I recall, I was inclined to disagree. I was pretty sure I'd seen God at least twice last Friday night.

'No, I know. And thanks.'

'You're welcome. Keep it on there for a few more minutes.' He checked his watch. 'Do you want a drink? I was about to ask you that earlier.'

'Thanks, that'd be really nice actually.'

'Coffee?'

'Tea please. White, no sugar.'

'Sweet enough, eh?' He rolled out the old platitude with a chuckle as the kettle finished boiling.

'There are those that would disagree with you, but that's the way of the world, isn't it?'

'It is. Can't make everyone like you.'

'Somehow I doubt you have much of a problem with that.' The words fell out of my head onto my tongue and launched themselves into the world without any discussion with my brain.

Finn turned, placing the tea on the worktop in front of me. 'What's that supposed to mean?'

'Nothing.'

'You don't seem the type of woman to say things she hasn't thought about.'

'Well, we both know that's not true.'

He threw me a frown. I did a quick scout with my eyes and lowered my voice. 'Saying yes I'd love to go back to your place didn't exactly go through a lot of thought processes.'

'Oh. I see. I did check with you several times.'

'I know. All of those questions bypassed security it seems.'

'Hence you disappearing Saturday morning.'

I took a sip of tea.

'I'm sorry you regret it.' He wiped over the worktop.

'It was my decision. You didn't make me do anything I didn't want to.' Oh God, that came out wrong! I risked a glance but Finn was focused on his coffee. 'It's just that...' He flicked his gaze up and met mine. He really was unfairly good looking but not in a pretty boy way. His face looked lived in – delicious but lived in. There were crinkles around his eyes that disappeared when he laughed, his nose had been broken at least once, perhaps twice and there was a scar on his chin that ran diagonally from one side to the other in a pale silver line.

'You're studying me like I'm one of your mummies.'

I sat back. 'Sorry. Occupational habit.'

He folded his arms across his chest causing the fabric to sit taut over his shoulders and pecs. I did my best not to think about those. 'No problem. And what is your professional opinion?'

'About?'

'Whatever it was you were putting under scrutiny.'

I opened my mouth to dismiss it but caught his expression and remembered from my limited experience of him that this man was a sharp crayon in the colouring box of life. Denying I'd had any specific thoughts was not only wasting both our time but also doing him a disservice.

'You have an interesting face. I was trying to decide whether your nose had been broken once or twice. I suspect twice.'

'Correct. Rugby the first time, trying to break up a fight the second.' I winced and he shrugged it off. 'What else?'

'The scar looks old but deep. You keep your face clean shaven. Is that from choice, or because the hair won't grow there?'

'I got it when I was twelve and my brother was nine. We were trying to outdo each other on our bikes doing wheelies and such like. I had a brain fart at one point and pulled my front brake accidentally. Sailed over the handlebars and landed chin first on the pavement.'

'Ah.'

'The beard thing is a bit of both. If I grow anything, there's a line in it which looks kind of weird and I prefer clean-shaven when I go out. Although full disclosure, if I'm just hanging around at the weekend, I don't shave. Does that answer all your questions?' His mouth was serious but amusement twinkled in his bright blue eyes.

'For the moment,' I replied, trying not to smile.

'Do I get a question?'

I swallowed. 'I suppose it's only fair.'

He glanced down to the ice pack on my hand. Lifting it off, he peered at my injury. 'It's taken the swelling down quite a bit already. That's good. I think it's an idea to tape it lightly to the next finger for now, just to give it some support.'

'I can't type like that.'

'Elizabeth, you're not going to be able to type with it anyway. This will just make it more comfortable.'

I huffed out a sigh.

He dug about in the first aid box next to him and within a couple of minutes, my finger was covered with fresh gauze and strapped neatly to the next one like a splint. I made to stand up from the table we'd sat at.

'I haven't asked my question yet.'

Damn, I was hoping he'd forgotten that. I sat back down.

'Why did you leave?'

I checked quickly around us. 'I don't think this is the best place for that subject.'

'There's no one here but us. I can see up the corridor.'

'Even so.'

Finn fixed me with a look that called BS on that reply.

'Because...' I swallowed and felt my chest and face grow hot. I tilted up my chin and faced him. 'Because I didn't know what else to do. I've never done anything like that before and I don't know how it's supposed to work. I certainly didn't want you waking up and there being a very awkward scene in which you attempt to find a polite way to ask me what time I have to leave. So I left.'

'I wouldn't have done that.'

'I'm not saying you would. I'm saying it was a possibility.'

'And I'm saying it wasn't.' Those eyes hooked my gaze and held on. 'Elizabeth—'

I jumped as the tap tap of heels echoed in the hallway. 'I need to make some phone calls. Thanks for this.' I moved my arm to indicate his handiwork and winced as I did so.

'Take some painkillers when you get back to your desk. Do you have some?'

'Yes.' I turned to go and then stepped back. 'I think it's best if we don't mention Friday again.' He went to speak but I got there before him. 'I made a mistake and we have to work in the same vicinity for a while so let's just move on.'

The tap tap tapping of the shoes was close now.

'If that's what you want.'

'It is,' I confirmed.

Finn met my eyes, hesitated a beat and then nodded just as Bella entered the room dressed the smartest – and sexiest – I'd ever seen her in the three years she'd been there.

'Hi, Lizzie. Do you want a drink?'

'Hi, no, I'm fine thanks. I've just had one. You look nice.'

Bella's smile widened. 'Oh thanks! I've been doing a wardrobe overhaul and found some pieces I haven't worn for ages. Thought I'd give them an airing.'

'Sounds a great idea,' I said, resting my good hand on her shoulder and deftly tucking the price tag under her cashmere cardi. She turned and caught the action, her eyes widening a little. 'I love this jumper. The colour really suits you.'

'Thanks, Lizzie.'

I stepped out into the corridor and turned towards my office, the conversation in the staff kitchen drifting out as I left.

'Oh hi, Finn. I didn't realise you were in here...'

I smiled to myself and headed back to set about some one-handed typing.

* * *

With so much planning to do for the exhibition and the many meetings that entailed, opportunity for conversation between Finn and I had been limited. On the odd occasion a moment presented itself, one or the other of our phones would ring and the chance would pass.

Bella had been a fixture in my office far more often than was usual, valiantly attempting to find an inroad with Finn. From what I'd seen, she didn't seem to be making much headway. He was polite but that appeared to be where things ended. Much to the obvious chagrin of Bella.

'Do you think he's gay?' she asked as she perched on the corner of his empty, but very tidy desk.

'Hmm?' I looked up from the email I was typing. 'Who?'

'Finn.'

'Oh... no, I, err, don't think so.'

I was pretty damn certain but I wasn't about to explain how I knew.

'I think he might be.'

'Oh... OK.' I carried on typing, only half listening as I composed my correspondence.

'I mean, there's been nothing back from him at all.'

I looked up again. 'Back from whom?'

'Finn!' She rolled her eyes at me. 'I've been flirting with him all week and there's absolutely nothing.'

'Oh, I see.' I scrabbled around for something useful to say. 'Well, it's his loss.'

This was true. Bella was a nice girl. Bright, witty and attractive.

'Thanks.'

'Isn't he... umm... a little old for you though?' I was pretty sure Finn had a good fifteen years on her.

She sat back and swung her long slim legs off the desk. 'I like an older man. Guys my age are so immature.'

'Ah.' I nodded, not really sure what else to say.

Clearly bored with my company, and realising that Finn wasn't returning any time soon, Bella slid off the furniture and clip clopped off up the corridor.

* * *

'So? How was your first week staring at the man who gave you the best sex you've ever had?' Colette asked in the same tone as if she'd just asked me what dressing I wanted on my salad.

'Shoosh!' I said, waving my hand for her to lower her voice although two women beside us had perked up and were attempting to pretend they weren't now ear-wigging on our conversation.

Colette took a sip of her drink, unconcerned and waited for an answer.

'I wasn't staring at him.'

She smiled. 'Not even a little bit?'

'Fine. A little bit. But that's all.'

Colette rested her chin on her hands. 'Would it really be so bad?'

'What?'

'Going out with Finn.'

'Yes.'

'Why?'

'For one, he hasn't asked. He's tried to be friendly but not *that* friendly.'

'And two?' she asked.

'Two, I'm not looking for a relationship. I've worked so hard in this field and I still haven't been given my own dig. I thought for sure I'd have been awarded leadership this time and still got passed over. So now I need to double down on my efforts to get noticed. I want that dig, Col. It's what I've wanted ever since I was eight years old, tucked away in a corner of the library reading about Nefertiti. Even all these years later we don't know for sure where she's buried. I don't expect to be lucky enough to find such an icon but I want the opportunity to search. I want to lead such an opportunity to search for more answers. And as gorgeous as Finn is, I—'

'You forgot fantastic in bed.'

'What?'

'Finn. How gorgeous *and* fantastic in bed...'

I rolled my eyes but neither of us bothered to hide our grins. 'Fine. No matter how gorgeous and fantastic in bed Finn is, I can't let myself get distracted. Not now. I need to keep my focus sharp and my name current by publishing papers and networking even more than I am now.'

Colette let out a sigh. 'Bad timing.'

I plopped my chin on my hands, mirroring my friend. 'Really bad timing.'

'Could you not do both?' She giggled. 'So to speak.'

I shook my head. 'He's a really nice bloke. He deserves someone who can give their full attention to the relationship.'

'Maybe that should be his choice? I mean, if you explain?'

'No, Col. It's not fair. Besides, like I said, he hasn't even asked. One night stands and full-on relationships are two very different things.'

'Are you going to be able to cope, staring over at that gorgeous face all day?'

'Next week will be better. I'm used to him now.'

'Is that so?'

'Yep.'

'Right.' Colette looked at me without the slightest hint of belief.

'Right,' I repeated more forcefully, attempting to stuff as much surety as possible into my own word because the truth was, much to my annoyance, I wasn't convinced I believed it myself.

4

As the next few weeks passed, I did my best to stick to the resolution I'd so adamantly defended to Colette. Bella's tactics, however, were pretty much opposite to mine. With a sigh, she stood and wandered out of my office having managed to make a two minute question expand into a twenty minute loiter. As her direct boss, I had gently hinted that perhaps she ought to be getting on with some work but I'd never been very good at people management. From what I'd seen, Finn had no problem with it – and people still liked him. A classic example of firm but fair. Maybe I should take some tips from him. But that would mean spending even more time in each other's company and I had a feeling that wasn't top of either of our to-do lists.

I watched Bella exit the room and head back to the task she was supposed to be doing – and was currently at least a week behind on thanks to the latest exhibit in our museum – Finn Bryson.

'Are you ever going to put her out of her misery?' I asked.

Finn looked up from his laptop screen and glanced across at me. 'Who?'

'Bella.'

He took off the black framed glasses and I had a sudden flash of Clark Kent lust. Finn looked hot without glasses but when I'd looked up and noticed him wearing them the first time, I'd had to make a swift exit to one of the temperature-controlled store rooms to douse the flames that had burst into life deep within me. Now, several weeks in, I was used to it. Sort of.

A frown creased his forehead. 'I don't understand.'

'Oh, come on, Finn. You can't be that naïve.'

He put the glasses on the desk and crossed his arms over his chest. 'Apparently I can.'

'I find that hard to believe.'

'I find it hard to believe you thought I wouldn't remember the first time we met. Life is full of surprises.'

I waved my hands about at him and put my finger to my lips. 'Don't blurt stuff out like that. Anyone could have been passing! Not to mention we agreed never to speak about that again.'

'I have a better view of the surrounding area from here, so I know there's no one in the vicinity. And I don't remember agreeing to that.'

'Well, you did.'

He shrugged which only highlighted the broad, muscular shoulders encased within a pale sage-coloured shirt. 'What did you mean about Bella? I wasn't aware that I'd upset her. I've barely spoken to her.'

I rolled my eyes at him. 'That's rather the problem.'

He breathed out a sigh. 'Elizabeth, could you stop talking in riddles and just tell me what I've done?'

'It's what you haven't done.'

He shot me a look that told me he was losing patience although it was a good job Bella wasn't here as the dark expression was unexpectedly, and annoyingly, sexy. 'Elizabeth...'

Finn, true to his word the first time we met, continued to use my full name. Thankfully the rest of the team seemed to have merely assumed that he was being polite and not taking liberties. Maybe he was. I certainly wasn't about to ask.

'Bella has rather the crush on you. You must have noticed!'

His frown deepened. 'Bella?'

'Yes.'

'Since when?'

'Since about two seconds after she saw you.'

'Oh.'

'Yes. Oh. Hence my question.'

'And why are you interested?' There was a hint of a smile now, his dark look turning quizzical.

I gave another eye roll. 'Don't flatter yourself. The only reason I'm asking is because she's spending so much time mooning over you that I'm only getting half as much work out of her.'

'So you thought... what?'

'If you ask her out, she might be able to concentrate more.'

'I'm not entirely sure I follow your logic. You think if I take her out, she will automatically be able to focus more?'

'Maybe. It might be worth a try.'

'No.' He picked up his glasses and slipped them back on his face, signalling that the conversation, as far as he was concerned, was over.

'Why not?' I asked. 'Are you seeing someone?'

'Nope,' he replied, typing away without looking up.

'So why not? She's really nice, intelligent, attractive and worships the ground you walk on.'

'She doesn't know me.'

'Apparently that doesn't matter but she will if you ask her out.'

'As I said, no.'

'Why not?' I asked again.

He let out another sigh, this time visibly more impatient than the initial one.

'Because,' he took off the glasses again and fixed his gaze on me, 'she's not my type.'

I opened my mouth to protest on Bella's behalf. As I saw it, it was the perfect solution. Bella finally gets the date she wants and Finn gets a date with a young, bright, attractive woman with legs up to her armpits.

'She's too young for a start.'

I shut my mouth. Momentarily.

'I did mention that and she said she didn't mind.'

'I wasn't aware you'd been discussing me.'

It was my turn to shrug.

'Did it occur to you that *I* might mind?'

Truthfully, it hadn't.

'That's what I thought.' He went back to his work.

'Why?' I was genuinely curious. I'd seen one man walk into the bottom half of a Colossus when Bella was nearby. In accordance with their name, these items were generally pretty hard to miss but he'd been too busy looking at Bella. And that had been in her previous, more relaxed sartorial choices. Had he been witness to her current bombshell look, it was likely he'd have given himself concussion.

'Because she's too young.' Finn repeated, giving me no new information whatsoever.

'For what?'

'For me! I'm guessing I've got about fifteen years on her and that, for me, is too much of a gap.'

'I thought it was most men's dream to have a young, beautiful thing on their arm boosting their ego.'

'My ego is fine as it is.'

Looking like he did, that actually made sense.

He dropped his gaze and shoved his glasses back on his face.
'You should tell her then.'

'Tell her what?' he asked, his keys taking a bashing.

'That you're not interested.'

He gave a humourless laugh. 'No thanks. That never ends well. She'll get the message.'

'She might not.'

'Then,' he said, pushing his chair back and collecting a couple of files from his desk. 'You can tell her.' With that, he walked out of the office.

* * *

'So, are you going to?' Colette asked as she took a sip of her cocktail. We were sitting in a new bar in Borough, the French owner of which, Colette had done work for. The cocktails tasted even better for being free.

'Do you think I should?' It had been over a month now and Bella clearly wasn't getting the message.

'Honestly?'

'Of course?' I said, taking a sip of my own cocktail, a Porn Star which Colette had ordered for me, a gesture which she thought hilarious.

'Don't get involved. It's between Bella and Finn.'

'He's not going to tell her and it's painful to watch her keep trying.'

'I agree with him. She'll get the message eventually.'

'I hope it's soon. It's not just that it's hard to watch her keep trying for him when he's apparently not interested, but her work is suffering and I'm already up to my eyeballs coordinating this upcoming exhibition.'

'So say something about that.' Colette had that innate confidence that French women often do, the suggestion tripping off her tongue as though it was nothing.

'I can't. I mean, normally she's really good.'

'But you were prepared to tell her that Finn wasn't interested in her?'

'God, no! I just wanted to ask whether you thought I should. Hypothetically.'

'Hypothetically you are too nice when it comes to doing the people side of management.'

'I know. But she's a good worker – usually – and Finn isn't going to be there forever.'

'More's the pity.' Colette grinned as she spoke.

'The sooner he's gone the better as far as I'm concerned. He's an unnecessary distraction.'

Colette placed her glass down on the green marble of the bar. 'For Bella, or for you?'

'Bella. Obviously.' I gave her a stern look and took a gulp of my cocktail. Shit, that was strong! I did that thing when you try not to cough and it immediately makes the situation twice as bad. The cough escaped and I did my best – which wasn't great – to choke in the most subtle manner possible.

'Hi.' Greg appeared behind us, leaning round and kissing Colette on the cheek. She turned and met his willing lips as she hooked her hands behind his neck. I, meanwhile, was still trying to die quietly and frantically trying to decide whether to ride it out here or risk attracting more attention by heading to the loos. The problem was I had no idea where those were and right now Colette was too busy to ask, even if I'd been able to form the words.

'Could we have a glass of water over here, please?' Finn's deep voice, together with a commanding tone caught the attention of the bartender, despite the many others vying for service in the throbbing bar.

'Here,' he said, his voice softer now but with that edge of order to it.

I took the glass from him and sipped, desperately trying not to cough it straight back out or even worse, expel it down my nose. These things never happened to Colette. I made to put the glass back on the bar but Finn covered my hand with his own. 'Try a bit more.'

I did so and felt things beginning to return to normal. I sipped again just to make sure. 'Thanks,' I said, placing the drink on the counter and faced him properly for the first time since he'd entered the bar. Greg said a brief hello before returning every fibre of his attention back to Colette, which she returned, pausing briefly to check I was still alive.

'No problem. You OK?' His face still showed some concern.

I waved it away. 'Yes, fine. No thanks to my best friend,' I said loudly enough for Colette to hear over the crowd.

Her smile was wide and teasing as she leant over and kissed me on the cheek. 'I knew you were in good hands.' Her eyebrows rose briefly as the private message was transmitted to me. That would teach me for declaring to Finn whilst under the influence, and within earshot of my friend, that he had incredibly nice hands.

I sent her a warning glare which she laughed off and kissed Finn hello on both cheeks and with as much subtlety as a hand grenade, began a conversation.

'I hear you have an admirer at the museum?'

Finn slanted his gaze to me. 'News travels fast.'

I took a sip of my cocktail, more carefully this time. This was obviously news to Greg and his antennae perked up. 'You never told me, mate.'

'I only discovered it for myself recently.'

I rolled my eyes. 'Even though everyone else in the entire museum and job site had already noticed.'

Greg nodded. 'Yeah. Our Finn is notoriously dim at picking up on things like that.'

'He picked up that Lizzie liked him.'

I shot Colette another glare as Finn shifted his glance to me.

'To be fair, I was doing most of the heavy lifting on that particular occasion,' he noted.

'An occasion we've agreed is in the past and not to be spoken of.'

'So you said,' Finn said, raising his hand to catch the attention of a member of the bar staff. As if by magic, one appeared, a wide smile on her face as she asked what she could get for him.

'Something tells me she has a few ideas of her own on that score,' Colette whispered.

'Shoosh!' I widened my eyes at her.

'She didn't hear. Stop worrying so much.'

Finn ordered a pint for himself and a glass of wine for me then gave my friend a patient look. He had definitely heard.

'I didn't know you were coming tonight,' I said to Finn once he'd got our drinks and I'd realised that I wasn't going to get any conversation out of Colette for a while.

'Neither did I but Greg's been away on a work trip for the last two weeks and apparently couldn't wait another minute to see Colette, who already had plans with you.'

'Ah. Hence you got dragged along so that I was less of a third wheel.'

He took a sip of his beer. 'Dragged is a little strong.'

'Well, don't feel you have to sit here and keep me company.'

'I don't feel I have to.'

'And yet, here you are.'

'Would you prefer I go somewhere else?' Azure eyes watched me over the rim of the glass.

'I think the bar maid would prefer it.'

He huffed out a chuckle. 'That's not what I asked.'

'I know Bella would.'

His laugh rang out as he took my hand and led me across the heaving room to a small corner bench seat that he'd spied was momentarily free. 'What's so funny?' I asked as I half ran to keep up with his long strides, following in the wake his bulk made in the crush of people filling the place.

'You,' he said, as I plopped down on the padded corner bench, glad to be off my feet. The heels I'd bought recently with Colette looked amazing but they were more what I called dinner shoes. Perfect only for sitting at dinner.

'Now what have I done?'

'Avoided the question. Twice.'

'I wasn't avoiding it.'

He turned to face me, preparing to speak when a group of lads next to us jostled each other roughly, knocking into our table, sending both Finn's pint and my wine into my lap.

'Sorry, love.' One of the group glanced over as I placed the now empty glasses back on the table.

'Are you OK? Did anything break?' Finn asked, his previously relaxed posture suddenly rigid and tense.

'No, it's fine.'

'It's hardly fine.'

'Calm down, mate. It was an accident.' The youngster turned back to his friends, pulling a face along with a smug smile.

Finn's face was dark as he moved the table back and stood. The man who'd tossed the casual apology over did a double take as he took in all six foot five of a very displeased Finn. After some simple maths he spoke again, this time with a little more respect in his tone.

'Bit cosy in here tonight, isn't it? I'll get you another round. What you having?' he asked, his smugness morphing into an attempt at pally banter.

'Thanks, but we're actually leaving now.' I wrapped my hand around Finn's and began to tug him away. After a moment of resistance, he let me do so. I found Colette and Greg crushed in another corner. Her eyebrows raised as she took in the joined hands.

'Tell you later. We're leaving.' I leant over, half shouting the words close to her ear.

'Ooh la la!' she replied, laughing.

'No. Definitely not.' I pointed at my soaked dress. 'I'll talk to you tomorrow.' I kissed her face, now set into a confused expression, gave them both a quick hug and then led Finn out of the bar.

The cool sharp air of the autumn evening was a shock after the warmth of indoors. Added to that, the fact that my dress was now sticking to my body and chilling my bones, it wasn't the ideal end to the evening.

'You're freezing,' Finn said, placing his jacket around my shoulders. Colette and I had got a taxi here and planned a taxi back so jackets hadn't seemed necessary. But then I hadn't planned on wearing my drink, much less Finn's.

'I'm fine,' I said, mentally having serious words with my teeth who were on the verge of going rogue and starting to chatter.

'You need to get out of that dress.'

I tilted my head up as he looked down, our eyes meeting. 'That wasn't what I meant,' he said, raising his palms towards me.

'No. I know.' What I didn't know was why I'd felt a stab of disappointment when he'd confirmed it. 'Look, why don't you just go back inside. I'm going to get a taxi and go home.'

'I've no inclination to go back in there and be, in your words, a third wheel.'

'Somehow I think you'd get your own wheel before too long.'

Finn gave me a patient look then curled his lips and let loose an ear-piercing whistle. A black cab cruising further up the street clicked off its light and pulled in to the kerb beside us. Finn opened the door for me and I gave the driver instructions, my voice faltering as I noticed Finn entering the cab behind me, closing the door after him. We pulled back out into the road and joined the traffic.

'I'm seeing you home, before you ask.'

'I don't need seeing home. I'm quite capable of finding it by myself.'

'I know but I'd feel better knowing you got to your door safe-ly.' He held up his hands. 'That's all. No ulterior motive, I promise.'

'Actually, that hadn't crossed my mind.'

He nodded in acceptance of this and then looked out of the window.

'I suppose the Christmas lights will start to go up soon.'

I gave an eye roll. 'Yes, I suspect they will. By the time it finally arrives, you're absolutely sick of Christmas, it's been dragged out for so long.'

Finn turned his focus on me. 'You don't like Christmas?'

I shrugged. 'It's just another day, really, isn't it?'

'No. Not really. Not to me anyway.'

'Oh.' For some reason this surprised me. I couldn't equate Finn's tidy mind – and apartment – with what I'd always associ-ated as the messiness of Christmas.

'Do you not celebrate it due to religious beliefs?'

'Not at all. It was just never really a big thing in our house. I suppose I've just taken that with me into adulthood.'

'Do you see your family for Christmas?'

'Sometimes. My parents retired down to Devon and it's a bit of a hike.'

'You could always drive.'

'Oh, ha ha,' I said and shoved against his arm with mine. 'Don't tell me, your side hustle is writing the awful jokes that go inside crackers.'

'I like to help out the elves in the workshop when they're swamped. That particular task is one of my talents.' He puffed himself up, his mouth tipping up on one side in fake smugness making me laugh.

'You in an elf costume must be quite the sight.'

His laughter wrapped itself around me and for the first time since he'd started at the museum, I felt myself relaxing in his company.

The cab indicated to pull in at the end of the road, where I'd asked him to and I turned to Finn. 'Are you taking this back home?'

'No, I'll get the Tube back.'

I handed over the fee, plus tip to the driver as Finn opened the door and held it for me as I stepped out. The cab pulled back on to the main road and I looked up at my unexpected escort.

'I'm OK from here.'

'How far is it?'

'Not far.'

'Would you mind if I walked with you?'

I didn't mind. In fact, I thought it would be rather lovely. But my door was where it was ending tonight.

'I can hear your cogs whirring. I promise I'm not after anything other than reassuring myself you're home safe.'

'I know. Besides, I haven't had enough alcohol this evening to think you're that hot.'

'Fair enough.' He looked down at me and grinned, immediately disproving my previous statement. We walked in companionable silence to my door.

'Greg seems very keen on Colette,' I said as we reached the house, giving myself the explanation that I was asking for the benefit of my friend rather than merely finding an excuse to keep Finn's company a moment or two longer.

He gave a short laugh. 'That's putting it mildly. He's crazy about her.'

'Is he?'

Finn leant against the door jamb of my pale pink front door. 'Completely and utterly. I've known him a long time and I don't think I've ever seen him this gaga for someone.'

'You don't look too pleased about that.'

'Don't I?'

'No, your nose went all wrinkly when you said it.'

'Well, that's something no one's ever told me before.'

'It wasn't a criticism.'

He gave a shrug, as though it wouldn't have mattered if it had been. I, on the other hand, probably would have spent the next three days turning the comment over in my head.

'You should get in and change out of that dress.'

'I bet you say that to all the girls,' I replied before my brain had had the chance to filter the words.

'Not really.'

He fixed me with a look. And then it struck me. 'Oh! God, sorry. You must be chilly!' I began hurriedly taking off the jacket he'd put around my shoulders and that I'd shoved my arms into during the short taxi ride, cosy in the oversized clothing that held the scent of the aftershave he used. Hints of cedar wood mixed with something else I couldn't name but combined to suit him perfectly.

'No.' He placed his hands on my arms as I made to hand the jacket back to him, his face serious now. 'That wasn't why I was hurrying you.'

'No... but still. You probably ought to get home.'

His mouth flickered a brief smile. 'Yeah.'

'Thanks for walking me back.'

'My pleasure.'

Then my mouth butted in, once again without asking permission from my brain to speak. 'Do you want to come in for a coffee?'

Finn hesitated and I panicked. 'No, sorry. Of course you don't. I'm sure you had a long day too and now you've come out of your way and probably just want to get—'

'I'd love to.' And then he smiled that 'what just happened to my knees' smile and I felt something inside me melt a little.

No, Lizzie. That can't happen again.

'Not for sex though!'

Finn gave a snort of laughter. 'Understood.'

I nodded. 'Good. OK.' I turned to unlock the door and lock my mouth before I blurted out anything else foolish.

5

'Wouldn't have had you pegged as a pink door kind of person,' he said as he closed it behind us, ducking under the lintel on his way in.

'Neither did I, really, but my grandmother chose it and she was very much of that ilk so I kept it. I thought I'd change it but it's grown on me.' I tilted my head to meet his eyes. 'I think maybe I like it because people don't expect it of me.'

'That's as good a reason as any. Go and get changed. I'm pretty sure I can find the kettle, if you're happy for me to do that?'

'Help yourself,' I said, dashing up the narrow stairs to my bedroom where I stripped off the dress and tossed it in the laundry bin before grabbing a snuggly jumper and matching jogging bottoms and scooting back downstairs.

'Better?' Finn asked, turning from the boiling kettle. 'You look like a little teddy bear!' he said, laughing as I came up next to him and began busying myself with mugs.

'It's warm and cosy.'

'It's cute. I like it. Again, maybe just not what I expected.'

'I'm full of surprises.'

'You certainly are. Ooh, loose tea. Very posh,' he said, leaning against the small island. My grandmother had extended out into the long garden, making the kitchen bigger and modern whilst retaining the sense of homeliness she'd always cultivated here. I'd loved coming here growing up and still had to pinch myself on occasion that it was now mine.

'Tastes better,' I stated simply. 'Would you prefer coffee?'

He shook his head. 'Tea is good, thanks, And I agree. I just don't know many people who use it.'

'I suppose I'm a little old fashioned but considering my job, I reckon I can get away with it.'

'I wouldn't say you were old fashioned. Perhaps you just appreciate the finer things.'

I plopped a tea cosy in the shape of the Great Pyramid on top of the teapot to let the tea brew which perhaps took the shine off his previous statement about my taste but I didn't care. I loved it.

'Cool tea cosy.'

I smiled as I often did when I used it. 'Colette had it made for me as part of a birthday present.'

'Thoughtful.'

'She is.'

'Has she spoken to you much about Greg?' Finn asked, taking the tray I'd loaded up with bone china mugs, milk and the teapot. I already knew from work that he didn't take sugar.

'A little,' I answered. 'Just through there is fine. Oh, hang on.' I scooted about quickly, removing papers and books from the sofa and clearing a space of the same on the coffee table in front of the squashy, overstuffed two seater sofa. 'Sorry. I wasn't expecting company.'

'Don't worry on my account.'

I tossed a throw over the pile I'd now made. 'I've seen your place, don't forget.' Admittedly I hadn't been taking much notice that first night but the following morning as I'd scrabbled around in the half light, trying to leave without waking Finn, it had been hard not to notice that his apartment was remarkably tidy and clean. 'It's like a show home.'

'It's also been called soulless so I suppose those two could connect.'

I plopped down on the sofa next to him and had the sudden realisation that Finn took up a lot more room than I did and I was almost wedged in. He made an attempt to move up but the fact was there wasn't any room to move to.

'Sorry. It's a bit snug.'

'Doesn't bother me but I can sit somewhere else if you'd prefer?'

'No, and as you can see, there aren't really many other options.' The only other chair in the room was also piled high with things I was in the middle of reading, doing or that needed filing away and I hadn't had the chance or energy to get around to doing so. 'I'm not naturally tidy like you, I'm afraid.'

'Elizabeth, stop apologising. You are what you are and I, for one, think that's pretty great. Shall I pour?'

I nodded mutely, his words dancing about in my brain.

'I do try. I mean... I actually prefer it when I can find things but I grew up in a kind of chaotic household and I suppose I tend to think of plenty of other things more interesting to do than tidying up.'

'I find it quite therapeutic.'

I turned towards him, genuinely interested. 'Really?'

'Yep. And I find I'm calmer and more productive in a tidy environment so it works well.'

'Oh God, you must be having kittens right now then!'

His laugh was as soft and warming as the fluffy lounge set I wore. 'Not at all.' His face was close, those lips, smiling now, within easy reach. If I just leant forward the tiniest amount I could—

'How long have you lived here?' Finn asked, turning his head and glancing around.

'About five years now. My grandmother left it to me.'

'Wow.'

'Yeah, I know. And yes, I do realise how lucky I am.'

'I don't doubt it,' he replied without turning. 'You don't come across as the entitled type.'

'What type do I come across as?'

The deep chuckle rumbled in his chest. 'I walked straight into that one.'

'Slap bang.'

He ran a hand across his jaw. 'OK, I need to be careful here, don't I?' There was a teasing note to his voice but when I replied, mine was serious.

'No, you need to be honest.'

'OK. Then I think you come across as highly intelligent and that can unnerve some people – men especially – who don't get you.'

Colette had suggested this exact thing before but I always dismissed it out of hand.

'I don't seem to unnerve you. Obviously you realise the highly intelligent thing isn't quite what it appears to be.' I tried to make light of his comment.

'No, it's exactly what it appears to be but for some reason you feel the need to excuse yourself for it and come out with daft comments like that.'

'Did you just call me daft?'

'I did,' he answered, clearly with no intention of apologising. 'Your intelligence is one of the things I admire about you. It makes you one of the most interesting people I've ever had the pleasure of—'

My head snapped round.

'Meeting,' he finished, a sparkle of mischief in his eyes.

'Hilarious.'

'I thought so. Your reactions are just too much fun for me to resist.'

'Try.'

'My apologies.' He smiled, looking anything but sorry.

'Go on then.'

'Are you sure you want me to?'

'You've started now. You might as well finish.'

'You're a terrible manager.'

'Pardon?'

He repeated his statement.

'No, I'm not! My staff like me.'

'Because they're allowed to do what they like.'

'They're good people and good workers.'

'Bella doesn't seem to do much work.'

'She did before you showed up!'

'So it's my fault?'

'Yes. The only thing that's changed is your presence, hence the fault lies with you.'

'And nothing to do with you not telling her that she has work to get on with rather than swinging her legs off your desk.'

'I knew you'd noticed her legs.'

He half raised one brow. 'I said I wasn't interested, not blind.'

'What am I supposed to say? Stop lusting over the project manager and get on with your work?'

'Something like that.'

I screwed my face up, horrified at the thought. 'I can't!'

'Why not? That's part of your job, isn't it?'

I remained silent.

'And that's the part you don't like. Dealing with people.'

'I'm not anti-people. I'm just more comfortable dealing with their problems when they've been dead a few millennia.'

'I can see how that might be easier.'

'Besides, I'm sure she'll get over you soon enough. You're not that great.'

'Should I have let Bella's attentions go to my head, at least I know where to come to be brought back down to earth.'

'I deal in facts.'

This brought a hearty laugh from Finn. 'No you don't. You deal in best and educated guesses.'

Annoyingly he was right. As archaeologists, that was exactly what we did. But that wasn't the point.

'Sometimes.'

He shifted position, his thigh sliding against mine as he leant back on the sofa. When I'd said that he wasn't that great, I may have been telling a substantial porkie.

'You OK?' he asked.

'Huh?'

'You had a strange look on your face.'

'Oh... yeah. No I'm fine. Miles away.'

Good one, Pinocchio.

'Were you?' Finn's eyes seemed to look right through into my soul and see exactly where my mind had been.

I attempted a laugh. 'Of course.' I tried not to concentrate on just how good it felt to have his hard, muscled body wedged against mine. However much I tried to rationalise what had happened that night, that I'd been in a vulnerable and low place mentally, and not in the best frame of mind for making sensible decisions, the fact remained that Finn was still the hottest man –

and the best sex – I'd ever had. And somehow I needed to find a way to forget both of those things entirely.

'This is a lovely house,' he said, long legs stretching out in contrast to mine which were curled up.

'Thanks. I do love it.'

'I can see why. It's got a great feel about it.'

'I like to think that's my grandmother, checking on me from time to time.'

'Do you believe in all that?'

'I suppose so.'

'How does that work with your job?'

'In what way?'

He shifted position. 'Your specialist area is Egyptology, right?'

'Yes.'

'So they believed that they needed all this stuff in the afterlife, right?' He seemed genuinely interested, unlike the few dates I'd had when Colette had convinced me to give Tinder a whirl.

'Yes. And that how their body looked at the time of mummification was how they would be in the afterlife. That's why they used tree sap to seal the cut they made to remove the internal organs rather than stitches. Did you know that?'

He shook his head. 'I did not. Is that a belief you share? Like if I went outside and dropped down dead now, is that how I'd look in the afterlife? If there's one at all?'

'Don't say that.'

'Say what?'

'About you dropping down...' For someone who dealt with the dead pretty much all the time, I still didn't have the best grip on it when it came to those I knew. And cared about.

'You don't like talking about death?'

'Not particularly, no.'

'Unless there's a lot of distance. Like thousands of years. I can understand that.'

I sat up a little. 'You can?'

Finn shrugged those wide, sexy shoulders and I tried not to think about them naked. 'Yes. You seem surprised.'

'I suppose I am.'

'People think that because you deal with the dead and the past all day, you're less affected by death?'

I swallowed, thinking back to how devastated I was when my grandmother passed away. How Friedrich had struggled to understand the depth of my grief. That should have been a clue that something wasn't right but I'd reasoned that everyone dealt with loss in different ways. And, as far as I knew, he was in the lucky position never to have lost someone he was close to.

'While I imagine you can get invested in a mummy or what-ever when you have a new discovery, for example if you're studying them over a long period, but it's still not the same as losing someone you've created memories with and loved.'

I could have kissed him right then and there. And not just because of the obvious. In one sentence Finn understood and conveyed what I'd tried to explain to my former fiancé time and time again. I'd lost my grandmother but she'd also been a friend, a mentor, a champion and a whole bunch of other things I couldn't even put a name to. The grief had swallowed me up like a deep, dark pit and the one person who I should have been able to turn to for support couldn't, and it seemed, had had no interest in trying to understand.

I stifled a yawn and Finn pushed himself up from the sofa, gathered our mugs and took them out to the kitchen.

'You don't have to do that,' I said, padding out after him.

'Habit,' he replied, glancing over his shoulder as he located the dishwasher and placed the two items in it. Neatly, of course.

'It's not usually this much of a mess,' I explained, as I followed him into the hallway. He turned to face me.

The corner of his mouth tipped into a half smile.

'Never apologise for being you, Elizabeth. You're perfect as you are. Don't let anyone tell you any different.'

With that he bent, kissed me on the cheek and twisted the lock of the front door, the chill air of the night causing me to shiver. I stood, waiting to see him off.

'It's cold. Get back inside and keep warm.'

I stayed where I was.

'Do you ever do as you're told?'

Without permission, my mind hurried off and helpfully fetched a memory of a time I'd done exactly as he'd asked. I was glad of the soft, low light of the outdoor lamp that hopefully hid my blush, and instead gave a shrug as answer.

'Night, Elizabeth.'

'Night, Finn,' I replied, looking up as I did so. There was a smile in his eyes now and I knew. His mind had gone to the same place. I gave a quick wave as he stepped away, closed the door, threw the bolts and leant back against it.

* * *

I turned over and looked at the clock. 3 a.m. Great. I'd gone to bed after Finn had left but sleep remained elusive. Instead my mind twirled with thoughts of his laugh, our conversation and occasionally – OK, more than occasionally – his body and the way he'd made mine respond so easily. Despite my instructional words to him this evening about no sex, the truth was I hadn't wanted him to leave. He'd been the perfect gentleman and I could have kicked him. My body wanted him to stay but the sensible, rational part of my brain knew that right now, any sort of distraction was a bad idea. I'd lost the opportunity I'd been sure I was going to get. I'd been the most qualified and best placed and still it had been awarded elsewhere. I was determined not to miss out next time. I'd study more, publish more papers and show them that I was the best, the only, candidate for the next one. I had to. Otherwise, what had it all been for? But that would take even more effort and determination than I was already putting in and I didn't have time for distractions. Even when they came in such a magnificent shape as Finn Bryson.

The expansion of the museum was several months' worth of work so avoiding him wasn't an option. Now I just needed to find a way to work alongside Finn for those months without my body trying to skew my plans for its own – admittedly pleasurable – ends. And that's when I knew I had it. The perfect plan!

6

Colette, when I told her, was less convinced of my brilliance.

'Why don't you just go out with him?'

'Because I'm too busy and frankly, after the whole debacle with Friedrich, I'm just not sure I want to go through any of that again. I don't need that in my life. And right now, I need all my focus on work and putting together another application for a leadership position.'

'A relationship doesn't stop you being able to do all those things. Not if it's with the right person.'

'And you think Finn is the right person?' I said, my tone suggesting we were definitely not on the same page when it came to this subject.

'He likes you.'

'And I like him, but I'm not in the market for a boyfriend right now. But Bella is. Specifically Finn.'

'But I didn't think Finn was interested?'

'He says he isn't but you've seen Bella. And I know he's noticed her legs.'

'It's hard not to notice Bella's legs,' Colette added.

'Exactly. And from little acorns, mighty oaks grow.'

Colette breathed out a sigh and took a sip of black coffee before placing the cup back delicately on the saucer. 'I don't think this is a good idea. Trying to set people up can backfire.'

'You've tried to set me up! With Finn!'

She shrugged my argument away. 'That's different. You have history.'

'A few hours is not history. Besides, like I said, Bella is interested. I'm not.'

'Is that true, though?'

'Yes!'

'But you said you had a nice evening when you left the bar.'

'He saw me home and had a drink. He wasn't even there that long.'

'But it was nice?'

'It was nice. But friends is all we can ever be. All I can afford it to be at this point in time.'

'And, if by some miracle, Finn goes for it, how are you going to feel seeing them together?'

'Fantastic. Everything will be back to normal. I get Bella doing her work again and I don't have to think about Finn.'

'So you admit you do think about him?' Colette's expertly shaped right eyebrow lifted a fraction in question.

'You know what I mean.'

'I do, Lizzie. That's what I'm worried about.'

* * *

'Hi.' I greeted Finn with a cheery smile and pointed to the mug of coffee steaming gently on his desk. 'Good weekend?'

He glanced at it, and then me before shrugging off his jacket and hanging it on the antique coat hook in my office along with the hard hat he was regulated to wear on site. 'What are you up to?'

I put all my effort into appearing taken aback and a little wounded but Finn wasn't buying.

'Thanks for the coffee, and yeah, not a bad weekend. Quiet.'

It occurred to me that I didn't really know what Finn filled his time with outside work. Maybe there was something there that could tie in with a hobby of Bella's.

'What did you do?'

He sipped the coffee and switched on the laptop he'd now unloaded from his rucksack, waiting for it to boot up. 'A bit of DIY for my parents, went for a walk, went to the gym.' He gave a shrug. 'Stuff.'

It didn't surprise me that the gym featured in his pastimes. His certainly wasn't one of those memberships that had been taken out with all good intentions and then left to gather dust after a few visits. From what I'd seen, and could see even in his everyday clothes, Finn got full value for money from his.

Nothing he'd said gave me a clue to link to Bella but I was still determined that this was a good plan, despite Colette's misgivings and Finn's previous comment that she was too young for him. Age was just a number after all, right? But I had to be clever about this. Finn was a man who knew his own mind so – as with most men – I had to make him think that it was all his own idea...

Bella, true to form, wandered into the office although today there was more of a strut to her walk which only accentuated her slim hips and the never-ending legs which were encased in tights and trendy, tweed shorts, topped off with a white shirt and heeled ankle boots. All of which made her about level with Finn's shoulder should he be standing and me with her boobs. I remained at my desk but hadn't missed Finn glance up as she entered and reply to her casual morning greeting. Interesting. It seemed like Bella had changed her tactics. Maybe this was going to be easier than I thought...

'Hi, Lizzie. How was your weekend?'

'Yeah OK. Quiet, thanks. Yours?'

'Busy! But great. Didn't you try out that new bar on Friday? How was it?'

Finn's gaze lifted momentarily before focusing back on his work.

'It was OK. Kind of loud and packed but it was opening night so I suppose that was to be expected.'

'Sounds amazing! Late night then? I'm not surprised you stuck with a quiet weekend.'

'Oh. Yes... but I actually left early.'

'Why? Oooh! Did you meet someone?' Bella's eyes widened and she plopped down in the chair opposite me, elbows on the desk, chin on hands, and waited.

Yes.

'No, I mean... no, not like that. I just... umm. I managed to spill my drink all over me and... well, I just felt like heading home.'

'Oh.' She sat back, clearly disappointed by the absence of excitement in my weekend. 'Lizzie, you really need to embrace life more, don't you think, Finn? I mean, who knows if this is the only chance we get. You have to grab life by the horns and ride it, right?'

Her last words had been directed with her focus fully on Finn and it was clear, to me at least, there was a double meaning there. Finn's expression didn't change but he was one of the most incisive men I'd ever met and knowing Bella already had a thing for him, I doubted he'd missed the inference.

'I think you have to do what you feel is right at the time,' he replied, standing and lifting his hat from the hook and grabbing a folder from his desk.

'Isn't that the same thing though?' I said, desperate to keep him in the room a little longer for Bella to work on as well as manufacture a connection between the two of them. Finn halted and Bella paused, one hip slightly thrown out as she leant against the wall looking like a model for a high-end English *Country Life* photo shoot.

'I suppose it could be, depending on the circumstances.'

'Sounds like you two have a similar outlook on life.'

Bella's studied pout slipped into a wide smile as Finn looked over her head at me, his face impassive as he gave the smallest tilt of his head to the side that was best interpreted as a maybe.

'Have you been to that bar, Finn? I'd love to try it but none of my friends are free this week.' Bella really was taking the bull by the horns and I'd barely had to do anything. This was perfect!

'I have been, yeah. Not really my thing, I'm afraid, Bella. I'm sure you'll find someone to go with you soon enough though.'

Bella covered her crestfallen expression quickly. 'Yeah, I'm sure. We're just all so busy, you know? Got to live life and all that, right?'

He nodded, an understanding smile on his face. 'Absolutely. That's what you should be doing at your age. Taking all the opportunities you can.'

Bella forced out a laugh. 'At my age? I'm hardly a teenager, Finn!'

'No, I didn't mean that. I just meant I'm older and tend to have a preference for the quieter things in life these days.'

'Oh my God, you talk like you're ninety!'

'Some days I feel like it.'

If his aim was to put Bella off, he was doing well – but then he gave that killer smile and all the words in the world melted away into nothing.

'I'm sure that's not true at all,' she said, moving towards him.

'Oh, believe me, it is.' He checked a message on his phone. 'Sorry, I have to go. Elizabeth, there's a query on site. Have you got a minute to come down and take a look?'

'Oh. Right, of course. Is everything alright?' This extension was hugely important to the museum. We'd waited for what seemed like forever for the funding and any hint of a hitch made my nerves spring as tight as violin strings.

'Yeah, I'm sure it is but I'd rather double-check before we go ahead, just to be certain.'

'Of course.' I pushed my chair out. 'Are you OK, Bella? Do you need anything before I go? I shouldn't be long.'

'I'm fine, thanks.' She gave us both a brief smile and headed out of the office, disappearing back to the area she was currently working in as Finn and I turned the opposite way towards the lift that would take us to the basement. He pressed the button and we stood in silence until the lift arrived, then he signalled for me to go first and pressed another button as the doors slid shut. I glanced up at the numbers until Finn's words pulled my attention.

'What are you up to?'

'What?'

'You. This morning. You're all cheery and then Bella comes in all guns blazing and you're there backing her up.'

'So saying good morning and getting a coffee for the person I'm sharing an office with as I'm already getting one for myself is now suspicious?'

'A bit, yes.'

'Fine. I won't bother again.' I turned away. The coffee thing actually hadn't been part of my plan. It had just seemed like a nice thing to do.

'It's not that I'm not grateful.'

'You could have fooled me,' I said, thankful for the lift reaching the basement and the doors hauling themselves open. The building was old and the lift had been installed decades ago. It was serviced but I still opted for the stairs as often as I could, just in case.

Finn caught my arm as I exited. 'I'm sorry. It just seemed like you and Bella were...'

'Well, we weren't.' Which wasn't a total lie. Yes, both Bella and I clearly had the same end game in mind but it wasn't the joint effort Finn was suggesting which I felt justified my mildly haughty exit, causing him to drop his loosely wrapped fingers from my wrist.

* * *

'Great, thanks, Lizzie.' Mike, Finn's second in command was a man ten years his senior with a cheeky smile and a broad, Northern Irish accent. 'It's good to double-check these things, just to be sure.'

'Definitely. Especially with my boss off. If something goes wrong on it now because of something I did or didn't say...' I drew a finger across my throat and hung my tongue from the side of my mouth.

'Ah, you're grand. Don't you worry. If she'd had any doubts, she wouldn't have left you in charge.'

'I don't think she had much choice.'

The older man gave me a wink. 'People always have a choice. Even if that's to make no choice, isn't that the truth, young Finn?'

'I suppose so,' Finn replied, his tone non-committal.

'I'll head back upstairs then, if that's all?' I said.

'You all good, Finn?' Mike asked.

'Yeah. If you're OK to get on with things here, I've got some stuff back at my desk that needs my attention.'

His colleague nodded and Finn followed me back towards the lift, our actions reversed from the trip down. We rode in silence for a few seconds and then Finn suddenly moved across me, his palm punching the button that halted the lift. We came to a shuddering halt and I felt a shiver of panic rush down my spine.

'What the hell are you doing?' I snapped, my hand already reaching for the controls, desperate to start the tiny metal box back on its journey so that I could escape from it. Finn caught my hand and then the other as I changed tactic, holding them either side of me.

'I could ask you the same thing.'

'You already did and I answered you. Nothing. Now please start this bloody thing again.'

'No. Not until you tell me why you're so desperate to set me up with Bella.'

'I'm not desperate. Don't flatter yourself,' I said, anxiety firing my emotions. 'She likes you and I thought it would be nice to help her.'

'Not when there's no chance of success. I already told you, I'm not interested.'

'Unfortunately, your smile says otherwise whether intentional or not.'

He shook his head, frustration tensing the clean-shaven jaw. I'd noticed it started the week like this, lasted a couple of days as dark stubble shadowed his jaw and then the next day appeared clean shaven again. I wasn't sure which I preferred. Both were pretty damn hot.

No! Lizzie! That wasn't the way to think. Not when this idiot had purposely trapped you both in a lift!

'Like I told you, she'll get the message, but not if you start suggesting that we have things in common and building her hopes up. It doesn't do her, or me, any favours.'

'I don't know what you're talking about.'

'Yes, Elizabeth, you do.'

'Oh, I do, do I?' I said, tilting my chin up defiantly to meet his eyes.

'Yes. And I'd appreciate it if you'd stop. I know what I want and it's not Bella. You stirring things is doing more harm than good.'

His gaze was steely, his voice harsher than I'd ever heard it. The little metal box fairly hummed with tension, our eyes locked, breathing heavy.

'Elizabeth...' He moved closer and my breathing hitched as it sped up. 'Elizabeth?' His expression softened and his hands dropped from my wrists and cupped my face as tears began to flow. 'What is it? Tell me?'

'I... I can't breathe! I can't...' The panic swelled and I pulled at the collar of my shirt. 'I need to get out of here. Get me out of here!'

His hand shot out and pressed a button and the lift shuddered into life. I felt the sweat running down my spine and under my arms, my face burning with a mixture of fear, anger and relief. Right now I wasn't sure which one was uppermost and I didn't care. All I cared about was getting out of that lift. The floor number shone in the digital window, the movement stopped and the doors opened. I pushed myself out of them and headed towards the women's bathroom, ignoring Finn calling my name.

When I returned to my office, Finn was nowhere to be seen. I noticed his rucksack had gone and I had no idea where to start with regards to the emotions that were flowing through my body. So I did what I always did when life threw unexpected balls at me, I got to work. Something I should have done the night that I found out I'd lost the dig to Friedrich instead of going out and getting plastered. And that, I decided, was the plan I needed to stick to.

I woke up my screen and checked my phone. Several emails about the exhibition to deal with. Good. That would keep me occupied. There was also a message from Finn.

Elizabeth. I'm so sorry. I had no idea you were claustrophobic. I was acting on instinct because I needed to talk to you and I didn't stop to think. I was hoping to apologise in person but I've been called to a meeting on the other side of town and won't be done until later. Again, I'm sorry. I never meant to frighten you. Hurting you is the last thing in the world I'd ever want to do.

See? Just as I steeled myself to ensure all our interactions were devoid of emotion, he steps in with his size thirteens and ruins it all by sending a sensitive, caring message. But no matter. This was it. I didn't need complications in my life. I'd made a mistake with Finn once before but I'd moved on and what or who he did was up to him. I had a goal to achieve. Friedrich had snatched it out of my hands this time but I was going to find a new project and it was going to be my team and my name on the papers. I'd worked for this as long as I could remember and I wasn't about to be distracted by a six foot five solid block of muscle with a face and body modelled by angels. Been there, done that. Moving on.

* * *

It was nights like this I loved being tucked inside my house. Outside the rain was streaking the windows, blown almost horizontal by the wind that was howling down the mews. I jumped as the doorbell sounded, looked down at my dinosaur pyjamas and sighed. Perhaps if I ignored it, they'd go away. The bell sounded again. I put down my book, pushed myself up from the comfy chair and plodded towards the door. Unlocking the bolts, I turned the key and pulled the door open to reveal Finn standing there, thoroughly soaked, raindrops running off his nose and chin. The lusciously thick eyelashes he'd been blessed with were plastered together and served only to highlight intense blue eyes which were serious beneath dark, frowning brows.

'What are you doing here?'

'My meeting just finished and I wanted to make sure you were OK.'

'I'm fine, Finn. You didn't need to come and check on me.'

'I wanted to.'

'Why?'

'Because I scared you and I've felt awful about it all day.'

I drew myself up and attempted to make myself look as tough as it was possible to look dressed in fleecy pyjamas and dressing gown. 'You didn't scare me, Finn. You weren't to know I don't like enclosed spaces and I got your message apologising. It's done. Just forget about it.'

'Right. Yes, I know. I wasn't thinking and stupidly, I'd assumed from the movies I'd watched about archaeologists that you were all up for crawling through small spaces to unearth treasure.' He gave an irritated shake of his head, sending raindrops in every direction. 'I really am sorry though. Again. I'll see you at work.'

'You're right. It's not an ideal phobia for someone in my line of work. Look, Finn, you're soaked. Why don't you come in?'

'No, I'm OK, but thanks. 'night, Elizabeth.' With that, he

turned and strode across the cobbles of the mews, their shiny surfaces reflecting the soft yellow porch lights of my neighbours. I watched him go before closing the door and returning to my book. Half an hour later, I'd read the same page twelve times, my mind instead drifting back to Finn standing at my door and the almost uncontrollable urge I'd had to drag him inside and kiss away that serious expression, to bring back that smile and hear the deep rumble of his laughter. I'd noticed at the bar he had a protective streak and today's visit was merely that showing itself again. Either that or he was worried I'd report him for – I don't know – stopping a lift against the wishes of another occupant. Who knew? Today's world was crazy and the museum construction job was a prestigious one. The last thing he'd want was a black mark against his name. I tossed the book on the sofa, gave up and went to bed.

7

'Hi.'

I looked up from the email I was reading on my phone as I walked to my office a few days later to see Finn heading the same way from the direction of the work site. He looked particularly gorgeous this morning with a fresh shave, a pale blue shirt and light tan chinos, topped off with work boots. He took off the hard hat he was wearing and tucked it under his arm.

'Oh. Hi.'

'I, erm, I picked this up for you. I thought it might be of help.'

I took the leaflet he proffered and scanned my eyes over it.

'My brother went there for a fear of flying. It really seemed to do the trick.'

'Hypnosis?'

'Worth a shot.'

'Why? Are you planning to mess about in the lift again?' I looked up at him, saw the thoughts that had suddenly shown in my own mind's eye reflected there and quickly looked away.

Silence settled again, broken only by the sound of my heels

clacking on the floor. I couldn't help wishing I'd worn quieter shoes.

'How's the project going?'

'Yeah, good, thanks. All on schedule so far. How's the exhibition planning?'

'Going to plan at the moment. Hopefully everything will tie up. I've got a meeting about it later online. If you're in the office, I can wear headphones so as not to disturb you.'

'You don't disturb me.' He glanced down, as I looked up and felt a bolt shoot through me. I took a quick scan of the corridor and then gave Finn a hefty shove into the room just down from my office which we used as storage. Thankfully he was off his guard as I'd have had no chance of moving him otherwise. He stumbled back against the shelving as I shut the door.

'What do you want?'

He gave his surroundings a quick survey before looking down at me, his face scrunched in displeasure. 'I want to be in a place that there aren't long-dead people peering at me.'

'Oh for goodness' sake, it's cleaning supplies. No one's about to mummify you.'

'You're saying I'm not important enough?' He flashed a smile. 'I've been reading up.'

I squashed the little glow that he'd taken the time to further his knowledge on the subject and concentrated on the task in hand. 'Finn, I don't know what you want and frankly it's driving me crazy.'

'Crazy in a good way?'

'No! Not in a good way!' I snapped back. 'In a bad way. In a messing with my head way. We agreed to never discuss what happened again and then you go around looking all hot in a hard hat – I mean you're supposed to look like Bob the Builder but you don't. It's not fair and you absolutely refuse to have a thing with

Bella which would be perfect as it would distract everyone involved and then you turn up at my door, acting all concerned and Alpha Male but then walk straight off.'

'That's not my intention, Elizabeth.'

'Then what is your intention, Finn?'

Finn sucked in a deep breath and tipped his head back as he slowly let it out before looking down and hooking my gaze onto his.

'You really want to know what my intention is?'

'Yes!'

There was a beat of silence between us and then Finn's hands were cupping my face, his mouth on mine, hard and desperate before suddenly pulling away. 'I'm sorry. I shouldn't have—'

I wasn't listening. I reached back up for his face, not wanting the kiss he'd begun to end. Finn responded immediately, his hands wrapping around my thighs to even the height difference as my own hands linked behind his neck and my legs hooked around his waist. He drew back for breath, his eyes shining with the same smile his mouth curved into now that it was free of mine momentarily.

'Does that answer your question?'

'To an extent.'

'I'm happy to explain further,' he whispered, his lips travelling down my neck.

I let out a sigh of pleasure and felt him smile against my throat. 'I love it when you make that noise.' His voice was low, gravelly and soft and I wanted this moment to last forever. To forge it in amber like some of the exhibits in our collection. Clacking heels outside dragged us both rudely back into reality.

'Bella,' I mouthed to him.

And then another thought hit me and I slid down his body, finding my feet once again. 'We can't,' I whispered.

'What?'

'This. I can't. We can't. Bella would be—'

I didn't finish the sentence because Finn kissed me again and any thoughts I had momentarily imploded in my brain, leaving nothing but dust.

'Bella would be upset? Is that what you were going to say?' he whispered, his hand still splayed on my hip, the warmth feeling sturdy and secure.

'Something like that.'

'As I seem to remember someone wise saying recently, Bella will get over it, I'm not that great.'

I looked up at him under my lashes. 'I might have lied about the last bit.'

'But you were right about the first bit.'

'She can't know. It'd just make things too awkward.'

Finn reached for my hands and held them in his own. 'And what is it that she isn't to know, Elizabeth?'

'This!' I whispered. 'You. Me. This.'

'And what is this?'

'Didn't we just have this conversation?'

'No. Because I couldn't stop myself from kissing you which is all I've wanted to do since I met you and every time I've seen you since. But I woke up that day and you'd gone and I didn't think I'd ever see you again so I convinced myself that I was OK with that. That it was a one night stand. Admittedly an amazing one but still just a night. Then I find out Greg is head over heels for your friend and I walk in here and see you. It means something, Elizabeth. This. It's more than just stolen kisses in a...' he looked around, '...a slightly creepy store room.' He looked down at our hands. 'You asked me what I want, and what I want is for the best night I've ever had to turn into the best thing in my life. But that, of course, depends on whether you want the same.'

'You know you're the first one night stand I've ever, ever had. I had no idea that... you know...'

He gathered me closer, his body warm, hard and strong. 'I know. But I don't want to be a one night stand. Not with you.'

I tilted my head up and everything else fell away. 'I don't want that either.' The frown smoothed out and his lips once again met mine. 'I mean it about Bella though. She can't know. I don't want her upset.'

'Fine. But we're not doing anything wrong here, Elizabeth.'

'Well, getting it on in a store room is probably against the rules at work.'

'Getting it on?' He laughed and I covered his mouth with my hand.

'Shoosh! Someone will hear us. And no, I have no idea why that particular phrase came to mind. This isn't a situation I've found myself in much before. I'm unfamiliar with the correct terminology.'

'Much?'

'At all.'

'Speaking of Bella. If you do actually like me which I'm getting the very relieved impression you do, why the hell were you so desperate to hook me up with Bella?'

'Because it seemed like a good way to get you out of my head. If you weren't available there was no point thinking about you.'

Finn's expression was puzzled.

'I have plans. Ambition. I didn't want to get distracted.'

'And you think I'd distract you?'

'I know you do,' I replied, unable to hold back the smile as his hand curved around my lower back, resting on the top of my bum.

Briefly he returned the smile but his features then settled into a more serious expression. 'But you know I would never try to stop you doing anything you wanted. I think you're amazing and I know you want to get that lead on a dig. I'm here for you, Elizabeth. Well, I want to be here for you. If you'll let me.'

I opened my mouth to reply but the steps in the corridor were getting closer and I snapped it closed again. They slowed as they got near and then stopped outside the store room Wide-eyed, I looked in panic at Finn. The door was old and didn't lock so, whilst it was easy to shove Finn in here for a private discussion, it also meant we couldn't keep anyone out.

'Shit!' I mouthed at him.

Almost silently, Finn switched us around so that he was against the door. As the person outside turned the handle, he leant his full weight back against it. A few struggling noises and a choice word came through slightly muffled from the outside and I felt the giggles build inside me. My eyes widened and Finn shook his head, his own eyes fixed on me, a silent warning in their expression but I couldn't help myself. With the hand that wasn't holding the handle in place, Finn reached out and pulled me back against him, his hard body pressed into mine, his free hand covering my mouth as giggles forced themselves out and I did my best to silence them with the help of a hand the size of a small excavator.

With one last rattle of the door handle and another swear word, the steps began again, moving away until they were no longer audible.

Finn dropped his hand and looked down at me. 'You are trouble.'

I tilted my chin up and studied the wide, handsome smile.

'You don't seem too upset about it.'

He caught my chin with his hand and stole another kiss. 'Not in the slightest.'

* * *

'But you can't tell Bella!' I said as I related the morning's exploits to Colette over a bottle of wine later that evening.

'You know she's going to find out at some point, don't you?' Colette pointed out.

'I know. I just...'

'Plus you knew him first.' She took a sip of wine. 'Intimately.'

I gave her a warning look.

'Several times,' she added, grinning now.

'Shoosh!' I flapped my hand at her, laughing as we sat in the bar.

'Seriously though. She's a big girl. She'll get over it. You have to put yourself, and Finn, first. He's definitely not interested in her?'

'No. He says she's too young.'

'Ooh, an older man...' She fluttered her hand at her chest. 'Ooh la la.'

'How old is Greg?'

'Same as Finn. They were in the same class at school. Known each other since primary school.' Colette rested her chin on her hand. 'Isn't that sweet? There's something appealing about that. The loyalty. That bond.'

'Yeah, I know what you mean.' I didn't know anyone from primary school. Or secondary to be honest and only kept in touch with a few people from university and that was sporadic. Even from an early age, I'd always found enough company in my books and studies, echoing my home life where my parents had little interest outside their academic circle.

'Do you know anyone from back then?'

'A few people, yes. We tend to get together when I go back to visit Maman and Papa.'

I nodded.

'Do you think I've missed out?'

Colette put her glass down and concentrated on me. 'In what way?'

'I don't know,' I said, running my finger against the twisted stem of my wine glass. 'I suppose my field of vision has been pretty limited most of my life. I don't have a lot of friends...'

'When it comes to friends, it's about quality, not quantity, *ma chérie*.' Colette laid her hand over mine, her dark eyes serious now. 'Do you feel you've missed out?'

'I don't know. I hadn't really thought about it until now. That's just how it's always been.'

'And are you unhappy?'

'No. I don't think so.'

'I think you think too much. Maybe just go with the flow sometimes?' My friend's accented voice was gentle.

I chewed the inside of my cheek.

'OK, so with your work, you don't always know the answer, right? You can make an educated guess about what might be in that tomb or this part of the country, right?'

'Yes, I suppose so.'

'You can't control the outcome?'

I laughed. 'No, unfortunately. I'd be a rich woman if I could.'

'Then perhaps learn from that. Life can't be controlled. It just happens. And we deal with what we find when we find it.'

I rested my chin in my hands, pondering her words.

'That's very profound.'

'I know. I'm rather proud of myself.'

'You should be. You're very wise.'

'This is true,' she replied with a nonchalant flick of her wrist.

A smile tugged at the corner of my lips. 'What would I do without you?'

'Luckily we don't have to find out because you are, how do you say, stuck with me.'

I reached over and hugged her. 'Good.'

'So when are you seeing Finn next?'

'I'll see him at work, of course, but other than that, we haven't really arranged anything. I'm just "going with the flow".'

Colette clinked her wine glass against mine. 'Make it soon. He's good for you.'

'You think so?'

'I know so.'

'We'll see.'

'We will indeed.'

* * *

Bent over an artefact that had recently come into our possession after the clearance of a large manor house, I became aware of a presence beside me. My boss was eager to report to the board any information we could gain about the item since we had little knowledge of its provenance and she had already been in twice this morning to see if I'd come up with anything.

'Still working on it,' I said without looking up.

'So I see.' Unless Inis had developed a severe throat infection, I was pretty sure that the deep voice didn't belong to my boss. The flutter in my stomach confirmed it.

'Hello,' I said, as I straightened from the bent position I'd been in and stretched my back.

'Hello,' Finn replied, smiling. 'Am I interrupting?'

'Yes, but it's not unwelcome. I could do with a break.'

'You free for lunch?'

I glanced at my watch. A basic one that told the time and did bugger all else, a fact that I liked very much. The thought of a smart watch pinging, buzzing and vibrating all the time when I was trying to get on with things gave me the shivers.

'I can be.'

'Good.' Finn glanced over his shoulder before bending and kissing me straight on the lips.

'Finn!' I stepped back. 'We said not at work!' My words were whispered but my tone was vehement.

He held up his hands. 'I know, I know. Sorry. But I saw that gorgeous bum and then that gorgeous face and...' He gave a shrug.

I did my best not to smile. The unexpected kiss had been the best part of my day and frankly I wanted nothing more than to kiss him right back. But I had meant what I said. Colette was right. Bella probably would find out we were seeing each other at some point but it wasn't only that. I wanted to keep things professional at work. Friedrich's appointment as dig leader still rankled and I didn't want anyone to find any excuse, no matter how pathetic or inaccurate to use against me when I put forward my application for the next opportunity.

'I really am sorry, Elizabeth.'

'I know.' I threw my own glance around, my voice still low. 'And don't think it's not that I don't... you know...'

Finn raised a dark brow, apparently amused by my current lack of ability to put into words anything remotely personal. I knew exactly where his thoughts had gone. That first night I'd had no problem at all with communication. Quickly I pushed those images and feelings out of my mind. If I didn't, I could pretty much guarantee I'd have been served with an 'inappropriate behaviour in the workplace' warning – at the very least. But looking up at that face and knowing the body that lay under the blue checked, brushed cotton shirt, I wasn't sure I even cared. I gave myself a mental kick up the backside into the present.

Finn stood there, looking patient and ridiculously hot. 'You don't what?'

'Like you.'

His smile broadened.

'What?'

'Nothing. You're just not great at this, are you?'

'No.'

'Then stop trying so hard. Come on, let's get out of here so I can kiss you properly.'

I frowned in consternation but the truth was I was of the same mind and he knew it.

8

The door to the car opened and a damp-haired Finn looked in.

'You alright?'

'Yep,' I said, looking up from my book.

'Watching rugby not for you then?'

I screwed up my face. 'No. Not really. The third time you disappeared under about seven other massive blokes I had to leave.'

'I'm fine.'

'Which I'm very glad to hear, but it's better for my stress levels if I don't witness the mauling in between. Also, that doesn't look like fine,' I said, pointing to where his eye was starting to close below a cut just above his brow, a bruise already flowering around the entire thing. He slung his bag on the back seat and then slid behind the wheel, flipping down the sun visor to study his injury in the mirror. 'Just a scratch,' he declared with a grin, knowing that I wasn't buying it for a moment.

'Where to?'

'I think we'd better get you home before that eye closes entirely and you can't drive at all.'

He made an attempt to roll his eyes with an exaggerated sigh as he shifted into first gear, the gesture rather weakened by the fact only one was taking part.

'How's it feeling?' I asked later that evening as I handed him a fresh ice pack, wrapped in a tea towel which he placed on the affected side of his face.

'You're fussing too much,' he said, catching hold of my hand and pulling me down beside him.

'Finn, you have a massive black eye and however macho you try to be, I know it's painful.'

'I'm not *trying* to be macho. It comes naturally.'

I gave him a gentle whack with a cushion, causing him to issue a deep chuckle and wrap his arms around me. 'I mean it,' I said, looking up at him from where I now sat, resting against his chest, my legs draped over his as they stretched out, his feet on the coffee table.

'I know you do, and don't think I'm not grateful. It's actually pretty nice,' he replied.

'So why are you complaining?'

'Who said I was complaining? You just don't need to fuss over me.'

'Maybe I wanted to.' The words came out without thought and for a moment, both of us just looked at each other.

'You seem surprised,' Finn said, his voice gentle, but with a hint of enquiry.

'It's not that. It's just that I'm not used to it. I've never really been in this situation before.'

'Previous boyfriend didn't get squished in the rugby scrum too often then?'

I remembered Friedrich's complete disdain for anything sport-related.

'He wasn't really the sporty type.'

'And what if you were ill?'

'I've never really been one to make a big deal of being poorly. My parents were quite serious academics so I tended to get on with things. Luckily.' I leant forward and touched the coffee table. 'Touch wood, illness isn't something I've had to deal with a lot.'

Finn was frowning. 'They felt their work was more important than the health of their daughter?'

'No! Not at all. That came across wrong. I just meant they're not the fussy kind which is fine with me. I hate being fussed over anyway.'

'Yeah, I think I've already sussed that out. But just to let you know, if you are poorly, I will be fussing.'

'You will not!' I said, laughing.

'Try and stop me.' He bent his head and nuzzled my neck then moved to kiss my temple. I knew I wouldn't try to stop him and the feeling that somebody might want to take care of me when I felt rough was a new experience. Friedrich had been even less interested than my parents were when I was ill. They had always cared about me which is why I'd been in such a rush to correct Finn. I didn't want him thinking badly of them. But Friedrich was a different matter. He really had no interest when anyone was under the weather; his disregard wasn't just limited to me. His excuse was that he didn't know what to do but it might have been nice if he'd tried on the odd occasion. Still, that was all in the past now. I pushed myself up on the sofa a little more.

'What do you feel like for dinner?'

Finn slid one muscular arm around me and pulled me tight against his hard body. 'I feel like ordering a takeaway so that you don't have to go anywhere.'

I snuggled into him. 'Fine with me.'

* * *

The cosy bedroom looked like a small grenade had gone off in it as I tried on the fifth outfit, which had also been the first. I turned this way and that in the mirror, stepped into my shoes, yanked at the dress and was about to change out of it again when the doorbell rang.

I sucked in a deep breath then blew it out. 'I guess this is what I'm wearing then,' I told my reflection then hurried down the stairs.

'Hi,' I said, wrapping my coat around me as I opened the door to Finn.

'Ready to go?'

'Yep.' I leaned over and grabbed my clutch bag from the side before stepping out and locking the door behind me.

Finn bent to kiss me, a little less far than usual, thanks to the heels I was wearing. His hand rested on my hip as he glanced down.

'Nice shoes.' The look in his eyes caused me to momentarily consider missing the party altogether.

'Behave,' I told him, unable to stop the smile entirely.

'Oh, sweetheart. Believe me, I am and I hope you appreciate the effort it's taking me to do so.'

I shook my head at him, laughing and took the hand that he offered. We walked to the car and I slid into the passenger seat as he closed the door after me.

Once behind the wheel he started the engine then paused as he was about to pull away. 'Is everything OK?'

'Fine, yes, thanks.'

'You've suddenly gone tense.'

'I'm OK, really.'

Finn wasn't buying it. 'OK,' he replied uncertainly, clearly realising that the conversation was over.

Instead he told me about his day as we drove towards the

restaurant that Greg had booked for his birthday meal. I was glad of the distraction. The truth was that I wasn't fine and as I surreptitiously wiped my sweaty palms on a tissue, I made a mental note to scoot to the toilets when I got there to mop up what currently felt like a very sweaty cleavage and underarms. Not exactly the cool, calm image I usually liked to project.

'You really don't seem yourself.'

I guess the conversation wasn't over then.

'I'm OK, Finn. Really.'

Briefly he swung me that look again. Did anything get past this man?

'Fine. I'm nervous, OK? I'm not very good at large gatherings and I don't know anyone.'

'You know me, and Greg, and Colette.'

'Well yes, obviously.'

'Then that's all you need to worry about. Believe me, everyone is going to love you.'

I gave him a side eye that conveyed my suspicion about that particular summation, but he merely smiled and put his hand on my leg.

'They will. I promise. How could they not?'

Having made an immediate trip to the loo as soon as I got there I then returned to where Finn was waiting, now joined by Colette and Greg. I unbelted my coat and Finn slipped it off my shoulders before handing it to the cloakroom assistant. As he turned back he stopped and stared.

'Wow.'

Colette turned around from handing her own coat to Greg and repeated Finn's exclamation.

'Is that new?' she asked, automatically touching the slinky red silk of my dress.

'No. I've actually had it for ages.'

'I've never seen it.' Bearing in mind how long I'd known Colette, it was easy to understand her confusion.

'No, I've never worn it.' I gave the butter-soft bias-cut dress an unnecessary smooth down, mostly as something to do, uncomfortable and unused to being the centre of attention. Finn gently took my hands within his own, his gaze running up and down my body.

'You look stunning.' His gaze settled now on my face. 'Seriously. You should definitely wear it more often. All the time if possible.' His eyebrows waggled mischievously.

I felt the heat in my face and dropped my head a little but that didn't mean I wasn't enjoying the compliment.

'He's absolutely right,' Colette added. 'You look amazing! How come I'm only seeing this dress now?'

I was prevented from replying by a group of chattering people entering the restaurant and surrounding us, wishing Greg happy birthday as the two men made introductions.

As the night wore on I began to relax, helped a little by a glass or three of champagne. Finn had been right. Their friends were lovely and welcoming, not hesitating to make Colette and I feel like a part of their group. With the dinner finished and people chair hopping, Colette came over to chat as Greg got pulled into another conversation. I had a feeling I knew what her first question was going to be.

'So? How come I've never seen this dress before?' She repeated the question I'd managed to duck earlier.

'You're not going to let this go, are you?'

'Not now I'm not. It sounds like there's a story here.'

I could have kicked myself. 'Not a very interesting one I'm afraid.'

'I'll be the judge of that.' She made a rolling motion with her hand indicating for me to start the story.

I sucked in a deep breath, let it out and took a swig of fizz. 'I bought it for an evening gala a few years ago. I know it's pretty far from my normal style but I kind of fell in love with it.'

'I'm not surprised. It's gorgeous! So you wore it to the gala?'

'I was going to. Friedrich was staying over as he was going to the event as well.'

Colette's smile faded several degrees. 'Oh yes?'

My friend had never really been a fan of Friedrich and I knew what I said next wasn't going to do anything to improve his reputation in her eyes.

'He didn't think the dress was appropriate for a work function.'

'But I'm assuming if it was a gala, the dress code would be formal wear.'

'It was. It was a big fancy do, basically trying to get rich people to sponsor research, etcetera.'

'So the dress was entirely appropriate then. Actually, quite understated.'

'I suppose I understood what he was saying at the time.'

'And what was that?' she snapped, her dark eyes flashing with fury. 'That he was afraid you'd get more attention than him and people would realise you're twice the archaeologist he is?' She took an angry swig of her drink.

My hand reached out and rested on her arm. 'I don't think it was about that.'

'Chérie, it *was* about that. *Exactement*! It's the perfect dress for an event like that and for tonight. You look bloody amazing in it and he knew it. Once again Friedrich put himself first.'

'You never did like him.'

'Believe me, it was a mutual feeling. I never thought he was good enough for you, and that he would tread on anyone to get ahead, including his girlfriend. He always wanted you to blend into the background so that he could be front and centre and make sure all the advantages came to him.'

'I think you're reading too much into one dress. Besides, I quite like being in the background, you know that.'

'I'm not, and I do. But sometimes we have to push ourselves out of our comfort zone. I know you say it's just a dress but I'm looking at it metaphorically.'

I squinted at her glass. 'How many of those have you had?'

'I'm still irritated by your ex so clearly not enough. And like I said, I'm not reading too much into it. I don't think you're reading enough into it. Don't you think him taking the lead on a project he knew you were up for says anything?'

I felt a fresh stab of disappointment in my stomach. Colette automatically reached out. 'I'm sorry. I didn't mean to upset you.'

'I know. But that was different. He was chosen by the board.'

'But it hasn't helped that you've always been in his shadow. He made sure of it.'

'Well, that was in the past. I'm not any more.'

'No, thank God. And I love this new look.'

I chuckled. 'Don't get too excited. I'm not sure there's a whole new look coming.' I paused for a moment. 'Why, do you think I need a new look?'

'No. Not if you're happy with the current one. So long as it's your choice and not someone else's.'

I took a sip of champagne and thought about what Colette had said. Had that really been Friedrich's intention? No, it can't have been. He had loved me at the time. We had supported each other. Hadn't we?

Colette patted my hand. 'Stop dissecting it now,' she said, reading my mind. 'It's done and over. And you've definitely upgraded.' She threw a glance towards Finn and my own gaze followed. He turned as though sensing he was being watched, the blue eyes fixed directly on me. He leant towards the person nearest him, said a few words and then headed towards us.

'Everything alright?' I asked.

'Yes, but I couldn't stand being over there when you're over here looking like that.'

'It's just a dress,' I laughed. 'It's going to come off later.'

'Even better!' Finn grinned. I flicked him on the arm with my clutch bag. 'That's not what I meant.'

'Too late. The image is in here now,' he said, tapping his temple. 'Firmly rooted and growing away happily.'

Colette laughed, then excused herself and went over to where Greg was standing. She snaked her hand around his waist and he responded by cuddling her close to him as she was brought into the conversation.

9

'What secrets are you hiding?' I asked. My companion remained silent. 'Come on. You can whisper it to me...'

'You free for dinner tonight or do you already have a date?'

I jumped as the deep voice broke into the conversation I was having with the mummy currently on loan to us and which we were hoping to get permission to do a CT scan on.

'Don't creep up on me like that!' I said, turning to face Finn. 'And lower your voice.'

Finn rolled his eyes. 'It's a good job I'm not the sensitive type. I might start thinking you were ashamed to be seen with me.'

My brow creased. 'You know it's not that.'

He gave a small shrug and turned his attention to the mummy on the table in front of me. Something told me he was more sensitive than he liked to let on. I reached out, my hand brushing his momentarily. 'It's not.'

'I know,' he replied, still not looking at me. 'So, who's this?'

I pulled my own gaze from Finn's face. His feelings were currently as hidden as the identity of the body in front of us.

'We don't know. It was part of a discovery made decades ago

when methods could be a little more... heavy-handed, shall we say? The sarcophagus was obviously incredibly fragile anyway and it didn't survive. Any clues that could have been gained from that are long gone.'

'So what's he – or she – doing here?'

'She. The museum has been loaned it as part of the upcoming exhibition but we're also hoping to try and use some modern technology to unlock some of its secrets.'

'A hospital scan?'

'Yes,' I said, smiling up at him.

'I saw a programme where they did that.'

'It's been successful in some other cases. But it depends if the owners will agree to it.'

'Why wouldn't they? Surely they're curious too?'

'They are but they're also quite rightly concerned about the possibility of damage.'

'Is that likely?'

'Of course we'd be incredibly careful. The last thing we want is for any damage to incur either but it has to be transported and with all the best will in the world, accidents do happen.'

'I guess that's true.' He looked at the mummified body. A tiny bit of the wrappings had been damaged in the original excavation, according to the notes. Finn bent a little closer, his face screwing up in concentration. 'Is that hair?'

'Yes.'

His nose remained screwed up as he looked at me.

'What?'

'I don't know,' he replied, straightening. 'It's just a bit... creepy.'

'Oh. I've never felt that way.'

Finn shoved his hands in his pockets. 'I probably shouldn't have said that.'

'Why not? I want to know what you think.' The words were out before my brain discussed them with my mouth. That seemed to be happening a lot lately.

He pulled his hands out of his pockets and then put them back in. 'Well, for one, it's probably not very manly.' His gaze darted to mine, the glimmer of a smile dancing in his eyes, threatening to tilt the corners of his mouth up.

'Believe me,' I said, moving closer to him, 'I already know you can be as Alpha as you – and I – want you to be.'

At this his face broke into a wide grin accompanied by a deep rumbling laugh. Quickly he craned his neck to look up the corridor then, seeing we were alone, apart from our aged companion, he reached for me and pulled me against him, my arms automatically reaching up to wrap around his neck as he looked down. 'I knew you liked that.'

'Oh, be quiet and kiss me if you're going to.'

'Yes, ma'am.' And then he did just that, so thoroughly that when we pulled apart, we were both a little breathless.

'OK, so we've established part one of your argument doesn't hold water. What was part two?'

'Give me a minute. My brain is still a bit scrambled from that kiss.'

My brain wasn't the only thing scrambled but if I let Finn know that, neither of us were going to get any work done this afternoon. Finn cleared his throat, stretched his neck one way, then the other and straightened his shirt.

'Right.' He looked down at the mummy, still with a hint of face scrunch, but also with a sense of curiosity and fascination that fought against the rest of it. 'I never want you to think that I don't respect what you do.' His gaze, intense this time, shifted to mine. 'I really do.'

'I know.' It was the truth. From the moment I'd met Finn and he'd discovered what I did, he'd been interested, asking questions and wanting to know about my day. He obviously still wasn't entirely comfortable with the idea that there was a dead body lying on the table in front of us but I understood that. Colette had been the same when she'd visited me one time and I'd been super excited about some new research and made the mistake of thinking she'd be as hyped as me. Her reaction had been similar to Finn's but multiplied. Had I thought about it, I would never have shown her. Colette had once passed out from a nasty paper cut. Explaining a particular aspect of mummification in order to set the scene probably wasn't one of my finest ideas. The first clue I'd got was when she'd begun to turn an unusual shade of green. The second was when she'd thrown up in my wastepaper basket.

Oh God.

'You're not going to throw up, are you?' I asked, glancing around in readiness to grab the nearest suitable receptacle.

'Not that I'm aware of,' Finn replied. 'Why?'

'I'll tell you later,' I said, recklessly snuggling against him for another cuddle.

He bent his head as his arms wrapped tighter around me, warm breath tickling my ear as he replied. 'I look forward to it.'

Footsteps in the corridor launched a massive pin into our bubble of contentment. As I pulled away, I caught a glance at Finn's face.

'I can't let them think I'm not professional,' I whispered.

Finn let out a sigh and I wasn't sure if it was directed at me, or the situation. Maybe both. Either way, I understood and frankly, felt the same.

'No one thinks that,' he said quietly. 'But you're allowed to have a life.'

'I do have a life,' I replied hurriedly.

Finn's eyes darted to the mummy. 'Outside work, I meant. With people who are alive.'

'So did I.' Our eyes met and for a moment there was nothing to say. 'I don't expect you to understand,' I whispered.

'I understand. I promise.'

The footsteps slowed as they got to the door and turned in to the room. Behind me, Finn brushed his fingers against mine, momentarily linking our little fingers and I felt a wave of tension release. I didn't want to argue with Finn. And, unlike Friedrich, I sensed that he meant what he said.

'Oh, hi, Finn.' Inis smiled as she entered. 'How are you?'

'Good, thanks. How's you?'

She glanced at her watch. 'It's past twelve now so I'll start to feel more human again soon.'

'Morning sickness can be rough from what I understand. I know my sister went through the mill with it. Anything you need? I'm heading out to get a sandwich.'

'Would you mind? I'd love some Peperami sticks.'

'No problem. Large pack?'

'Could you get me three large packs?'

Finn's laugh wound around my senses and ended up in areas it had no place being during working hours. 'That's quite the craving.'

'You think? They'll be gone by the end of the day.' She handed him a bank note from a pocket in her dress.

'Consider it done. Do you want anything, Elizabeth?'

I shook my head. What I wanted wasn't something you could buy and certainly not something I could say in front of my boss. But apparently I didn't need to voice that to Finn, he could see straight through me, and the private smile he gave me as his back turned briefly to my boss confirmed it. I only hoped that Inis couldn't read me as well. Finn nodded and left the room.

'Well, that's brightened up my day.' Inis laughed. 'What was he doing down here?' Her question sounded innocent but I had an underlying feeling that it was as loaded as Tutankhamun's tomb back in 1922.

'Just querying something about a display area on the plan.'

Inis nodded. I was such a shit liar. 'Bella has quite the crush on him.'

'Mmhmm.' I was ostensibly concentrating on the exhibit but in truth trying to regain my studied air of calm.

'Personally I think she's a little young for him. And I get the feeling he has the same opinion.'

'Oh?' I said, trying not to sound too interested when in fact I wanted *all* the gossip she had.

'Don't you think he would have reciprocated the attention if he was interested? It's pretty hard not to notice she likes him.'

'Maybe he just wants to keep things professional at work,' I said with a casual shrug.

Inis sat down with a relieved sigh. 'I wouldn't have any objections to it, so long as it didn't interfere with work.'

'I'm sure it wouldn't.'

'I agree. And Finn seems like the sensible type.'

'Yes, I suppose so.'

'He's very nice. Thoughtful. Did you know he had a sister?'

'No,' I replied. I knew a whole lot more intimate things about him but that was something he'd yet to share. Was that odd? I'd told him about my parents and he'd made a comment about us being a very cerebral family, teasing me that I might be ashamed of dating anyone without an Oxbridge education. But was he keeping his own secrets from his family? See? This was why I'd been determined to avoid relationships. They messed with your head – and heart. I redoubled my efforts on my studies, taking notes and comparing them to those that had already been made on the mystery mummy.

'Lizzie?'

I jumped, caught up in my own muddled thoughts.

'Sorry!' I straightened quickly, for a moment forgetting my boss was there.

'Perhaps it would do you good to have some distraction?'

My brows pulled together.

'All work and no play, Lizzie...' She let the sentence hang. 'You're an excellent archaeologist and a wonderful curator.'

'I sense a but coming.'

Inis smiled. 'But... it's OK to have interests outside work too.'

'I do.'

My boss's eyebrows raised in suggestion that she thought I may be telling a porkie.

'I do!'

Inis raised her hands in a calming motion. 'I'm sure you do. I suppose what I'm trying to say is that life is about more than work.'

'I know. I just happen to enjoy my subject very much. I know reading and taking trips to study one's area of expertise outside work may not seem like fun to some people but it is to me.' My tone had switched to defensive and I wasn't entirely sure why. It's not like Inis was the first person to make such a suggestion but I would have thought she'd have been the first to understand.

'I know. And believe me, I'm eternally grateful you chose to come to work here. Especially now. I know that whatever happens, things are in safe hands.'

Something in her tone made me look up. I crossed to where she was sitting and plopped myself down on the floor in front of her. Without thinking, I took her hands. 'It's going to be OK you know. You're strong and this baby has yours and Eric's genes. He or she is a tough cookie and it's all going to be perfect. OK?'

Inis nodded, a smile flashing briefly on her elfin face. I couldn't pretend to know what she was going through worrying about the baby. The midwife had done her best to reassure the couple but it was only natural they'd have concerns, especially as it was their first baby and Inis had joked she was the oldest in the pre-natal classes they'd been attending. She'd made light of it but in that moment it was clear that being an 'older' mother was another layer of anxiety.

She squeezed my hands before releasing them to wipe away a tear with the back of her hand. 'Sorry. Not very professional of me.'

'Don't be daft. We're human first, professionals second.'

Inis looked at me for a couple of beats before taking my hands again. 'Thank you.'

A knock at the open door made her start but I placed a light pressure on her hand, conveying the message to stay where she was.

'It's only me. Am I interrupting?' Finn's voice was hesitant.

I looked back to Inis. She turned and waved him in. 'No, I'm just having a moment. But you're not allowed to tell anyone.'

Finn handed her the bag with her goodies in it and the change before holding up a hand in a boy-scout salute. 'My lips are sealed.'

'Thanks, Finn.'

He shifted his weight, glanced at me then back to Inis.

'Whatever it is, spit it out, Finn.' Inis laughed.

'OK, stop me if I'm overstepping any boundaries but I've seen this before. My sister wanted to try and do all the things she was doing before, but she was pregnant and suffering with bad morning sickness and got exhausted. You're growing a human –

that's no small feat! It's OK not to do everything. You know what's important.' He finished talking and let out a breath through his teeth. 'Feel free to put in a complaint about me.'

Inis made to stand and Finn put out a hand which she took willingly. Behind her, I pushed myself up off the floor and dusted off my bum automatically despite the fact that the place was kept meticulously clean for the exhibits.

'The only reason I will put in a complaint is if you don't give me a hug right now as you've made me cry. Again.'

Finn obeyed and Inis caught his face between her palms as she stepped back. 'Your sister is lucky to have you.'

'I'm pretty sure it's the other way around but thank you. Now, do you need a lift home?'

'No, but thanks. I am going to go home though, if that's alright, Lizzie?'

'Of course it is. How are you getting there?'

'The train. I'll be fine. The walk to the station will do me good.'

Finn's dark brows drew together. 'I'd really rather take you.'

'Finn, you've done more than enough. I'm sure you have plenty to do here.'

'Nothing that can't wait.'

My boss hesitated for a moment as the faint rumble of thunder drifted through the single pane glass of the old building.

'It's supposed to pour with rain,' I added.

'Fair enough. You two win. Although how you got the weather to collude with you, I don't know.'

Finn tapped the side of his nose. 'Some things have to remain a secret.'

'Are you sure you don't need me for anything, Lizzie?'

'No, I'm fine. I'll message if I do. But please go home and rest.'

As she nodded, Finn and I saw tears glistening in her eyes.

'Bloody hormones,' she said as she rummaged in a pocket then dried her eyes and blew her nose with the tissue she'd pulled out, giving me a wave as she did so. As they left, Finn glanced over his shoulder and gave me a wink.

'Right,' I said, turning back to my 3000-year-old friend, 'you need to help me knuckle down here and distract me from perhaps the hottest man I've ever met.'

Still nothing.

'Yes, OK, *the* hottest man I've ever met.'

* * *

You never answered me.

I was typing up my notes when my phone lit up with a message.

About what?

I felt the smile on my face at the simple communication. This was ridiculous, I told myself. But I didn't stop smiling.

Dinner. Tonight.

Oh. Yes. Well we got a bit distracted...

Finn sent a little devil face emoji followed by a winky one.

Dinner sounds lovely. Thanks.

Great. I've got a meeting off site this afternoon but I can pick you up after that. Seven?

I can get the Tube.

I'd rather pick you up. It's gives me more time with you.

OK. Thank you.

A row of grinning faces appeared before his next message.

Have a good afternoon. See you later xx

And you. Hope the meeting goes well.

Xx

* * *

'No Finn this afternoon?' Bella asked, glancing over at the empty desk as she waited for me to look over a query.

'No,' I replied without looking up. 'Some meeting or other.'

She plonked herself on the corner of my desk. Her sartorial choices today were more casual than they had been since Finn had started and I wondered if she was, hopefully, turning her attentions elsewhere. I still felt awkward whenever I thought too much about the fact that Finn and I were seeing each other, knowing that Bella was interested in him. Both Colette and Finn had told me I was worrying too much. He wasn't interested in her, and rationally I knew that, but I'd be happier if she decided he wasn't all that great after all. Even though I knew for a fact he most definitely was – and more.

'Do you still see Friedrich?'

I paused momentarily in my work, surprised by the question.

'Umm, no, not really. Why do you ask?'

'I just wondered. I know you were together for a while and then he got the lead in that dig...'

I looked up at her, waiting for her to continue. She slid off the desk and made a point of peering at some old photographs on the wall, her back now to me. 'Everyone knows you have a huge amount of expertise in ancient Egypt. I didn't know if he'd approached you to be on the team.'

'I see.' I didn't really but then again I also knew that it didn't matter what kind of workplace you were in, gossip would always be there. Academic circles were no different. 'No. He hasn't.'

'Oh. Right.'

'This is fine,' I said, handing back the document. 'Thanks.'

Bella took it and turned to leave. As she got to the door, she paused. 'You know we all think you should have been given that dig.'

I gave a brief smile. 'Thanks, Bella.'

Obviously I did too, but had I been chosen, it was highly unlikely that I'd have got as ravingly drunk as I had that night so that none of the events that had followed during the course of the evening would have happened. And although part of me was still steaming from being passed over, there was, much to my surprise, another part prodding at me that perhaps, just perhaps, I wasn't meant to get that role. Perhaps I was meant to go out, get drunk, have my first (and likely last) ever one night stand and meet a man who, in any other circumstances, I wouldn't have considered. Not because there was anything wrong with him – far from it! But because he wasn't an academic. I'd gone through university and my career only ever taking an interest in men from that small pond. It had seemed the natural way. We would have things in common, plenty to talk about and understand each other's careers and the pressures involved. And maybe deep down there was another reason that I didn't like to think about. The possibility that anyone outside that circle wouldn't be interested in me. That I'd be back to being the swot, the boring one, the one that didn't get invited to parties because they 'didn't think I'd be interested'. But one drunken night when I'd thrown all my caution to the wind and champagne, things had changed for the better. I was having my eyes opened to new things. Colette had done her best but she'd always known that I had my comfort zone and hadn't wanted to upset me by pushing me out of it. But Finn hadn't been aware of the barriers, limitations and rules I'd set for myself. He'd just walked in and begun turning everything I thought I knew about myself upside down. And I loved it.

10

'You look beautiful,' Finn said, his eyes roving over me as he bent to kiss my neck while I turned to lock my front door. 'And smell just as good.'

'It's a new perfume. Do you like it?'

'Very much so,' he replied.

'Good,' I grinned as his lips left my neck and closed in on mine.

After my epiphany in the office, I'd stopped at Boots on the way home on a whim to buy myself a bottle of expensive, luxury perfume. Colette didn't even go to the corner shop without a squirt of Chanel No.5 but I'd always made do with a can of Impulse. She'd tried many times over the years to convert me. To explain that it's not just about smelling nice. It's the treat. The self care. The 'I'm not going anywhere and I'm still going to wear expensive perfume because I can'. I'd never been convinced.

But then the moment I sprayed the perfume on my pulse points this evening, I got it. Colette had been right. I wasn't doing this for Finn. I knew myself well enough for that. But it gave me a boost.

'How did the meeting go?' I asked when Finn slid behind the wheel, having opened the door for me and snuck another kiss before closing it.

'Good, thanks. It could be a real opportunity but it's early days yet so I'm not going to focus on it too much.'

'I get that.' I'd spent months focusing on the possibility of finally getting to lead a dig and look where that had ended. 'I'm glad it went well for you though.'

'Thanks,' he said, glancing momentarily across before focusing back on the slow traffic in front of us. Was it me, or had there been a shadow in his eyes when he'd turned.

'Is everything alright?'

'Yep.' He turned briefly again, this time his beautiful smile at full wattage. 'How was your afternoon?'

'OK. Nothing extraordinary.'

'No mummies rising from the dead and reincarnating themselves by sucking the life out of hapless museum staff?'

I shook my head. 'I can't believe that's your favourite film.'

'*The Mummy*? It's brilliant. And don't you think it's kind of serendipitous? You working with them and me loving the film.'

'There's really not a lot to correlate with what's in that film and what I do for a living.'

'Did you watch it yet?'

I shook my head. 'Not yet.'

'You have to! I reckon you'll love it.' His boyish enthusiasm made me laugh. 'OK there's a lot of belief to suspend, especially for you, but you'll get all the references about Egypt and the history stuff. And it's funny.'

I remembered Friedrich's disgust whenever he caught sight of clips of, or adverts for, any such films.

'It's a serious subject. They're just making a mockery of it all. It's pathetic.' He'd sniff and dismiss them. As he didn't own a television, something he seemed rather proud of, luckily the conversation didn't come up too often but I did remember one poor date of Colette's get short shrift from him when he'd mentioned being a fan of the same film in a vain attempt to find some sort of connection on a double date. Colette had been livid and I'd been mortified. I'd pulled Friedrich aside and attempted to explain that his comments had, and I was sure in error, come across as rude but he'd been unapologetic. It was moments like that that I'd had doubts about our relationship but for the most part we had surrounded ourselves with like-minded people and for them, Friedrich was charm itself. It wasn't surprising that he and my best friend hadn't got along. Something I'd regretted constantly. But in the end, after years together and subconsciously accepting that we were a permanent thing and one day, when our careers gave us time, we'd likely make it official, I'd discovered that Friedrich had been seeing a young intern on the side and that had been the end of that.

'You're quiet over there. You OK?'

'Yes, sorry. Miles away.'

'Anywhere interesting?' Finn asked.

'No,' I answered. 'Nowhere important at all. So where are we eating?'

* * *

'Here?' I peered at the cosy, romantic restaurant tucked down a lane. I'd held on to Finn's hand as he took us this then that way before we ended up at the small, brick-fronted building with large, filigree frosted windows. Old-fashioned gas-style lamps burned outside casting puddles of warm light onto the cobbles.

'Is that OK?' Finn looked down at me, his expression serious.

'Yes! I've always wanted to go here.'

The frown cleared and the smile returned. 'Oh, good! I thought I'd messed up.'

'No, not at all. I just... my previous boyfriend thought it was "too romantic".'

Finn let out a surprised laugh then quickly cut it short. 'Sorry. I didn't mean to laugh. It's just that... how can something be too romantic? Isn't that the whole point?'

'That's what I thought but I suppose it depends on who you're talking to.'

I moved towards the door but Finn held back. 'What's wrong?'

'If this place brings back unpleasant memories, we can go somewhere else. Selfishly, I don't want you sitting in there thinking about your ex.'

I reached back and took his hand. He let me pull him closer. 'That is most certainly not going to be the case.'

The smile I knew that I was falling in love with tilted his mouth. 'I'm very glad to hear that.'

'Come on,' I said, tugging his hand. 'I'm starving.'

Finn reached over me to push open the door and we entered into the cosseted, intimate feel of the restaurant.

'Room for pudding?' Finn asked once the main course plates had been cleared away.

I shook my head. 'I'm so full already. Everything was delicious.'

'Want to share something?'

'You really want pudding, don't you?' I laughed. 'It's fine to have one without me having one too.'

He gave a little wiggle of his head and wrinkled his nose.

'It is!' I said, laughing as I reached for his hand resting on the crisp white linen tablecloth. His hand turned, enclosing mine within it, his thumb gently brushing against my palm.

'I know. But it's nice to share.'

'OK then.' I'd seen some desserts passing by and they did look incredibly tempting. Everything with Finn was so much more relaxed. So easy. Before I'd met him, my life had been totally structured. I wasn't hungry so I didn't need the pudding. But what about the occasional indulgence? That was OK, wasn't it? Was I really going to lie on my death bed thinking, I'm so glad I didn't have that melting chocolate pud that time? The more likely scenario was quite the opposite. What was it they said? It's the things you didn't do you regret, not the things you did.

'I just need to nip to the loo. Choose whatever you want.'

'I'll wait until you come back. We can choose together.' His hand released mine and I grabbed my clutch and headed towards the back of the restaurant. I could feel the smile on my face and had no interest in trying to cover it. But then I saw something that wiped it off completely. I dipped my head and hurried on my way.

'Lizzie?' Friedrich noticed me as I made my way back towards Finn. I drew on all I could remember from senior school drama class and acted surprised at the sound of someone calling my name.

'Oh. Hello.' I turned towards his table. 'Hi, Bella.'

'Hi, Lizzie,' she replied. She'd drawn herself up from the intimate attitude they'd both been in when I'd passed earlier, so absorbed in their conversation – and apparently each other – that they hadn't noticed me. But I didn't miss the flicker of insecurity behind her eyes as she greeted me.

'I didn't expect to see you here,' Friedrich said.

I could say the same.

'Turns out it's a lovely restaurant,' I replied, unable to restrain the opportunity for the dig.

'Yes, it is. You look well.'

'Thanks.' He was clearly waiting for the compliment to be returned but I didn't feel the need. I could be civil but it was there I drew the line. I'd had the time and distance now to see that our relationship, although long, hadn't actually been all that good for me. I'd been a supporting role to Friedrich's lead. And then with no warning, it was over leaving me to find a place to live and rearrange my life whilst still trying to keep on top of my job. I was past caring now. But the arrival of Bella onto the scene had me intrigued. It did, however, explain her apparently random question about him earlier on today. Perhaps not so random after all.

'Well, have a nice evening,' I said, nodding to them both.

'Who are you here with?' Friedrich asked as I turned to leave. Bella looked up, also interested.

'A friend.'

'Anyone I know?'

'No.'

He looked surprised at this, and a little disbelieving. We operated within a relatively small field; he, like I, had only really ever dated within this circle. But frankly, I was pretty damn happy I'd broken out into the wider world.

'Bye, Friedrich. See you tomorrow, Bella.'

She nodded and gave a smile that did its best to hide a tinge of awkwardness. I wasn't always the greatest at reading people – at least not ones that hadn't been dead a few thousand years – but even I could tell she wasn't as sure of herself as she was trying to pretend.

'Do you mind if we leave?' I said as I sat down.

'Er, no. Not at all,' Finn replied, already signalling to a waiter for the bill. Another difference. Previously I'd have had to give a dissertation on my reasons. But Finn just read my face and acted accordingly. 'Are you OK? Are you ill?'

I shook my head as I reached into my bag to retrieve my credit card.

'I'm getting this,' Finn said. I met his eyes and saw he wasn't prepared for it to be a discussion.

'Fine. But I'm getting the next one.'

'Maybe,' he said with a wink.

'The world's moved on, you know.'

'I know,' he replied calmly. 'And I know you're fully able and prepared to pay. I just want to. It makes me happy to spend money doing nice things with people I... care about.' I saw his Adam's apple bob as he spoke and felt a strange feeling in my stomach. Had he been about to say something else? Had I wanted him to? I gave myself a mental head shake. We'd only been seeing each other a short time. I was being ridiculous. Seeing my ex and Bella together had scrambled my thoughts. All I needed was some fresh air and a little distance between them and me.

The waiter retrieved our coats and Finn took mine from him, holding it for me to slip my arms into before putting on his own charcoal grey wool pea coat. He took my hand and we headed out of the restaurant.

'What's up?' Finn asked when we were outside, a few steps away from the doorway.

'Finn!' Bella's voice carried on the crisp, cold night air.

Finn turned towards the call. 'Hi, Bella.' His eyes darted briefly to me as he replied, a question in the depths of the blue. Friedrich followed her out and was now standing behind her, his pale eyes roving over the scene, scanning me, then Finn before he took a vape stick from his jacket pocket and began puffing away like a wiry German dragon, clouds of vapour engulfing him periodically. He made no attempt to introduce himself to Finn.

'I didn't expect to see you here,' Bella said pointedly. 'We saw Lizzie inside but she didn't mention she was here with you.'

A tiny muscle in Finn's jaw flickered as his face tightened. He gave a non-committal half smile, half shrug in answer.

'So how long has this been going on?' Bella asked, clearly not intending to give up that line of questioning just yet. There was a hint of something steely beneath the apparently jovial tone.

'Not long,' Finn and I replied at the same time, although my response had a touch more hurry to it. The jaw muscle twitched again.

'Well,' Bella said, turning to me. 'You kept that quiet. Does Inis know?'

'Yes,' Finn answered before I had a chance to.

It took all the effort I had not to spin my head towards him. *Does she?*

'Oh...' Bella said, momentarily knocked off her stride before changing tack. 'I guess it's just me that's been kept in the dark.' She turned to her date. 'This is Finn. He's working at the museum.'

Friedrich's eyebrows rose the smallest amount as he finally deigned to speak. 'Not like you to mix business and pleasure, Lizzie.'

I liked Bella but I'd had just about enough of her stirring while she was stood there with my ex. I didn't care who Friedrich – or Bella – dated but being made to feel like I was doing something wrong was getting on my nerves.

'And how did you two meet?' I asked with a smile.

Bella faltered for a moment.

'I contacted Bella.' Friedrich announced airily. 'I remembered her from when you and I were together.'

Beside me, Finn shifted his not inconsiderable weight and I felt his glance slide to me.

'I expect you heard I got the lead on a dig next year.'

Of course I had, just as he would have heard it was one I'd applied for.

'I did. Congratulations.'

'Thank you. I'm putting together my team.'

'I see.' I wasn't the slightest bit interested in what he did and right now just wanted to get away from both of them. What had been a lovely evening now had a mile wide streak of discomfort and awkwardness running through it. The sooner we left, the sooner Finn and I could attempt to claw back the cosy, romantic atmosphere that had surrounded us prior to my trip to the Ladies. Although I got the feeling he would have questions. 'Well, we'd better—'

'That's why I contacted Bella.'

Bella threw him a wide smile, snuggling closer. To my surprise, he accepted the attention. He'd never been one to show emotions publicly. PDAs were common and unnecessary he'd told me once when I'd been excited about something and given him a hug when he'd met me from work.

I knew I should leave now. But he'd dangled the worm, knowing I wouldn't be able to resist biting and be reeled in.

'Oh?'

'Yes. You always said she was a useful and knowledgeable archaeologist. You were absolutely right.'

'I'm going to be on the team!' Bella squealed excitedly, unable to contain her delight.

She missed the sharp look Friedrich threw her as she broke the news before he could.

'Oh...' For a moment I was lost for words.

'Inis doesn't know yet. I'm going to speak to her tomorrow.'

'I hope you don't mind,' he said, a cool smile accompanying the words.

Mind you poaching my staff, and taking them to a restaurant you refused to take me to?

'Not at all,' I said. 'It's a great opportunity, Bella. Congratulations.'

'Thanks. I was going to tell you tomorrow too. Obviously.'

'Nice to see you, Bella.' Finn stepped into the conversation. 'Our parking is about to expire so I'm going to have to steal Elizabeth away.'

'Oh.' Bella looked put out. 'Right. I thought maybe we could go for a drink all together.'

Friedrich looked momentarily horrified. He never had mastered, or even attempted, to keep his thoughts to himself.

'That sounds great, but maybe another time,' Finn said, a note of steel to his voice that brooked no argument.

'Yeah. That'd be fab.'

He nodded and Bella sent him the full wattage smile she'd given my ex earlier. 'Lovely to see you. We missed you at work today.' She gave him a wink before wrapping her arms around his neck for a hug. Finn accepted the hug briefly before gently stepping back. Bella's slight sway on the four inch heels suggested there had been some celebrating this evening already.

'Ready, Elizabeth?'

More than ready. I turned away from the two, wrapping my coat tighter around me as I did so. Finn took my hand and we walked away.

* * *

He didn't speak until we were back at the car. The northerly wind had funnelled down the street straight at us, taking our breath away and clouds were building, covering the full moon that, away from the light pollution, was likely casting its ethereal light over the landscape, shimmering in lakes and rippling on the sea.

'So that's your ex.'

'Yes.'

'Quite the charmer.'

'Not really.'

'Bella seems quite taken with him.'

'Well, he can be charming when he wants something.'

'You were together several years, you said. And planned to get married.'

'We had a lot in common.'

'Right.'

'That was a very loaded word.'

Finn ignored my reply. 'Are you upset about him and Bella?'

I turned from watching the rain that had begun to streak the windows, the raindrops chasing each other, racing to be first to the bottom.

'No, not at all.'

'So why did we have to leave the restaurant so suddenly?'

'It wasn't because of that.'

'So why not come back and just tell me that you'd seen them? I thought we were staying for pudding and coffee.'

'Are you angry?'

'No.'

'You sound angry.'

His voice was calm but there was a tension to it that I hadn't heard before. 'I'm confused.'

'About what?'

'I just told you.'

'Finn, I'm tired. Can we talk about this tomorrow?'

'At work? Or do you want me to meet you three streets away in a café no one from work will ever go to?'

'What's up with you?' I snapped.

'I'm fed up of not knowing where I stand with you.'

'What's that supposed to mean?'

Finn pulled the car to the side of the road before turning to face me. 'You wanted to get out of there tonight so that Bella wouldn't see us together.'

I opened my mouth to reply.

'The truth, Elizabeth.'

'OK, yes. I did.'

'Why?'

'I already told you.'

'No, you didn't.'

'It's not professional.'

'I don't even work for the museum!' He threw up his hands. 'There's nothing in your contract to say you can't date colleagues anyway, even if I was.'

'How the hell do you know what's in my contract?'

'Inis told me when I took her home that day.'

'Why? And while we're on the subject, who the hell gave you permission to tell her about us?'

'I didn't. She's not stupid. She knew.'

'How?'

'I don't know, but she did. And you know what? I'm glad.'

'Well I'm not!' I snapped out before thinking.

Finn's brow flickered into a frown before his face cleared of all expression and he turned back to the wheel. 'I'll take you home.'

My stomach twisted and I felt the deliciously rich food of earlier now sitting leaden in it.

'I didn't mean that the way it sounded.'

'It's fine, Elizabeth. It's been a long day and I get you're upset about your ex fiancé and Bella.'

'My very *ex* fiancé and no, not in the way you think.'

'How do you know what I think, Elizabeth?'

'What do you mean?'

'Have you any idea what I think about things? Or do you just assume that I couldn't possibly understand that you're upset because, not only has your ex been selected for a position that you feel should have been yours, but he's also rubbed it in by offering a place in the team to a member of your own staff. And done so by charming her at a restaurant he refused to take you to.'

I stayed silent.

'Just because I'm not an academic doesn't mean I don't understand things.' He turned back towards the wheel and started the engine. 'In fact, I think I understand things pretty well.'

The rest of the journey was undertaken in a silence so thick I could have cut it with a spoon. Finn pulled in to the parking area for the mews and turned off the engine.

'I'll walk you to the door.'

'You don't need to do that.'

'I'd rather.' He got out before I could argue any further. Finn pushed the door closed after me and beeped the car locked before ramming his hands into his pockets. The short walk to my front door was again made in silence. The cobbles beneath our feet were shiny from the rain that had now stopped.

'I'm sorry the evening turned sour.'

Finn shook his head. 'These things happen. I am sorry you were upset though.'

'I'm not really. Just surprised. I thought Bella might have told me she was having a meeting with him. She asked if we still saw each other earlier today.'

'And what did you say?'

I tilted my head back to meet his eyes. 'The truth. That we didn't. And before you ask, or don't ask, I prefer it that way. I thought it was a bit of a random question at the time but it certainly all makes sense now.'

'But you wanted a place on the team?'

'I'd rather perform self-mummification!'

Finn let out a bark of laughter before his features settled back into their previous serious expression.

'That's a hard no then?'

'I know it probably seems petty to you. And it will be a great experience for Bella. Yes, I would have liked to have been told that she was meeting him, but then again perhaps she just thought it was a date.'

'I've a feeling Bella is smarter than that.'

'I was trying to give her the benefit of the doubt. But I have no desire to be working underneath Friedrich.'

'So to speak.'

I gave Finn a look.

'Sorry. Open door. My level of humour.'

Splats of rain began to bounce on the floor around us. 'Do you want to come in?'

Finn shook his head. 'No, thanks. It's been a long day. Probably best if I get home.'

'Right.' Disappointment flooded through me but I did my best to keep any trace out of my voice. 'Finn?'

'Yes?'

'I've never thought you, or your intelligence, is any less just because you don't work in the same field as me and I'm sorry if I ever did anything that made it appear that way.'

'OK.'

'I've worked hard to get where I am and I didn't want to give anyone an excuse to think I'm doing something that could be classed as "unprofessional".'

'Like seeing someone who isn't an archaeologist?'

'No!' I replied, automatically reaching out and closing my hand around his arm. 'Not at all! I just don't want people thinking I'm not entirely dedicated to my work.'

Finn swallowed, his Adam's apple bobbing. 'Right. Well, I

don't think anyone thinks that in the slightest, but I'm not stupid. I do understand why you might have concerns that women can still be judged, or held to different standards and something tells me the academic world probably isn't the most advanced when it comes to sexual equality.'

'Depends who you speak to. I'm lucky to have Inis as my boss but... I guess the decision by the board to give the lead position to someone else – particularly Friedrich, is still stinging more than I thought.'

'I get that. And I'm sorry if anything I've done has made things difficult for you.'

I shook my head, my hair slowly plastering itself to my head. I needed to get this misunderstanding with Finn sorted. All my life I'd been led by my head. Made the sensible decision. Until the night I'd met Finn.

That night I'd followed my heart. Admittedly that heart was pumping blood heavily diluted by alcohol but even so. For once, I hadn't taken the prudent path. And although I'd regretted it the next morning (God knew I hadn't regretted a single second that night), that feeling of regret hadn't lasted long. And then I'd done it again. I'd said yes to going out with Finn. Even though the sensible, steady part of me was kicking and screaming that this wasn't the right decision, the other part of me had told it to sit down and shut up and stunned, it had obeyed. The result was that I'd been enjoying myself more than I had in years.

My life had begun to expand outside my career. Colette had teased that I had a glow about me. I'd laughed it off but maybe she was right. Looking at Finn now, I realised how it had seemed from his perspective. He'd done his best to understand but trying to shove him furtively out of the restaurant tonight had been a step too far. Right now, both my head and my heart were telling me that there was every chance I had messed up the best thing that had happened to me in years.

'Night, Elizabeth.' Finn bent and kissed my cheek and I knew for sure. What I didn't know was how to fix it.

'Please don't leave, Finn.'

He turned back to face me. It was hard to see his expression now, his face in shadow. 'I think it's best.' He reached for my hand and held it for a moment. 'Go inside now. You're soaked.'

'I don't care.'

'But I do.'

'Do you?'

Finn faced me, shifting as he did so. Now I could see his expression and it was incredulous. 'You really don't know me at all if you think I can switch that off after one evening, Elizabeth.'

'I don't want you to switch it off. I want to fix this.' I swallowed but the lump in my throat refused to shift. 'But that depends on you. If that's something you want too.'

Finn let out an audible sigh.

'Elizabeth...' Finn shook his head and I felt my stomach drop and steady, sensible Lizzie was shoved unceremoniously out of the way by the woman who had for once thrown caution to the wind and found a glimpse of happiness not only when she wasn't looking for it, but without a clue that she was even missing it. But now I'd had a taste. The door was open and I was terrified it was going to shut and I'd be forever looking through the glass at that sliver of delight I'd had the chance at and thrown away by worrying too much what other people thought.

'Finn, I—' I didn't get to finish the sentence because he'd placed his hands either side of my face, his gaze locked on mine, intense and serious.

'I've wanted this, you, since I first met you. You're completely different from anyone I've ever met and I *feel* completely differ-

ently about you from anyone I've ever met. I don't do this. I don't
do one night stands and fall in love there and then. I don't get
hurt because I start thinking I'm not enough for that woman—'

'You are! You're more than—'

Finn's lips were on mine and I wriggled my arms free to wrap
them around his neck, pulling him as close as I could. His words
were flying about in my head but I'd deal with those in a
moment. Right now I just needed to know that I hadn't lost the
best thing that had ever happened to me. Slowly the kiss broke
apart.

'Enough.' I smiled, finishing the sentence I'd begun.

'Sorry. I couldn't wait.'

'I'm not complaining.'

'Always good to hear.' He chuckled and I bumped against him.
'Finn?'

'Yes?'

'Did you say... that... umm...'

'I love you? Yes. Are you freaked out?' We'd both squeezed
under the tiny porch of my front door now although it was more
for aesthetics than function.

I gave the tiniest head shake. 'No. I'm not.'

'Good. I hadn't intended for that to come out just yet but I got
carried away.'

I pushed myself up on to my toes and kissed him. 'I'm so glad
you did,' I whispered. 'Now will you come in?'

He shook his head and I pulled back far enough to see his
face.

'Don't look so worried. Although, don't get me wrong, that
look is doing great things for my ego. But I have an early meeting
tomorrow.'

'I don't care.'

Finn rested his forehead against mine. 'But like I said before, I do, and you need your rest. I'm at the site in the afternoon so I'll see you then, if that's OK with you.'

'Yes. It is. Definitely.'

'I'd better go because otherwise I won't.' He kissed me hard and quick once more before pulling away and striding back to the car. I stood watching, both of us drenched and neither of us caring.

—————

11

'Hi.' Finn dropped his bag on the floor. Dressed in a pale blue shirt, light tan chinos and a navy blazer, he looked edible.

'Hi,' I said, making no attempt to cover my wide smile at seeing him. The reaction caused the corners of his own unfairly sexy mouth to turn upwards.

'How was your meeting?'

'Good, thanks.' He glanced around. 'How's today been?'

I knew what he was referring to. 'I haven't seen her yet.'

'Is that unusual?'

'Not especially. I've been in a meeting for much of it. We got the go ahead to have our new friend scanned so now comes the hard bit – arranging it all to the nth degree.'

'That's great news!' Finn said, coming over. 'Are you excited?'

'I am. That probably seems a bit weird to you.'

'Not at all. I know what your work means to you.'

I nodded. 'But there's more to life than work.'

'That there is.'

Admittedly this was a new concept to me but I was willing to learn. Especially if my teacher was volcanically hot!

'You two seem pleased with something.' Bella's voice cut into our little bubble, popping it sharply.

Surprised, we looked up. Ooh, someone was dealing with a monumental hangover. Perhaps that was part of the reason I hadn't seen her so far today. Finn laid a hand briefly on my shoulder.

'I'll see you later.' He gave Bella a nod as he passed and left us alone in the office.

'Hi, Bella. Are you OK?' I asked.

'Fine. Have you seen Inis?'

'She's working from home today but said to call if we need her. I've got some work to do for the exhibition so you can have the office to yourself if you want to call her about your news.'

Surprise mixed with a flash of insecurity shadowed her attractive, but clearly tired face. I didn't want to know the reasons for the tiredness. I didn't care. And I didn't want either Finn or Friedrich to come between my relationship with Bella as a colleague I both valued and appreciated.

'Oh right. I thought you might have told her already.'

I frowned. 'Why would you think that?'

She gave a Millennial's shrug. 'You didn't look that thrilled about me and Friedrich last night.'

'Bella, I have no axe to grind with you. I am truly pleased for you. Friedrich is an accomplished archaeologist and I'm sure you will get a lot from the experience. Obviously I will be sad to lose you from the team but we all have to do what's best for us.'

'And for you, that seems to be Finn.' She raised an eyebrow and I concentrated on keeping things professional.

'Your news is for you to discuss with Inis. As your direct supervisor, I admit I hoped you'd feel that you could come to me if you'd been considering a move.'

'And I'd have thought you would have told me that you were seeing Finn instead of letting me think he was available.'

'That's personal, Bella. I was referring to work.'

'It's personal with me and Friedrich too, so I guess we're even.'

'I'm sorry that you think it's a competition. Perhaps we could move on now?'

'I suppose.'

'I'll let you have your privacy,' I said, standing from my desk, taking what I needed and heading out of my office. I stopped at the ladies to splash my face and wrists with cold water. My face felt flushed with discomfort from the confrontation. I liked Bella although she had been known to take offence at the slightest thing on more than one occasion and now she was upset I hadn't called her into the toilets to gossip about Finn. But that wasn't me. Colette always said getting anything out of me was like getting blood out of a stone, unless it was quite literally ancient history. Besides, what would I say? Oh Bella, you know the guy you're lusting after, well, a) he thinks you're way too young for him, and b), we're seeing each other after I met him at the pub when I was very drunk and went back to his place.

Yeah, that was never going to happen.

I walked out of the loos, head down, lost in thought and bumped straight into a familiar, very solid chest that smelled like heaven.

'Oh, sorry!'

Finn looked down. 'You were miles away.'

I shook my head as I began walking towards my destination in a different part of the museum. Finn fell into step beside me. 'Bella.'

'Oh, for God's sake, what's her problem?'

'You, I think for the most part.'

'Oh?'

'I told you she had the hots for you.'

He gave a shrug. 'Not my type, like I said.'

'What is your type, out of interest?' I asked, looking up at him.

'Honestly, I don't think I have one. I've no idea why I said that. But the end result is that it isn't her I'm interested in.'

'See? That's the problem.'

'What about old Friedrich?'

I shrugged. 'Don't ask me. Strangely, I don't think the fact she's seeing someone is relevant.'

Finn let out a sigh. 'Some people need to wake up and realise that life isn't fair. We don't always get what we want and that's just how it is. Not everyone gets a trophy.'

I frowned as I looked back up at him. The conversation seemed to have touched a nerve.

'Is everything OK?'

'Yeah, sorry.' He made a comical little hop to the side. 'Off the soapbox now.'

Laughing, I brushed the side of my hand against his. Almost instinctively he caught his little finger around mine. 'I'm assuming from the fact I didn't get a kiss when you walked into my chest, that we're still doing the "not at work" thing.'

I curled my finger tighter, squeezing it for a second. 'I'm more than happy for people to know, if they happen to find out.' Finn pressed a button on the wall to call the lift down to the basement. 'I just value my privacy.'

The lift arrived, the doors opening with a sigh. Finn waited for me to step in first, followed me in and pressed the button for the basement. After my meltdown last time, I trusted him to let the thing proceed on its way this time. In theory, getting stuck in a lift, which I knew had no cameras, with this man could have been undeniably hot and sexy. I really needed to do something about my claustrophobic tendencies.

'I know.' He took a step closer but without touching me. I tilted my head back to meet the blue gaze. 'I'm sorry if I over reacted last night. I had some stuff on my mind and—'

'You didn't. Once I considered it from your perspective, I could see how it might have looked.'

'Yeah, but stuff like that doesn't usually bother me. People can take or leave me. I don't really care either way.' His chest expanded with a breath. 'Until I met you.'

The lift pinged to announce our arrival and Finn stepped back, his eyes still focused on me.

'So you're saying this is my fault?'

One side of his mouth quirked up. 'Entirely.'

'Hmm,' I said, heading out of the lift. 'I'm not sure I agree. Perhaps we could take up this discussion later?'

'I'll have to check my diary.'

'You do that.'

We walked together into the building site which would eventually be the new exhibition area. Scanning over the state of it right now, it was hard to see how the mess would ever transform into the sleek, clean vision that the digital pictures displayed upstairs for visitors promised.

'Don't look so worried, love,' Mike said with a wide grin as he approached us. 'Our Finn here's got it all under control, haven't you, lad?'

'Absolutely.'

'I'm sure he has. It's just...'

'A little hard to picture right now?'

'Exactly.'

Mike shoved a stubby, flat carpenter's pencil behind his ear and surveyed the scene. 'Yep. I can see why. But it'll be grand, don't worry.'

'That's great.'

The fact that there was a hefty penalty for any delay in the completion of the project went some way towards assuaging that fear. But even meticulous planning couldn't entirely rule out the possibility of a rogue spanner in the works.

'Come on,' Finn said, 'I'll show you how the space is coming together up the other end.'

To my eyes, the other end looked as much of a tip as this one but Finn assured me it was ahead of schedule.

'That's good to hear. Inis will be pleased. Any positive news I can report back to her is appreciated.' A gentle ring echoed around the site as I finished speaking and I pulled my phone from my pocket. 'Speak of the devil.' I showed him the screen with Inis's name displayed. 'Thanks for the update here. I'd better take this.'

'No problem. I'll catch up with you later.'

I nodded as I pressed answer at the same time and made my way back out into the main building. 'Hi, Inis.' I took the stairs back up, chatting as I did so.

'Did you know?' Inis said. Preamble had never been her way.

'I assume we're talking about Bella?'

'Yes. Did you know?'

'About which bit?'

'There's more than one bit?'

Bugger.

'Umm, well no, I mean.'

'OK, I'll tell you what I know and then you can fill me in.'

By the time I was back in my office, thankfully now vacated by Bella, Inis had had a full rundown of the evening's events.

'So you had no idea Friedrich had been snooping around our staff?'

'Nope. We're not exactly chummy.'

'I don't blame you. I feel the same way. Although I suspect if I am ever in a position to be useful, he may be less cool in his manner towards me.'

She had a point.

'Sorry. I shouldn't be bitching about him. Blame it on the hormones.'

'Bitch away.' I laughed. 'I'm long past caring. I was initially annoyed at him poaching staff but the truth is, Bella would be daft not to take the opportunity. I just don't need the drama that appears to have come with it.'

'Ah yes, well, you've ended up with a prize she had her eye on.'

'Not intentionally.'

'No. But perhaps the universe finally took things into its own hands.'

I rolled my eyes.

'I heard you roll your eyes.'

'You know I don't believe in any of that,' I replied, laughing. 'And neither do you.'

'No. Not really. But either way, Finn's lovely. And gorgeous. It's about time you were appreciated by someone for something other than your academic writings and ability to do your job to a brilliant level.'

'Thanks. I'm not sure I'll be getting top marks on the staff management part of my annual review this year.'

Inis made a dismissive noise. 'From everything I've heard it sounds like you've acted completely professionally. Bella's going to face more competition and far more people willing to escalate, rather than try to dispel, confrontation as she goes further in her career. You know what academics are like.'

I did.

'And in life in general.'

'Funny. Finn was saying something very similar earlier.'

'He's got a good head on those delightfully broad shoulders.'

She paused then let out a laugh. 'Yes, your shoulders are lovely too, my darling. Men are so insecure,' Inis said, returning to our conversation after teasing her husband, amusement still in her voice.

'How are you?'

'I'm fine. Finn was, annoyingly, right about not overdoing it. The midwife said the same thing the other day. So I've been perfecting my epic nap technique.'

'I'm glad to hear it. Don't try and do too much. Everything's under control here. I've just been down on site and it's all coming along nicely.'

'It looks like a bombsite, doesn't it?'

'Yes. But I'm reassured it's coming along nicely anyway.'

She laughed again. 'Good.'

I glanced at my watch. 'I've got a meeting about the loan mummy's scan shortly so I'd better go and get prepared.'

'OK. Thanks for keeping it all together over there.'

'I'm doing my best although I already seem to have lost us a staff member.'

'It was inevitable.'

'Are you going to hold her position open?'

'Did she tell you that's what she wants?' Inis asked.

'No, she didn't tell me anything.'

'She didn't say specifically one way or the other but it's a conversation I need to have with her. I thought it was better to do that face to face. I'm hoping to be in tomorrow so I'll do it then. OK, I'd better let you get on.'

'Thanks, Inis. Look after yourself and the bump.'

'I will. Speak to you later.'

I ended the call then turned my attention to the pending pile on my desk, pulled out the pertinent file and logged into Teams, ready for my meeting.

*   *   *

It was about a week later when I looked up from my desk to see Bella hovering in the doorway, her face bare of make-up and an unsure expression in her eyes. Finn was at his desk, headphones on, engrossed in an online meeting. I say engrossed. Five minutes ago he'd made what was obviously a deliberate act of knocking something from his desk. Whilst bent over, he'd shot me a look and then pretended to fall asleep before straightening and reassuming a serious, studious expression.

'Hi. Did you need something?' Bella had mostly kept her distance since we'd run into her and Friedrich at the restaurant but we worked together and it was inevitable that we'd need to interact at times. When we did, I'd kept it professional. Bella had been cool but I'd pretended not to notice. Inis was less than impressed and had made noises about speaking to Bella but I'd asked her not to and hoped things would settle in time.

Bella looked over towards Finn briefly before back at me. I shook my head.

'He's preoccupied with his meeting. Come in.'

Finn hadn't actually moved in the last few minutes and I had begun to wonder if he had mastered the art of sleeping with his eyes open. If so, I needed to know the secret. I had plenty of my own calls when that would be a handy skill.

Bella gave him another quick glance but Finn didn't react in the slightest and I encouraged her in again with a wave.

'What's up?' I asked and indicated she take a seat the other side of my desk.

From the corner of my eye, I saw Finn glance up, shift a look between the two of us before returning his concentration to the screen in front of him.

'I didn't mean to disturb you...' This Bella was certainly more subdued than I could ever remember seeing her. I was curious as to the reason but didn't rush.

'Not at all. What's up?'

She unfolded a piece of paper she'd been holding. It was a little worse for wear where she'd been fidgeting with it.

'It's just that... well... I've...' She cleared her throat. 'I've had this and I was sort of wondering if you would be able to help.' She slid the piece of paper across the well-worn but highly polished teak desk.

The desk had belonged to an amateur but highly skilled and unusually ethical adventurer from the golden age of archaeology. His family had donated it to us a few years ago. It was such a beautiful piece but it weighed a tonne. Probably literally. Every time I sat down at it, I felt that sense of past and couldn't help but wonder what notes and sights had been journalled here by the original owner.

'I wasn't expecting it to be honest. Not at all.' Her words were coming out in a rush now even though I hadn't yet finished unfolding the piece of paper. 'I went to Inis but she said that it would be best if I asked you.'

Reading the words, I nodded without looking up. Now the reason for Bella's hesitance was plain.

A potential position on the dig team... suitable reference... competition for places on the team, as I am sure you understand...

Good old Friedrich. Wielding any little bit of power whenever he got the chance was one of his favourite pastimes. Thankfully I hadn't been in a situation where it affected me during our time together but on the odd occasion he'd done it in my company I had, tactfully, tried to get him to tone it down. He'd always laughed it off and said I'd imagined it but I hadn't. And here was the proof in black and white.

'It's not what he said on the...' Bella swallowed and shifted in her seat. 'The evening he asked me to dinner. He said I had a place on the team. I've told everyone and handed in my notice! What am I supposed to do if he decides on someone else instead now?' Her face was flushing pink with panic and distress and although I hadn't appreciated her manner recently, it was hard not to feel sorry for her.

'I didn't realise you planned on leaving us entirely. Inis was prepared to keep your position open.'

Bella let out a sigh laced with misery and regret. 'Friedrich also promised me a position as a research assistant for him when we returned from the dig. Said it would be better paid and...' She looked back down at her lap, one thumbnail worrying the skin on the other before she raised it to her mouth and gave it a quick, nervous chew. 'And more interesting,' she finished.

'Oh?' I laid my hands on the email print-out and met Bella's eyes. 'Have you been bored with your work here?'

'No!' she replied, the word rushing out quicker, and louder, than either of us expected. Finn looked up (or woke up!) and Bella hastily turned so that her back was towards him a little more. 'Sorry. I didn't mean to blurt it like that.'

I smiled. 'That's OK. I'm just glad to hear it. I'd hate to think that you'd been bored all this time and never said anything.'

Bella let out a sigh. 'No. Not at all. I love it! Actually, I'm beginning to think I've made a huge mistake.' Her eyes filled as she pulled her sleeves down over her hands, wiping her eyes with her jumper. She looked up. 'I'm sorry I was such a bitch to you. And I'm not just saying that to try and get you to do me a good reference. I don't blame you if you don't.'

'Personal life and work are two different things, Bella.'

'That depends, I guess,' she said. Her eyebrows flicked up briefly, before her head snapped up. 'Oh God. I didn't mean anything by that. I mean, I did, but not about you and Finn. Honest.'

'Is there anything else you want to talk about?' It was obvious something was on her mind and, whatever happened, Bella would still be working with us for some time yet. I wanted to know about any problems and attempt to fix them, if I could.

She shook her head, her nail once more in her mouth. 'Not really. I mean...' Bella looked up, her face a pure picture of misery.

'Bella. Just tell me,' I said, softly.

'I slept with Friedrich.' Her words poured out in a hurry, racing to beat the outburst of tears that followed immediately afterwards. With perfect timing, Finn's meeting wrapped up and he removed his headphones just as Bella blurted her confession. The young woman's hands were currently over her eyes so she missed the surprised look Finn sent my way.

'You OK?' he mouthed.

I returned a faint smile and small nod, a rush of warmth flooding through me at his concern before I turned back to face my colleague as she removed her hands from her eyes, misery showing there. I handed over a box of tissues I kept in my drawer to save her jumper any more soaking.

'Thanks. I hadn't planned to. It kind of just happened.'

Like I'd told Finn, my ex could be quite charming when he wanted to be.

'I was just so excited about the dig position which now doesn't even seem like it's definitely going to happen and the possibility of a move up in my career.' She swallowed. 'I want to ask you something but it feels so weird.'

'OK.'

'But you probably know him better than anyone else.'

I waited and she let out another wretched sigh as she started on another nail.

'Do you think he offered me the position just to get me into bed?'

She was right. It was a bit weird. But only because I'd never been confided in like this before. I'd always kept myself to myself, even as a child. Colette confided in me but that was different and she knew that if anyone could keep a confidence, it was me. I considered my reply. I could go for tact, or honesty. In the end, I aimed for something that, hopefully, encompassed both.

'The truth is, Bella, I don't know.'

The tears made a reappearance and I put my hand across the desk towards her. 'But.' I had to raise my voice to be heard above the sobs. Her wet eyes met mine. 'But,' I repeated. 'The truth is that you will be a great asset to that, or any other dig team. You're knowledgeable, bright and quick to learn.'

She gave a sniff and took another tissue. 'I've certainly learned from this.' Her tone was gloomy but there was a hint of light back in her eyes now.

'I will, of course, write you a reference. Nothing that's happened will make any difference to what I put in it.'

'Lizzie, I'm so sorry.' She glanced over towards Finn but he'd immediately put his headphones back on and was tapping away at the keyboard, concentration fixed on the screen. 'I don't know what I was thinking. I don't usually drink that much.' She gave an empty laugh. 'There have been quite a few lessons from that night actually.'

'We all do things we regret, Bella.' I cleared my throat. 'Would you like me to speak to Inis about the situation? I know the position hasn't yet been advertised.' I looked towards my in-tray. It was the only way I remembered to get things done. I was still a paper girl at heart. Or papyrus girl as my father liked to tease. The request to begin a search for Bella's replacement was currently sitting in the pile.

Bella's gaze flicked up and locked on to mine. 'Really?'

'If that's what you want, yes. But you, and we, have to be sure that is definitely the path you want to take.'

Bella opened her mouth to reply but I continued. 'Why don't you sleep on it and come and see me again tomorrow.'

'OK. Thank you so much, Lizzie. I'm so sorry again. I just—'

I waved the rest of it away. 'We've moved on now. Right?'

She nodded enthusiastically. 'Yes. Definitely.'

12

I got in the car, one hand tucked around the present I'd bought and the other holding a brolly over me as biblical rain teemed from the sky. I'd told Finn to message me instead of getting soaked himself coming to the door.

'Hi!' I said, a little breathlessly as I shoved the wet umbrella into a plastic bag I'd brought along for the purpose.

'Hi,' he said, waiting patiently while I faffed. Having finished, I leant over and kissed him quickly before he steered out into the traffic.

'Are we going to be late?'

His posture was relaxed and I could see a gentle smile resting on his features as he shook his head, eyes still focused on the trail of red tail lights in front of us. 'It's fine. Strict schedules aren't really a thing in our family.'

'I did try to get away on time but then a phone call I'd been waiting for came in. Isn't it typical? They'd had all day and then chose to ring when I had one foot out of the door.'

Finn pulled the handbrake on as we sat in traffic.

'You OK? You seem a little flustered.'

'Me? No, not at all.'

One dark brow twitched ever so slightly as he threw a brief glance my way.

'OK, yes. I am if you want to know the truth.'

'I always want to know the truth with you. What's up? Is it work?'

'No. It's this. Tonight.'

The dark brows drew together. 'Why? Did you not want to come?'

'I'm just a bit nervous.'

'They're going to love you, just like our friends did. And Colette and Greg will be there too, so it's not like you won't know anyone.'

'Did you say your parents are going to be there too?'

'Yep. They're looking forward to meeting you.'

I curled my toes in my shoes and felt the tension in my neck tighten.

'Oh good. No pressure.'

'No,' Finn repeated, his left hand coming to rest on my thigh. 'That's right. There is no pressure, Elizabeth. It's just a fun evening celebrating my sister's birthday. Nothing more.'

'Of course. Yes, I know that. I didn't mean... it's just the whole meeting the parents is made out to be this big thing, isn't it? Even though I know this isn't that, not in that way but still.' I sucked in some air having gabbled the previous sentence without taking a breath.

'What have you got there?' Finn wisely decided a change of subject was in order and indicated the present sat wrapped on my knee.

'Birthday present. I've no idea if she'll like it.'

'Am I allowed to know what it is?'

'A luxury spa day voucher and some goodies from the same spa.'

'Alice has two kids. I can guarantee she will love it. Thanks. You didn't have to get anything.'

'Of course I did. She was kind enough to invite me.'

'Yeah, because they're nosy.'

I grinned. 'Fair enough. I'd probably have been the same if I'd had siblings.'

'Do you miss not having had any?'

I shrugged. 'I don't know any different and I've always been pretty good at entertaining myself.'

'Yeah, I guess you don't miss what you don't have. I can't imagine not having my family close.'

'No, they're obviously a huge part of your life. I think it's lovely. I'm ridiculously nervous but I'm also looking forward to meeting them.'

My comment appeared to please Finn as the faint smile he'd been wearing spread into a grin. He took advantage of a pause in the traffic to lean over and kiss me.

* * *

'Come in, come in!' The family resemblance was obvious in the woman who opened the door. Her blue eyes shone with laughter and the wide, bright smile was welcoming and warm. 'You must be Elizabeth,' she said, having hugged her brother tightly. 'I'm Alice. We've all been so looking forward to meeting you,' she said as Finn took my coat and I was suddenly enveloped in a hug. Her speech had a distinctive pattern to it and when she stepped back, Finn tapped her on the arm to get her attention.

'Elizabeth brought you something.' His hands signed the words as he spoke them and Alice turned back to me. 'You didn't have to do that,' she said, now using both methods, as her brother had, her hand reaching for mine as soon as she'd finished. I smiled and handed over the present.

'I wanted to.'

Alice studied me as I replied and I guessed she was reading my lips. 'That's so kind.' She took the present and then linked her arms around mine and her brother's and led us through to where everyone else was gathered.

'Lizzie!' Colette wrapped me in a hug, careful not to tip the champagne she held in one hand down my back. 'I was worried you weren't coming.'

'Yeah, sorry. I saw your messages. Work went a bit mad and I didn't get a chance to reply.'

Colette gave a dismissive wave with her free hand. 'You're here now. That's what matters.'

I got the impression that Colette had been here a while and that most certainly wasn't her first glass of fizz.

'They're the nicest people. Alice was so sweet when I made my rather clumsy attempt at signing that I was happy to meet her.'

'I didn't know you could sign?'

Colette took a sip of drink before replying. 'I can't really. Greg can though. He's known Finn for so long. I think he learned with the rest of the family when Alice lost her hearing.' She tilted her head. 'What is it?'

I glanced around quickly and leant close to my friend. 'I didn't know any of this. Finn didn't say a word.'

'Oh. I know they don't make a thing of it. I just wanted to make an effort.'

'Yes, I know. That's really thoughtful. I just... I wish Finn had mentioned it.'

'It doesn't matter though, really, does it? She's still the same woman.'

'No, of course! I didn't mean like that. I just would have perhaps liked to have at least known how to say hello or something too.'

'Don't worry. From what I hear, Finn's been singing your praises so highly, I don't think anything else you do could possibly endear them any more to you.'

'Oh God, has he?'

Colette laughed. 'Yes. And he's absolutely right to.' She reached out and hugged me again, Greg appearing at just the right moment to take her glass as the contents swilled up the sides of it. 'You're lovely, Lizzie. It's wonderful to see you with someone who actually appreciates it.'

'Thanks, Colette.'

'Talk of the devil...' Colette reached out her arms to Finn who returned the hug and then gave his mate a similar one. His hand then slid around my waist. 'Sorry, got caught up.'

'Don't be silly. It's your family.'

'I know. And they're dying to meet you.' He looked over at Colette. 'Mind if I steal your friend for a while?'

'Not at all. Just make sure you look after her. She's very precious.'

Yep. Definitely not her first champagne.

I felt Finn's eyes on me and looked up. 'I promise,' he said, his gaze hooked on mine.

'Awww!' Colette and Greg cooed at the same time. Finn threw them both a look, grinned, then slipped his hand around mine and led me away.

'What would you like to drink?' he asked.

'Anything with alcohol.'

Finn looked round at me, half smiling, half bemused. 'Everything OK?'

'Yeah.' I tried to laugh it off. 'Just more people than I thought and...'

'And?'

I faltered in my words. 'Nothing.' Suddenly my insecurity felt silly.

Finn waited a beat, poured me a champagne and then led me through to a quiet spot in the entrance hall. My eyes drifted from the black and white tiles to the large gilt-framed mirror which was reflecting a huge bunch of white lilies, their scent filling the space. I took a sip of my drink.

'So, what's up?'

'Nothing, honestly,' I said, looking up at Finn. 'It's just nerves.'

'Is it about Alice?'

My treacherous cheeks flamed, giving him an answer.

'What's the problem?' There was a hint of defensiveness in his voice and the usual warmth in the blue eyes cooled. My free hand reached out to touch his hand.

'There isn't one, honestly. I just...'

He waited while my mind scrambled around trying to find the best words to put in the right order.

'I just wish you'd been able to teach me a couple of signs so that I could have said hello and happy birthday.'

'Alice lip reads.'

'Yes, I guessed that but... I would have liked to have made the effort. She's been kind enough to invite me to her birthday party so it would have been nice if I could have signed a few basic words as a thank you.' I raced through the sentence then downed a good portion of the glass for Dutch courage. Then slugged a bit more for good measure.

Finn's eyes were still fixed on me. Suddenly the warmth I was used to flooded back in as his fingers took my drink and placed it on a side table before wrapping his arms around me and pulling me close.

'Believe me, nothing you could do would make them like you more.'

'They haven't even met me properly yet,' I said, feeling myself relax within his embrace.

'They will be as nuts about you as I am.'

I tipped my head back, feeling more comfortable now, although whether that was from the sudden hit of alcohol or the feeling of security from being wrapped in Finn's arms and pressed against his muscular body. Possibly both.

'I think you're just nuts.'

'Not the first time I've had that accusation levelled at me, but this time I'm in a position to accurately refute it.' He shifted position and his smile faded a little. 'It didn't occur to me to tell you about Alice because it's not something any of us think about and neither she, nor the family, want her to feel she's being treated any differently.'

'No! That's not what I meant. I—'

'I know,' he said, squeezing me a bit tighter to reinforce his words. 'I realise that now. And, if you want to learn some sign, I'm more than happy to teach you.'

'Thank you.'

'It'll probably be a doddle to someone who reads hieroglyphics like they're reading a book written for toddlers.'

'I've been doing it a long time.'

'I still think it's fascinating. Just like I think you are.' He bent and nuzzled my neck. 'But much to my chagrin right now, rather than discovering just how fascinating you are, we have to go and be sociable.'

'Maybe we can pick this up later?' I asked, emboldened by

downing a glass of champagne on a stomach that hadn't seen food since I'd hurriedly scoffed the last Weetabix this morning. I made to pull away but his arms tightened.

'Nope. You need to stay there for a minute.' His head was tilted up as he apparently studied the chandelier with great interest.

'But I thought we had to go and mingle.'

'Yes, in a sec,' he said, still not looking at me. The penny dropped.

'Ohhh.'

'Exactly.'

I giggled.

'It's not funny,' Finn returned in a pained voice.

'It is though,' I said, giggling even more and I felt the rumble of laughter through his chest as he finally looked down.

'You're going to pay for that.'

'Is that a promise?' I said, teasing as he pulled away.

'Definitely.'

I flashed my eyes at him. 'I can hardly wait.'

'Stop it or we're never going to get into this party.'

After several drinks and letting go of my panic at being in the midst of a large family gathering where it appeared I was one of the main attractions, I'd sat down with Alice and got quietly, or not so quietly, drunk with her. By the end of the evening, she'd taught me how to sign all the rude words I'd ever need. We'd hugged goodbye like old friends before Finn and I folded ourselves into a taxi and headed back to my place, Finn arranging to return tomorrow to collect his car.

* * *

'Finn?'

Silence.

I wriggled closer. 'Finn? Are you awake?'

'No. I'm having a nightmare that my girlfriend won't let me sleep.' Finn's head moved on the pillow. The ultra blackout blinds he'd fitted for me made seeing anything impossible but I heard the pillow scrunch with the movement.

I kicked him in the shin and he wrapped his legs around mine so that I couldn't do it again. Maybe I should have kicked him earlier...

'Can you teach me some sign language tomorrow?'

'Of course.'

'I already know all the rude words.'

The deep laugh reverberated through his chest and I felt it within my own body. 'Then you've got a good grounding already.'

'We could start now.'

'Elizabeth. I'm knackered and I can't see my hand in front of my face.'

'There is that I suppose.' Apparently I wasn't quite as sobered up yet as I thought I was.

His hand drifted a little lower. 'I'm having to do everything by touch at the moment.'

'Something you appear to be rather skilled at.'

'It's always good to get practice in though.'

I caught his hand and laid my own on top. 'I'm serious.'

'So am I. But yes, I'll teach you. Just not right now.'

'Thank you.' I shuffled, snuggling close, my body moulding to his side, his shoulder acting as my pillow. 'So Alice wasn't born deaf? Is that OK to ask?'

'Of course it's OK to ask. I didn't tell you because I'm ashamed of her, or because I want to keep things from you. It's just the norm for us. But no, she wasn't. When she was in her last year of university, she contracted bacterial meningitis.' I felt his body tense as the memories returned.

'If you don't want to talk about it, I understand.' My hand reached for his and he wrapped his own around it, lifting it gently to his lips so that he could kiss my fingers.

'No, sweetheart. It was just a tough time and I still get frustrated that I couldn't do anything for my little sister.'

'You're only human, Finn.'

'I know. But that knowledge doesn't help when you know that you'd give anything, do anything, to fix things.'

I moved and kissed his shoulder, understanding the need to want to relieve suffering for someone you cared about. Finn responded, dipping his head to kiss the top of mine.

'She was OK initially and we just thought she had the flu. Mum and Dad drove over to the university to see her and ended up bringing her back with them. The following night she deteriorated rapidly and Mum noticed the rashes. She got a glass and pressed it against Alice's skin. When they didn't disappear, Dad scooped her into his arms and they broke all the speed limits to get her to the hospital.'

'I can't even begin to think how frightening it must have been for you all.'

'Dad rang me and my brother from the hospital and I went and picked Henry up and then we all just sat and waited.'

I remained silent but gave our still joined hands a gentle squeeze. There were no words to say.

'Eventually Alice came round and, obviously, we were all over the moon. But then we saw this look of confusion on her face. She was just staring at us. For a minute we thought she didn't know who we were but then she touched her ears, as though she thought there was something in them. When she realised there wasn't, she started crying. Mum was trying to comfort her but

Alice was sobbing her heart out and almost screaming that she couldn't hear us.'

'That must have been so much for her, and you all, to deal with.'

'I think initially they were hoping it might be temporary but they did a whole barrage of tests and came to the conclusion that the damage was permanent.'

He cuddled me closer and I wrapped myself around him as though if I got close enough, I could meld into him and absorb some of the pain. The room was like pitch but the pain in his voice was obvious.

'Alice had been studying music at university.'

'Oh God...'

'Yeah.' The sadness was palpable. 'She's really talented. Wrote all her own music, lyrics, has a beautiful voice to accompany it all. Then, just like that, she couldn't hear any of it.'

I thought about what to say. 'I hope this isn't insensitive, but there have been some deaf musicians, haven't there?'

'There have. But Alice wasn't interested. The music itself was what moved her. What made her tick. What she loved. If she couldn't do it the way she wanted, she didn't want to do it at all.'

'Life is so cruel at times.' I cast my mind back to a previous conversation with Finn. 'So that's what you meant before about life not being fair. You're right, of course, and I can see now why you were so outspoken about it.'

'There are examples every day if we take the time to see them.'

'Yes, I suppose there are. Life is a strange thing.'

'That it is.'

'I do still wish you'd told me about Alice though.'

'I don't.'

I shifted up to look at him, even though the darkness

prevented me from doing so, the movement was almost automatic.

'Why not?'

'Because she met the real you.'

'I don't understand.'

'A couple of previous times, I'd told girlfriends the situation beforehand and it freaked one out, I've no idea why, so clearly that relationship wasn't destined for the long term and another one just bellowed at Alice.'

'Really?'

'Yeah. So weird. Alice wasn't fazed obviously, but from the way we all jumped she got the idea what was happening. As you've already discovered, she's got a great sense of humour. Afterwards, she said seeing us all flinching with the noise, she was quite glad she couldn't hear her.'

'Oh dear.'

'It was mortifying.'

'But not your fault, Finn.'

'No, I know but still.'

'You felt responsible.'

'I guess so, yes.'

'You didn't need to, and Alice obviously knew that. People react in the way they're going to react. We have no control of how others behave. It's not your fault if they don't act the way you'd hoped.'

'But you did. You were just perfect, even though I dropped you in at the deep end.'

'Thanks. Good to know you weren't curling up in a corner from mortification.'

'Far from it. The fact that you and Alice hit it off so well just goes to show that you're as great as I thought you were from the very first moment I met you.'

'You're very romantic when you're tipsy.'

'I'm very romantic when I'm not tipsy.'

A few minutes later, my brain clearly unwilling to go to sleep despite the insistence of my body which was entirely knackered, I piped up again.

'How long did it take you to learn sign?'

'God, woman, why aren't you asleep yet? You drank enough wine between you to sink a battleship.'

'We did not and alcohol is a stimulant. So that's probably part of the reason. Also, don't be rude. You don't normally complain when I'm awake.' I teased.

A low, throaty laugh wrapped itself around me in the darkness. 'True, but that's because I've generally got more energy than I have right now.'

I prodded him in a stomach that was annoyingly firmer than my own. 'So? How long?'

'A while, but we learnt as a family. No one wanted Alice to feel left out and obviously we wanted to hold conversations in the easiest way possible for her. It was natural that we'd all begin learning as soon as she did. Greg's known her since she was a kid so he was up for it too.'

'I suppose that made it easier to practise? Any language gets rusty when you're not using it.'

'Exactly. We made a point of getting together every single day if possible to work on it. It wasn't always easy, especially when I was away on a job but then we did it on video.'

'That's dedication.'

'If something's important to you, you make time.'

'I'm not sure how good a student I'll be but I'm eager to try.'

There was that laugh again. He needed to stop doing that or he was going to have to find some of that energy he'd just denied having. 'Sweetheart, like I said, you read bloody hieroglyphics like it's a comic book. Believe me, you'll pick it up just fine.'

I kissed his chest lightly and his arm trailed along my hip.

'Elizabeth?'

'Yes?'

'Do you have any more questions or could I please, for the love of God, get some sleep now?'

I let out a long-suffering sigh. 'I suppose so.'

Finn's hand slid over my waist, tightened momentarily and then rested there. Within a minute, I felt it relax and his breathing grow deep and steady. I closed my eyes and soon joined him on the night bus to the land of Nod.

13

‘Sssh!’ was the first thing Colette said when I video called her the next day after Finn had left. She held the forefinger of her free hand to her lips as she rested the phone on the duvet.

‘Having a duvet day?’ I whispered.

‘*Oui*,’ she replied, too hungover to not revert back to her native language as she adjusted herself in the bed to get comfy. ‘How come you’re not feeling like I am?’

‘I am. I’m just better at hiding it.’

She gave me one of those Gallic shrugs she was so good at and snuggled down under the duvet. ‘Did you enjoy yourself?’

‘Yeah, actually. I did. Once I got over the whole terror of meeting all his family in one go.’

‘Perhaps it was for the best?’

‘Maybe.’ I mimicked her shrug without the easy looseness she managed.

‘They seem lovely though. And it looked like you were getting on well with Alice… from what I remember.’

‘You were there too,’ I reminded her, laughing. ‘She was teaching us rude words in sign language.’

Colette's pixie-like features wrinkled in what I assumed was an attempt at recollection, but it could have been the hangover. 'Was she? *Merde*. I can't remember any of them! You'll have to reteach me when I'm recovered enough.'

'You're assuming I remember.'

'I know you do. Drunk or not you have an uncanny ability to remember anything you learn whereas for some of us, it seems to drop out of our ears when we're not looking.'

'Oh, rubbish.'

Colette pouted. 'Please tell me you remember some. It's definitely going to come in useful as a way to vent my feelings in certain situations without getting into trouble.'

'I remember some.'

A hand wiggled out from under the bedclothes and she made a circle with her thumb and forefinger before pulling it back into the warmth of the duvet.

'I'll leave you to sleep.'

Colette's eyelids looked heavy and her pallor had a tinge of green.

'*Merci, ma belle.*'

'Message me later when you're feeling better.'

'You assume I will.' She summoned up enough energy to send me a tragic look.

'I'm sure you'll drag yourself through it. If not, I'll make sure the funeral is magnificent.'

'I knew I could count on you.'

I grinned and she responded with a watery smile, the most she could apparently manage but I appreciated the effort.

'Get well soon. Love you lots.'

'*Merci. J'aime aussi.*' Her eyelids drooped again. Suddenly she forced them open. 'He's good for you, you know. Finn. He's good for you.'

It was hard to disagree but Colette seemed to take the hesitation before I replied as such.

'He is. I know he's not your usual type but that's not a bad thing. He's widening your horizons – and I mean that in a good way. Not everything is about academia.'

'I do know that.'

She gave me a look that suggested she thought otherwise.

'I do. It's just hard. I've had that all my life. I suppose it was just what I knew.'

'What was safe,' Colette added.

'Maybe.'

'I really like him. And I really like him for you.'

'I really like him too.'

'Is he there?'

'No. He had to go and get his car from his sister's and then meet up with some friends.'

'What are you up to?'

'I'm going out to try and clear my head.' I held up a large water bottle. 'And dilute my blood back to a level where it doesn't feel like it's 80 per cent proof.'

'I know that feeling. I'm hoping to do that by sleeping. Your way sounds like far too much effort.'

'Let's hope both ways work. I'll let you sleep. Talk to you later.'

She snuck a hand from under the duvet again, waved sleepily and I hung up.

* * *

'You look nice.' Finn smiled as he greeted me on the steps of the stately home hosting tonight's book launch.

I looked down at the basic black dress I'd chosen. It was functional and plain and, I knew, boring. But it suited me and the image I wanted and perhaps felt I needed to portray. Sensible. Serious, and to be taken seriously.

'Thanks,' I said as I handed over my coat to the cloakroom. I caught a glance of other guests in far more sophisticated dress and felt an unexpected stab of envy. Colette had made several attempts to get me to 'lighten up', as she put it, my sartorial choices but I resolutely stuck to my guns. I couldn't help but wonder though, as a historian I recognised from telly swished by in a hot pink, bias-cut silk gown, her hips swaying, the fabric rippling sensuously as she walked. What would it be like to step out of this look I'd cultivated for myself. Could I take the chance? The woman in pink flashed Finn a smile. I gave myself a mental kick, told myself my clothes were perfectly adequate and folded my arms across my chest. Finn placed his hand gently at the small of my back and we entered the room.

'Are you OK?' I asked sometime later in the evening. Normally laid back and chatty, Finn had been unusually quiet this evening.

'Yeah. Probably just a bit tired. Sorry. Long day.' There was a tightness about his mouth and eyes that I had rarely, if ever, seen.

'We can go shortly. I promise.'

His hand drifted to mine. 'Don't leave early on my account.' He raised his glass of beer. 'I'm fine. You keep doing your thing.'

An hour later, we were still there as I got caught up in various discussions and debates about aspects in the book which led to other subjects. Finn remained beside me for the most part but said nothing.

'And what do you think of the book?' Friedrich asked, directing his pale gaze at Finn who took a moment to realise he was being spoken to. Everyone in the small group turned to face him.

'I'm afraid I haven't read it.' Finn gave a shrug and took a large swig of his drink.

'Really?' Friedrich asked, apparently all astonishment as he looked around. 'I have to say I'm surprised, knowing you were invited to such a prestigious launch.'

'He came with me, Friedrich,' I said, flashing my ex a warning glare.

'Still, I'm sure there are others who would have appreciated the opportunity to attend. Those who perhaps might have actually taken the time to read the book we're all here to celebrate.'

Finn finished the rest of his drink in one go and gave the group a sharp nod. 'Excuse me.' He turned and walked calmly away, placed his empty glass on the bar and continued out of the door.

I threw Friedrich a furious glare and turned to follow Finn but instead walked slap bang into one of my old university tutors. Fifteen minutes later I finally managed to excuse myself and hurried out of the venue, looking for Finn. I scanned the street and spied a familiar shape sitting on a bench.

'Finn,' I called, but my words were carried away by the noise of an ambulance, hurtling up the street, sirens wailing. 'Finn!'

He started at the sound of his name. The collar of his coat was turned up against the cold, his hands rammed deep into his pockets. 'What are you doing out here?' I asked, hurrying up to him.

He gave a mirthless smile. 'It's warmer out here than in there.'

I shook my head. 'I'm so sorry. I'm livid with Friedrich for acting like that. I don't know what he thought he was doing.'

'Belittling people, Elizabeth. I guess it amuses him and his literary cronies.' He looked up at me properly. 'Bloody hell, what are you doing? You haven't even got a coat on!'

'I was looking for you! I got stuck talking to an old professor. I'm so sorry.'

He stood and wrapped his arms around me, transferring his warmth.

'Let's go home,' I said, my words muffled as I spoke them into his chest.

'Sounds like a bloody good idea to me. But let's get your coat first so I don't have to call that ambulance back here to thaw you out.'

I grinned up at him. 'I'm pretty sure you have much more interesting ways of warming me up.'

His arms wrapped tighter. 'Now that,' he said, 'is something I really am an expert on.'

* * *

A pigeon who was clearly regretting the fact that his species didn't elect to head to warmer climes for winter sat clinging to a skeletal branch of a London plane tree as it whipped around in the gale. All week the nation had been warned to batten down for severe winds in the usual dire, apocalyptic tones adopted by the media for such circumstances. I blew in through the heavy, Victorian oak doors of the museum and headed up to my office.

Somewhere along the way, I must have taken a wrong turn because this was not my office. The bones of it seemed familiar but in its place was a Christmas grotto so spectacular, or gaudy, depending on your opinion, that it made me wonder if Selfridges was missing a large part of their festive display.

'Hi!' Finn bounced into the room, apparently as full of the joys of the season as my office. 'What do you think?'

'Umm...'

'I asked Inis if she thought you'd mind.' He took in my face. 'I'm beginning to think she might have been wrong.'

'Oh!' I looked up at the handsome, and currently crestfallen, face. 'No, it's just...'

He held up his hands, palms towards me, a smile that was a

mere shadow of the one that had been there moments before fixed on his face. 'I'm sorry.' Finn scanned the office. 'I guess I got a bit carried away. I love Christmas.'

'I would never have guessed.'

His cheeks flushed. 'I'll take it down.' He reached for a thick strand of tinsel that outlined the top of the door frame and I stilled his hand.

'No,' I said, pulling him gently back. 'Leave it.'

Finn turned to face me, his free hand cupping my cheek. 'Elizabeth, that's kind of you but it's pretty obvious from the expression of pure horror on your face that this is not your idea of the perfect seasonal decoration. Like I said, I got a bit carried away.'

'And maybe I should let myself do that a bit more often too.'

Finn waited.

'You're right. This isn't how I'd do things but that's because I don't do things. If I'm honest, the season mostly passes me by. I'm not a complete Scrooge in that I do go to the Christmas do and stuff but at home, the break was mostly considered free time to spend even more time reading, writing and researching academic papers.'

'Did you miss it?' Finn had seen straight through my smile. He rested his bum on the edge of his desk, tugging me gently to follow.

'You don't miss what you don't know you're missing.'

'But you must have had some idea.'

I gave a shrug.

'Not especially. We just didn't do it so it was the norm. To be honest, there were always so many books and research material in our house that there wasn't a lot of room left for an elf let alone a Christmas tree!' I laughed but now I looked at it from a different perspective; it might have been nice to have had a Christmas like the other kids at school had.

'Does that mean you're not going to your parents' for Christmas?'

'No, probably not.'

'Then I'd love you to spend Christmas with me and my family. Although I will warn you, it's like this,' he indicated Santa's grotto around him, 'and more.'

'I'm not sure it's possible for it to be any more "more" than this.'

Finn gave a deep, rich laugh and gathered me in close. 'Oh, you have no idea.'

'Wow.'

'Yep. But if it's too much, I get it.'

'No...' I cast my mind back to the quiet Christmas holidays I'd had over the years. They'd seemed typical at the time – for us at least. But now there was that feeling inside me again. That tug to do something out of the norm, the same feeling that had led me into the very situation I was in now. That's when I decided.

'I'd love to.' Following my heart once had definitely paid off and looking around my unrecognisable office right now, I felt the joy emanating from the décor's creator. Yes, it was garish and overwhelmingly 'extra' but wasn't that what Christmas was about – unless you were religious of course.

'You would?' Finn repeated.

'I would. If it's not too much trouble? I don't want to get in the way.'

The laugh rumbled again. 'You definitely won't. I can't wait to tell Alice. She's going to be so excited!'

'I'm excited too. I think!' Maybe it was time for me to add a bit of 'extra' to my life.

Finn pulled me back against him as his eyes darkened with

heat. His head bent and I lost all thought of professionalism as warm lips brushed my neck and that now familiar but ever exciting thrill rushed through my body at his touch.

'Elizabeth,' he whispered.

'Yes?' I replied, tilting my neck for easier access.

'I—'

The remainder of the sentence was lost as the phone on my desk rang loudly, rudely interrupting something which right then was far more important than anything anyone else could possibly have to say. I pulled myself away, reluctance equal on both sides and reached over to answer it. Finn's eyes remained upon me for a moment until his own phone stole his attention.

* * *

'Wow! This is quite something!' Inis said, looking around as she entered the grotto later that afternoon.

Laughing, I looked up from my desk to greet her, taking in the décor anew as I did so. 'That's one way to put it. I thought you had seen it. Finn mentioned that he'd asked you about it before he set to work.'

'No,' she said, picking up a snow globe and tipping it up to set the flakes in motion before replacing it on Finn's desk. 'He asked if you'd mind and I didn't think you would but I was more imagining a Christmas tree and a few bits of tinsel, not Santa's workshop on steroids.'

'He has apologised for going overboard.'

Inis laughed. 'I hope you told him he had no need to. This is absolutely joyful!' She turned back to me. 'Don't you think?'

Inis had hit upon the right word. That was exactly it. Joyful. Just as Finn's appreciation and excitement about the season appeared to be. And it wasn't just Christmas. It was his approach to life, something he appeared to share with his family and I loved how it was infectious and bringing out a side of me I hadn't even known existed. He was considered but also impulsive. Serious when he needed to be but silly when he wanted to be. His job meant a lot to him but it wasn't his entire world. When he wanted, he could switch off. I'd thought talking about work and my field of interest with my partner was the ideal but now I was beginning to question that. That wasn't the only thing I was questioning. I'd thought archaeology was the most important thing in my life – if not the only thing I needed, then very close to it. But Finn was opening doors that not only had been locked, but that I hadn't even known were there.

* * *

'Am I dull?' I asked Colette that night when we got together for a meal and a catch up.

'What? No! Not at all.'

'Even before I met Finn?'

'No.'

'But?'

'But what?'

'I can see there's a but there.'

'I don't know what you mean,' Colette replied, her face a picture of pure innocence. I had, however, known my friend for far too long to be lulled into the sense of reassurance she was obviously hoping for.

'Tell me.'

'*Merde*,' she mumbled. 'You know there are distinct disadvantages to having known people for as long as we have.'

I shrugged. 'Spill the beans.'

'First, no, you're not boring. But you have been, at times, rather singular in your focus.'

'Work you mean.'

'Not just work, but the subject itself. I mean, I know that it's your passion but until recently, I have wondered at times if it was to the detriment of other aspects of your life.'

'Ah.'

'And of course your parents didn't help.' Colette, having at first been reluctant to say anything at all now seemed disinclined to stop. 'I always thought it was a bit unfair that you didn't have any Christmas decorations up but that they wanted you to be there for Christmas.'

'We did exchange gifts. They just didn't go in for the whole decoration thing. I don't think it was a failing. And I wanted to be with them.'

'No, but I wish you'd come to France and celebrated with us when you were younger. It might have made you more inclined to come when you were older rather than always making excuses not to.'

I sat up. 'I haven't made excuses.'

Colette speared a fried halloumi stick and bit into it, fixing her eyes on me as she did so. The expression in them suggested that she and I had differing opinions on this.

'Is that what you think?'

She gave me a maybe yes, maybe no look as she drowned another stick in chilli jam and popped it in her mouth.

'I know you didn't like Friedrich and I felt I ought to spend it with him too when we were together. The last thing you would have wanted was for me to ask you to invite him.'

'You're right, he would definitely not have been invited. I'm just glad you didn't marry him. That would have been awkward.'

'He wasn't quite as bad as you think he was.'

'Lizzie, I met him enough to form an opinion and I didn't care for his attitude on a lot of things, including the way he always stole any glory he could from you.'

'I'm not sure he did, Col. We're just in the same field so there are going to be comparisons and linked stories.'

'Funny that, without fail, those stories turned into ones about himself.' She stabbed another stick, this time with such force I half expected the plate to be on the end of the fork when she lifted it.

'You should have said something.'

'I didn't want to upset you, or us to fall out. And to be honest, you always seemed content to stay home around Christmas anyway.'

Echoes of my conversation with Finn floated back to me. The very thing I'd told him about my parents, the hint of criticism I'd made about them was now the same one being levelled, and likely accurately, at me by my friend.

I reached across the table and covered Colette's free hand with my own. 'I'm so sorry. I never knew you felt that way.'

She swallowed the mouthful of cheese and took a sip of iced water. 'I know. And yes, you're right. Perhaps I should have mentioned it to you before. It's easy to get into the habit of not saying anything and just accepting the status quo.'

'You're right. I sent my parents a picture of the office after Finn had decorated it.'

Colette's hand paused, her wine glass part way to her mouth. 'And?'

'They asked me how I felt about it.'

Colette took a delicate sip. 'And?' She repeated.

'And I told them the truth. That it had been a shock initially but that actually I was loving being, quite literally, immersed in the spirit of the season.'

'Did they say anything else?'

I took a sip of my own wine. 'Just that they were glad I was enjoying life and that I seemed happy with my "new chap".' I made the shapes with my free hand. 'I haven't told them much other than I met someone.'

'I'm glad you're happy with your new chap too.'

'Thanks. But, like I told them, it's still early days. We are pretty different.'

'Opposites attract.'

'So they say.'

'Maybe you just didn't give them a chance to before.'

'I think the bottles of fizz were heavily instrumental in giving this one a chance.'

'They merely gave you a nudge in the right direction. You followed your heart for once instead of your terribly clever but eminently sensible head. And I, for one, am glad. And I think you are too.'

'Alright, smarty pants.'

Colette giggled at the term. It was one that had always tickled her.

'I am.' I paused. 'He's asked me to spend Christmas with him and his family.'

Colette's eyes shone with happiness. 'He has? And what did you say?'

'I said yes. But now I feel bad knowing that you asked me and I never agreed!'

'Oh, pfft.' She made that classically dismissive French sound. 'That is in the past. Perhaps next year you can come out to Paris and we will do it then.'

'Oh, Colette, that would be so lovely, thank you.'

'But in the meantime, I'm thrilled you're going to be spending this one with Finn and his family.'

'Me too. I was thinking of asking Alice if she wants to meet for coffee sometime. Would you come too?'

'Sounds perfect.'

Since the party, Finn and Greg had been teaching us both sign language. We weren't great but had at least added a few more useful words and sentences to our repertoire than just excellent curse ones. And, as Finn had explained, Alice did lip read too. I'd run the idea of coffee past him first and he'd assured me that his sister would be thrilled to be asked and, if needed, he could always go over and babysit.

* * *

Friday had rolled around faster than expected and a tap on the open door of my grotto that afternoon pulled me from my spread-sheet. Spreadsheets were the bane of my life. But spreadsheets on a Friday afternoon was just wrong. There ought to be a law against it. The distraction was, therefore, much welcomed and I looked up to see Bella. She was back to the original, more relaxed sartorial style she'd favoured before Finn had entered into our midst and she seemed happier, and more at ease, for it. The fact that Inis had agreed to hold her post open while she was on the dig, which she definitely was now to be part of, I knew was also a weight off her mind. I'd suggested, strongly, that she secure confirmation from Friedrich in writing and after a momentary look of horror she'd hurried off to do so. Bella was a knowledge-able member of the team and we'd miss her. Despite the original drama, or perhaps because of it, our own relationship was now more relaxed than it had been too.

'You have visitors,' she said, grinning again at my unrecognis-able office. 'You know, I think things definitely worked out for the

best. I'm not sure how this would fit into my minimalist decorating aesthetic.'

'The one thing it's not is minimalist,' I replied, laughing as I
rose from behind my desk to go and greet the visitors she had
alerted me to. I wasn't expecting anyone so I hoped I hadn't
missed putting anything vital in my diary.

'I hope you're not disparaging my masterpiece,' Finn
responded as he came along the corridor, the heels of his smart
shoes clicking on the flooring as he walked.

'Would we?' I asked, eyes wide with innocence.

'If you thought I was out of earshot, quite possibly.'

I reached up as he stopped in front of us. 'Not at all,' I said
and kissed his cheek. Past me had been so worried about what
others thought, what was thought professional. But there was
more to life, and finally, I got that. If anyone had a problem with
me giving my boyfriend a quick peck on the cheek, after the
amount of hours I put into this job, then they might well be the
one with a problem. I'd never been arrogant, but I did know that I
was damn good at my job and should I need to find another, it
was unlikely to be as hard for me as it would be for the museum
to find someone who was as dedicated and conscientious for the
same salary.

'There's someone waiting for me in reception. See you in a
bit.'

Bella walked part of the way back with me. 'You make a really
cute couple.'

'Thanks,' I said, my laugh slightly breathy. It was certainly
new to be referred to as part of a 'cute couple', but Bella hadn't
been the only one to say so now that we'd met more of Finn and
Greg's friends. My colleague turned to head back to the archive
where she'd been working.

'I'll see you later.'

I walked on towards the marbled reception area of the museum. Curly-haired men stared down from two plinths, wantonly uncaring that their bits and pieces were on show and had been for centuries. Admiring one of them with a surprising degree of intensity was my mother.

'Mum?'

'Oh, there you are! Hello, my love. How are you?' She reached out and I went to her for the brief, perfunctory hug that was our usual greeting and was therefore surprised to find that this time she wrapped her arms closer around me and held me tighter for longer before letting go.

I stepped back. 'Oh my God, you're dying.'

14

Mum looked confused for a moment, then shook her head. 'No darling, I'm not dying.'

'Then it's Dad. Dad's got something awful!' I felt the tears pricking at my eyes. I knew I should have made more effort to get down to Devon but I'd always harboured a niggling fear that they might slightly resent the intrusion into their quiet, retired but still resolutely academic, life.

My mother reached and took my hands in hers. I stared down at them.

'Look at me, Lizzie.'

Reluctantly I raised my eyes to meet her own bright blue ones, framed by a pair of trendy new specs I didn't recognise.

'We are both fine. Fit as the proverbial flea.'

'Are you sure?'

'Yes,' she pressed my hands gently in reassurance, 'I'm sure.'

'Then why are you here?'

Mum tilted her head to the side and the tears that had now subsided from my own eyes appeared in hers. 'Oh dear. We really have made a mess of our relationship with you, haven't we?'

'What?' I squeezed her hands back, probably a little harder than I meant to but the crack in her voice reverberated deep in my soul.

'We're your parents, Lizzie. There shouldn't have to be a reason for a visit.'

'No, no I know. It's just, well. Devon's not exactly round the corner.'

'We came on the train last night. It was really rather lovely. We never should have left it so long.'

'I should have come down to you more often.'

'You're working, darling. It's not as easy for you. No,' she said, her manner determined. 'The onus was on us and I'm sorry we haven't made more of an effort.'

'What's brought all this on, Mum?'

'Hello, my bright button!' Dad's voice boomed around the marble, echoing off the surfaces. Bob, the security guard, threw me a grin and I knew exactly how I would be greeted the next time I came in. Not that I minded.

'Hello, Dad!' I said, hugging him close. 'It's such a lovely surprise to see you both.'

'It's been far too long.' He exchanged a look with Mum. 'This health scare has really made us sit up and reassess how we've been living our lives.'

My eyebrows flew to the top of my head. 'What health scare?' My voice pitched up an octave, possibly two. Mum shot him a look.

'William,' she sighed. 'I've just spent the last five minutes convincing the poor girl that she has nothing to worry about in that regard. You can't just go blurting things out.'

Dad winced, his expression contrite. 'Sorry.' He turned to me. 'There really isn't any need to worry.'

I heaved out a breath. 'It sounds like there's a lot to talk about.

Why don't you come up to my office and have a cup of tea and I'll see if I can get off a bit early.'

'We don't mean to interrupt your day, darling. We can just arrange to meet later if that's convenient?'

'No,' I replied. 'Some things are more important than work. It's not like I don't put the hours in.'

'No. You always were so conscientious.'

'I had good role models.'

Mum gave a little head wobble, apparently doubting my claim.

'Come on,' I said. 'Let's go up to the office and get a drink. I'm pretty sure I saw Finn had biscuits so we can swipe some of those too.'

'Who's Finn?' Dad asked as we made our way along the corridors, both of my parents peering at the odd exhibit that had been strategically placed to add visual interest to the passageways.

'He's the project manager for the new exhibition space.'

'Ah OK. Going well, is it?'

'Well, it was kind of unexpected and it's early days really, but yes, I think so.' It was only when I went to speak again that I realised my parents were no longer beside me. I stopped and turned.

'What?'

'I was talking about the exhibition space build,' Dad said. He exchanged a look with Mum and a grin slipped onto his face. 'But it seems there is something far more interesting in your life than that?'

'Oh! Yes, well no. I mean, that's a major thing of course. The build. It's going to be such a boon to the museum and the plans for the first exhibition are going great. There are still some things to iron out, of course, but there always are.' I was well aware that a), I was jabbering and b), neither of my parents were buying it.

'That's good to hear,' my dad said after a moment or two of silence.

'As is the fact that said project manager is the chap you mentioned. Is that how you met?' Mum's eyes twinkled behind her lenses. 'I do hope this one is worthy of you.' She never had been one to beat around the bush.

I skimmed over the details of how Finn and I actually met. Some things were best kept from your parents! 'Friedrich wasn't that bad.' A small part of my brain was sat in the corner, legs crossed, chin resting upon its hand, pondering why I was always so ready to defend Friedrich.

'Oh darling, he was rather a know-it-all and I was never keen on how whenever you had a particular achievement he always felt the need to pipe up about some marvellous thing he'd done.'

My mind recalled how Colette had recently said the same. 'You never said anything.'

'No.' She cast her eyes down momentarily. 'I didn't really know how to. I know I can be rather blunt at times but we thought you were happy. Your dad did want to mention it but I'm afraid, despite years of dealing with students, neither of us had a clue how to say the right thing to our own daughter. Something we now regret most bitterly.'

Instinctively I reached over and hugged them both in a group hug. 'Don't worry about it. It's all ancient history now.' I paused. 'Well, not ancient in the manner we're used to but you know what I mean.'

She dragged up a half-hearted smile. 'We do.'

'Come on, let's get you that tea.'

'Oh my word!' Dad exclaimed as we turned into my office. Mum's mouth was open. Finn's décor had apparently rendered her speechless.

'The picture I sent didn't really do it justice, I'm afraid. You

can really only get the full experience in person.' I looked around
the room now, tinsel wrapped around any available post or table
leg, festive garlands edging both of our desks, enough fairy lights
to illuminate a small country, a highly decorated tree and a three
foot tall, once laughing but now silent, Father Christmas. That
particular display had lasted about half an hour before I'd
removed the batteries. I had my limits.

'This is... ummm...'

'A touch over the top?'

Mum and Dad remained speechless, apparently unwilling to
say anything about what they obviously thought was my own
handiwork. It occurred to me that I hadn't explained in the
attached message that I'd personally had nothing to do with the
new look my workplace was now sporting.

'No, I mean, it's... very... umm... Christmassy.'

Giggles bubbled up inside me and I could no longer contain
them.

'It's fine. You can't offend me. I felt exactly the same when I
walked in to find it like this.'

'Someone else decorated your office?'

'Yes.' My parents looked horrified. 'But,' I hurried on, 'it's OK.
I'm sharing it at the moment and they did check with my boss
before they did it.'

'But surely they should have checked with you?'

'They wanted it to be a surprise.'

Mum looked around. 'I can imagine it was certainly that.'

'I'm actually rather fond of it now,' I assured her, realising as I
said it that I truly was.

They both nodded, once again temporarily at a loss for words.
I took the opportunity to sit them down before I nipped off to the
kitchen to make some drinks, suggesting they make themselves at

home as I did so. Both turned to me with mirroring expressions of stunned bemusement and I left the room, chuckling quietly to myself.

When I returned, three museum-branded mugs balanced precariously on a tray, my eyes glued to them as I tried not to remember my one and only attempt at waitressing years ago, I heard laughter drifting out from the office and wondered if Inis had run into my parents. But then I heard the familiar, deep tones that always sent darts of heat to places that should remain resolutely cool during work hours.

'Hi!' Finn was already up, crossing the office in a couple of strides and lifting the tray from me.

'Sorry. I didn't realise you were here or I would have made you one.'

'No problem. I've just had one downstairs.'

I handed out the mugs. 'I see you've met Finn.'

'Yes,' Mum said, all smiles. Finn could charm the apples off a tree. 'We were admiring his choice of décor.'

Finn let out a chuckle. 'I'm not sure admiring is the right word. They were both sat here open-mouthed when I walked in.'

'It's quite something.'

His eyes roamed around the grotto tableau he'd created. 'I guess. But Elizabeth was great about it. And I think it's grown on her.' He looked down at me before his eyes drifted to the Father Christmas figure. 'Most of it anyway.'

'That's true. Although I fear it's going to look terribly bare when it all comes down after Christmas.'

He shrugged. 'It's always that way with decorating at Christmas though, isn't it? Just makes you look forward to the next one even more.'

Both my parents suddenly found great interest in their tea

and I studied a vital Post-It note on my desk as I moved around to sit down on my chair. Even that had tinsel on the gas strut. Honestly, the man had covered every single inch. It was probably a good thing I hadn't been in here at the time. If I'd have stood still for a couple of minutes I'd have been decorated too!

Finn crouched down beside me, one of his knees clicking as he did so, the noise sounding loud in the momentarily quiet office. 'Why do I get the feeling I just put my size thirteen in something?'

My hand automatically slid to where his was resting on the edge of my desk, balancing himself. 'You didn't.'

Blue eyes met mine looking entirely unconvinced and, rather sweetly, bearing in mind the size of the man, a little insecure.

'Nothing to worry about, Finn.' Dad broke the atmosphere that had descended over our small group. 'I'm afraid Lizzie's mother and I were rather more occupied with our studies than with making sure our daughter was surrounded by the warm, festive feeling you've created here.'

'Dad...' I shook my head.

'No, Lizzie.' Mum joined in. 'He's right. As your dad said earlier, we've had the opportunity to reconsider various choices we made in the past and have found some of them to be wanting.'

Finn stood. 'This sounds like a private discussion. I'll get out of your way, but it was a pleasure to meet you.'

'Please, Finn,' Mum said. 'Don't leave on account of us. You're most welcome to stay. I can see now why Lizzie was smiling when she mentioned you even before we knew you were the one.'

'I didn't say you were the one!' I squeaked before clearing my throat. 'I didn't,' I said, turning to Finn to reassure him, this time at a more normal pitch.

The broad shoulders gave a shrug.

'Sorry. Poor turn of phrase.' Mum spoke up. 'Although...' she looked from me to Finn and I gave her a warning glare in return. 'But in all honesty, even if you hadn't accidentally told us, the way both your faces lit up when you came in from the kitchen was enough to give even us two a sign that there's something special between you.'

I don't know what Finn had done to me but my previous ability to filter out everything but work had been decimated. I caught a glance at him, and at my parents' faces, now creased gently with concern.

'We're honestly very pleased, Lizzie. From the short acquaintance we've had with you, Finn, you seem very lovely and even just seeing Lizzie downstairs, it was obvious that something had changed in her life. Something for the better.'

'What do you mean?' I asked, frowning at her.

Mum tilted her head to the side. 'You were always so serious, my love.' She held up her hand as I opened my mouth. 'And I know we, if not wholly, then at least had a large part to play in that. Other relationships seem to have compounded that, but it appears that Finn here has brought out the fun, lighter side of you that we never took the time to nurture.'

The scene in front of me blurred as tears sprang to my eyes. This was another new aspect to my personality. I'd always been able to keep a lid on my emotions before, at least until I was sure of privacy. The man might be hot as lava, sweet as chocolate and bloody amazing in bed but I could have kicked him for this. A tissue appeared in front of me, attached to a large hand. I grabbed for it, wiped my eyes, gave a hearty blow of my nose and tossed the tissue in the bin.

'This is your fault,' I said, craning my neck up to look at Finn who was standing beside me looking for all the world like he'd rather be anywhere but here.

'Yes, I was getting that feeling.'

'Why don't we all go to dinner this evening?' Dad suggested, 'If you're both free? I know it's a bit short notice and all that.'

'I'd love to,' Finn spoke first. 'But I'm afraid I'm chief babysitter for my sister tonight.' He looked down at me. 'Sorry.'

'That's OK. Say hi to Alice and everyone for me.'

He squeezed my shoulder. 'I'd better get back to work. Thanks very much for the offer,' he said, looking back at my parents now. 'It was really nice to meet you.'

'And you, my boy.' Dad said. 'Hopefully we can do it another time before we head back down to Devon.'

Finn's smile was genuine and wide. 'That would be great. Thanks.' He bent quickly and dashed a kiss on my cheek. 'Talk to you later,' he said, his voice soft and close to my ear. Then he straightened, grabbed his laptop from his desk and strode out of the room.

'He's lovely, Lizzie.'

'Thanks. Like I said, it's still early days.'

Mum appeared to receive the message and decided against pushing for more information, and instead changed the subject. 'Are you free for dinner tonight?'

'Yes, I am. Let me just finish up here and I can sneak off a bit early.'

Finn was hardworking, but he was also a bad influence. Prior to meeting him, I'd probably have sat here until at least seven before dashing off to meet my parents for a hurried meal. Then again, I thought, taking in the faces I'd only seen via a video screen for far too long, perhaps he wasn't such a bad influence after all.

* * *

'So, basically all was well in the end. Just put the wind up us both for a bit.' Dad finished recounting the health scare about his heart that had prompted their desire to begin making some changes in their lives, and that apparently included making amends for what they felt were inadequacies in raising me.

'Honestly, you're overthinking it all.'

'We're not, darling. Believe me, we've taken a good hard look at the way we've lived our lives and found ourselves rather wanting.'

'I really wasn't bothered about not having a tree, or decorations, for Christmas. And, as you saw today, I've been more than compensated in one year for any tinsel deprivation!' I laughed but the most Mum and Dad could do was raise weak smiles. 'Honestly, you're worrying too much.'

'If we could do it all again, we would and quite differently,' Mum said, her eyes casting downward.

'Well, we can't,' I replied, shrugging. 'And I hate that thinking about it all is making you both unhappy. I've never felt like I missed out. Yes, ours was different from some other houses and some other families but you encouraged me to read and question things. That's something I've never forgotten and it helped me in achieving my goal to work in the field I am. I could never get back the hours and years of encouragement to study and without that I wouldn't be where I am now.'

My parents exchanged a look.

'Please,' I said, spreading my hands on the table and taking one of theirs in each of mine. 'You need to let this go. But I would love to see you more so let's all just agree to make sure that happens. Deal?'

The smiles returned. 'Deal.'

'So what else are you doing whilst you're up here?'

'Tomorrow we thought we'd take another step to our new start.'

'Oh?' I said, leaning forward, intrigued.

'Yes. We're going to hit the shops and stock up on Christmas decorations.'

Even hearing my dad use the phrase 'hit the shops' was extraordinary but I felt a happy warmth envelop me at the enthusiasm behind the words. I hadn't been lying when I said that I was grateful for the way I'd been brought up. Yes, perhaps it would have been nice if we'd spent more time outdoors and doing more traditional family things from time to time but as I'd said, would I be in a job I loved in a field of study I was passionate about if I'd had a different upbringing? I might not have been to Disney World but we regularly had family excursions to bookshops and frankly that was a far better deal in my eyes.

'Have you got any ideas where we should start?'

'I'm afraid you're looking at the wrong person, but I do know someone who can probably give you some tips.'

By the next morning, Finn had supplied my parents with a list of shops that included the greats like Liberty and Selfridges, but also some small boutique places tucked away from the main tourist areas, which stocked different pieces made in small amounts by artisan glass-blowers and the like. Having met early for breakfast before I started work, they were raring to go, filled with an enthusiasm that I hadn't seen in years. The thought of my parents going through Dad's health scare upset me, especially as they hadn't told me because they 'didn't want to worry me'. I was incredibly glad, of course, that the outcome had been benign but also grateful for this new lease of life it appeared to have instilled in them. They were heading back to Devon on the early train tomorrow but we made arrangements to video call in a couple of days and set up a proper visit.

* * *

'If you want to spend Christmas with your parents, that's totally understandable,' Finn said a couple of days later over the heavenly spaghetti carbonara he'd cooked.

'No, it's fine. I said I'd already made arrangements and when Colette and I met Alice for coffee the other day, she was so excited.'

'But she'd understand,' he said, expertly twisting the pasta onto his fork.

Resting my own cutlery on the plate momentarily, I took the white linen napkin from my lap and dabbed at my chin where I had just slapped myself in the face with a strand of spaghetti. 'Not the point.' I shook my head as I resumed my meal. 'I'm looking forward to it too.'

'Good.' He grinned, wiping his mouth before taking a sip of the full-bodied, fruity red wine he'd served with the dish. 'Because, selfishly, I'm looking forward to waking up to you on Christmas Day. That's probably the best present I could think of.'

I finished my last mouthful before raising my eyes to his, the hint of a frown creasing my brow.

'Probably?'

He stood and then bent over my chair from behind, his warm breath tickling my ear as he spoke, arms with corded muscles wrapping just tight enough around my shoulders. 'Most definitely the best present ever. In fact, I might even have to unwrap it early.'

Some time later that evening, Finn was watching a documentary on bridges which was, surprisingly, far more interesting than it sounded. The book I'd been reading now lay closed on my lap.

'You'd be good at doing programmes like this.'

Finn laughed as a commercial break came on. 'Me? I don't think so.'

'You would. You know your stuff, although that's not always necessary as I guess these things are scripted, but you do, and you have the enthusiasm as well as that knowledge. Plus you're pretty to look at. I'm sure the latter would be enough of a draw for a lot of people.'

He gave me a brief, sceptical look.

'It's true. Whether you believe it or not.'

'Thanks. I'll bear it in mind for my next job.'

I shuffled on the sofa, snuggling in more towards Finn, who responded by wrapping his closest arm around me, laying the other across my legs which were now hooked over his long, outstretched ones.

'What is your next project, do you know?'

There was a pause before he replied, and he shifted position slightly. 'No, not really. There's a few things I'm looking into that have been floated in my direction but I'm undecided at present.'

'Do you mind that?'

'What?'

'Being a contractor? Self-employed. Would you rather have the security of a set position within a company?'

'Is that any more secure these days?' he asked, flipping the TV back off mute now that the adverts were ending.

'I suppose not.'

'I like the variety. I get to pick and choose to work on whatever project interests me the most. It's good.'

I leant my head against his chest, listening to the slow, steady rhythm of his heart. 'I'm glad you chose to do your current one.'

Finn's cuddle tightened around me. 'Me too. This has been the most rewarding and interesting job I've ever had.'

I smiled against him and focused back on the enthusiastic engineer on the television, currently swinging underneath a bridge on a harness and appearing to love every moment of it.

Rather him than me I thought as I snuggled deeper into Finn and closed my eyes, soothed by his heartbeat.

15

'How do you feel about a weekend away?'

I looked up from the screen, having just hung up from yet another Teams meeting. Video calls were all very well and did save time and travel when the participants were remote but nothing was quite as good as being in the same room together. It was certainly harder to build a rapport with people through a screen than it was when meeting in person.

'Huh?'

Finn placed a much-needed cup of coffee in front of me and then rested against the edge of the desk. He took a sip from his own mug before he spoke again. 'A weekend away. You and me. What do you think?'

'When?'

The broad shoulders shrugged. 'This weekend?'

My brows raised. 'Not one for planning things in advance, are you?'

'I spend my working life planning things to the nth degree. Outside of that, I'm inclined to be a little more spontaneous.'

'I suppose that makes sense.'

'So?'

I made some notes from the meeting before looking up again. 'Umm, yes I guess.'

Finn gave a chuckle. 'Don't sound too enthused.'

I laid down my pen and concentrated on him. 'Sorry. My mind was elsewhere.'

'Everything OK?'

'Yes, just coordinating the items we're getting on loan and we've just agreed to lend an exhibit to the Met in New York so there's rather a lot on at the moment.'

'Sorry.' He pushed himself up off the desk. 'I'm disturbing you. We can talk about this later.'

'No.' I caught his hand. 'Tell me what you were thinking while I have this,' I said, raising the coffee to my lips. Finn rested back against the desk.

'Sure?'

'Yes. I've just sat through a two-hour meeting. I need the break. So, what were you thinking?' I asked again.

'Ever been to Bath?'

'I have but it was ages ago. Colette and I went to see the Roman Baths and I'd planned a tour but I could see she was flagging after the Baths so we ended up at the hotel bar for the rest of it.'

Finn grinned. 'There are worse places to be.'

'That's true. And we still had a lovely time.' I frowned. 'From what I remember.'

'They have an amazing Christmas market there. I thought perhaps we could go for that?'

'Are you sure you're not an elf in disguise?' If he was, it was a bloody good disguise. I doubted there were many six foot five, built-like-a-brick-outhouse helpers up at the North Pole.

'Not always in disguise,' he replied cryptically.

I put my mug down, my eyes fixed on him. 'Now that sounds like a story.'

'Let's just say I got the short straw. I was aiming for Father Christmas.'

'Please tell me that there are pictures.'

'Not that I'm letting you see.' He laughed. 'I've got an image to maintain.'

Leaning down, I grabbed my phone out of my bag and tapped out a quick message.

'What are you doing?' Finn leant over to see the screen but I tilted it away from him.

A few moments later, my phone beeped with the reply. 'Oh my God! Your face!' I said, laughing. 'You look so pissed off.' He made a swipe for the phone and I let him have it.

'My sister is such a traitor.'

'You look so cute!'

Finn's mouth was set in a line. 'I wasn't going for cute.'

'Even so, you nailed it.'

'Thanks.' There was a glimmer of amusement in those sexy eyes.

I leant closer. 'Do you still have the outfit?'

'Why?'

I wiggled my eyebrows and Finn burst out laughing. 'You're a very strange woman.'

'Thanks.'

'Although it is, of course, up to the elves to tell the big man who's been naughty and who's been nice.' He returned the tease.

'Hi, Finn,' Bella said, striding in and screeching the conversation to a halt, which was probably just as well.

'Hi, Bella. How are you?'

'Not bad, thanks,' she said, placing a folder back on the shelf to the side of his desk. She swung a glance as she turned back, checking him out as she did so. I couldn't blame her. Although she seemed over her initial crush, as an archaeologist and a lover of history, she was an admirer of beautiful things. Finn most definitely fell into that category. Even when dressed as an elf.

* * *

The drive down to Bath had been surprisingly free flowing and I teased Finn that he must have used some of his elf magic to ensure a good journey. He'd shaken his head, mumbling something about how he wished he'd never opened his mouth but the smile on his face told a different story. I loved that I could tease him, and that he in turn did the same back. I'd never laughed as much in the whole time I was with Friedrich as I had in the last few months with Finn. My world view was so much wider and this spontaneous trip was another new experience.

'This is gorgeous,' I said, dropping my handbag on the side as I nosed about the hotel room.

'Glad you like it,' Finn said, following me in with the luggage.

'I love it!' I replied, throwing him a smile as I pulled back the sheer curtain to look at the view. The city spread out and away from us, the vista expanding to the hills beyond. 'Thank you.'

'I thought you'd like a boutique hotel rather than one of the larger chains.'

Once again, he'd read me right.

'Not a bad view, eh?' Finn said, coming to stand behind me at the window, his arms slipping around my waist, his body pressed close to mine.

'Wonderful.'

'It'll be nicer if it stops raining. I was hoping we might get a walk around this evening, but the weather seems to have other ideas.'

'That's OK. I'm pretty tired from the journey anyway. You've had a full day and a long drive too. We've got the next two days to explore.' I tipped my head up and he kissed my forehead, his lips curved in a smile. 'Ooh, what's the bathroom like?' I wriggled out and headed off to investigate. Pushing open the door, I was met with a scene of pure indulgence. White marble streaked with delicate strands of black glistened around the sink and shower, the enclosure of the latter frosted in parts in the angular Art Deco style all accented by brass fixtures. I walked over to the elegant free-standing bath, across which sat a bamboo bath rack. I picked up the scented candle it held and gave it a sniff. Lavender, sage and a hint of geranium made a soothing combination. I couldn't wait to light it. The floor was dark slate and the room itself was painted in a deep, rich green as were the sides of the bath. The final touch was the plethora of greenery. Frothy ferns spilling over their containers, a large hammered-brass pot that held something with banana plant-type leaves and several others, all crammed together, which enhanced the décor perfectly.

Finn leant on the doorframe. 'You want to spend the rest of the weekend in that bath, don't you?'

I laughed, nosing at the free smellies lined up on the marble counter, unscrewing one of the lids to take a sniff. 'Isn't it heaven though? Ooh, smell this.' I held the little bottle up to his nose.

'Nice.'

'Thanks for arranging all this, Finn.' I followed him out to the main room which followed the same theme. All luxury and indulgence. 'It's perfect.'

Friedrich and I had taken holidays but they were always to sites of rich history which was fine. As much as Finn teased me about wanting to wallow in the tub, I was looking forward to having the chance to explore Bath and visit the market, just as he was. But that was the difference. Looking back now, previous breaks were more akin to school trips. It was all study, all learning. Don't get me wrong. I loved to learn, to absorb the history of places and its people. That would never change. It was part of who I was. But life was about balance and so were holidays. I worked hard for those breaks but it had apparently never occurred to me, or previous companions, that when we ventured to a different location we could loosen up a bit. Enjoy the surroundings on a more superficial level as well as the deeply historical one.

'You're deep in thought over there.'

I'd wandered back to the window, looking out on the steady rain that had started about halfway into the journey and showed no signs of stopping any time soon.

'Not really,' I replied, turning back from the window. The light was fading and I pulled the heavy velvet curtains across, the room now bathed in soft, warm light from the bedside lamp Finn had switched on.

'Fibber,' he said, a smile teasing those just full enough lips. 'Come here.'

I padded over, having immediately kicked off my shoes the moment I found the hotel slippers. I'd be snuggling into the soft, white dressing gown with its embroidered logo on the chest shortly too. Finn had laughed at my little squeal of delight upon finding them both. It turned out I was fairly easy to please.

Clambering onto the bed, I wiggled myself next to Finn and he laced his fingers through mine.

'What were you thinking about?'

I opened my mouth.

'And don't tell me nothing.' His free hand reached over and with the gentlest of touches, hooked under my chin and tilted it to meet his eyes.

'I suppose I was just thinking of missed opportunities.'

'Anything I can do?'

Smiling, I shook my head. 'No, but thank you for wanting to.'

He leant forward, placing a light kiss on my lips. His voice was low when he spoke. 'I will always endeavour to keep that beautiful smile on your face.'

'You know, you were right.'

'About what?'

'You are romantic when you're sober too.'

'Told you. Now, if that was your stomach I just heard, I think we need to decide what to do about dinner. We can go and find something or,' he scooped me towards him, 'as I saw your eyes lingering hungrily on that cosy dressing gown in the bathroom, we can always snuggle in for the night here and order room service.'

I leant my head back against him. 'That sounds absolutely perfect.'

'It does, doesn't it?' He leant over, grabbed the in-room dining menu and leaning it on his flat stomach, opened it for us to peruse.

* * *

Bath in full seasonal dress was stunning. The hotel Finn had booked was perfect. Boutique, stylish and with just enough of a country feel to it to remind us that we were most definitely not in London. I'd woken early and looked out of the window to see a sleeping city. Without the hustle and bustle of the day, it was easy to imagine it at its height of popularity when carriages would be returning their owners home right about now after a night of dancing at a ball. I'd climbed back under the wonderfully soft duvet, snuggled up to Finn and drifted back to sleep dreaming of times past. A leisurely, and delicious, full English breakfast began the day well, our enjoyment enhanced by the inclusion of proper fried bread. None of that toast substitute for this place. The rain had passed through in the night, and filled to the brim, we wrapped up against the bright, but bitterly cold day and headed out, ready for me to experience my first ever Christmas market.

'These are beautiful,' I said, tugging Finn over, my gloved hand wrapped in his own, my eyes drifting over the handmade glass stall. Beautifully displayed amongst delicate seasonal garlands and fairy lights were ornaments, artwork and jewellery. 'Look at this one,' I said, pointing to a delicate fuchsia pink flower encased within a clear star-shaped pendant. 'Do you think Alice would like it?'

'She would. It's just the sort of thing she'd choose herself. Except she wouldn't because she's great at spoiling everyone but herself.'

'I think lots of people are like that, especially if you have children, I'm sure.'

'Sometimes it's good to spoil yourself though. Life's short and you never know what's around the next corner so, if you have the money, then why not?'

Until my parents' visit my thinking had been more in line with Alice's. But Dad's health scare had given us all a much-needed shove out of our complacency. As Finn had said, and had experienced, you didn't know what life held in store. Alice had pulled through, thank goodness, albeit not without cost. At the thought of something being wrong with Dad my body had flushed with pure, cold dread and panic. I couldn't begin to imagine the terror that Finn and his family had gone through, seeing their daughter, their sister, swamped by a hospital bed and equipment, the final outcome unknown. Finn's words now resonated loudly in my mind.

'I agree. Shall I get it for her Christmas present?'

'Elizabeth, you don't have to do that. No one is expecting anything from you other than your,' he nuzzled my neck, 'very delightful company.'

'Your nose is cold!' I said, laughing as I rearranged my scarf.

'I was warming it up on your neck,' he said, pulling me closer.

I leant back a little so that I could see him. 'I'd like to get this for Alice though.' Excitement whooshed through me at the thought of the present buying. A lot of people appeared to find it the bane of their lives but I'd always enjoyed the task. Thinking, researching, hunting out just the right thing. Of course, until now I'd only had Colette and my parents to cater for. Friedrich had told me, after I'd been Christmas shopping the first year we were together, that he felt the whole thing was just the chance for capitalism to make a grab for people's wallets. A roundabout way of telling me not to expect a present. I'd donated his to a local charity Christmas drive and never bothered again. But he hadn't quashed the desire. And now, with the prospect of spending the day with Finn's family, I was loving the opportunity to go all out.

'She'd love it,' he confirmed and I grinned, handing it to the stall owner and adding another bag to our growing collection.

As darkness fell on the city, the Christmas lights took over, adding an extra layer of festive joy to the whole experience.

'How have I never been to one of these before?' I asked Finn as we found a bench and sat down, hands wrapped around a mug of real hot chocolate, topped with swirls of proper cream and finished with a flourish of mini marshmallows. It was likely a whole day's calorie allowance in a cup but I didn't care. It was bloody delicious and warming me from the inside.

'I don't know,' Finn said, having temporarily relinquished his job as pack horse, bags piled next to him on the bench as he sipped his own extra large version of the drink. 'I guess if it's not your thing then it's not something you'd be seeking out.'

'But I'm loving it! I can't tell you how much.'

Finn scanned the bags. 'I can hazard a guess.'

I gently bumped him with my shoulder, careful not to spill either drink. 'I don't just mean the shopping.'

He grinned at me with a fresh cream moustache which I managed to quickly snap a picture of before he wiped it off. 'I can put that one in pride of place alongside the grumpy elf one.'

Finn gave a shake of his head. 'I'm beginning to wonder if introducing you to my sister was such a good idea.' But the smile on his face spoke the truth.

'Too late. Anyway, like I said, it's not just the shopping. It's, well, this, for a start,' I said, indicating the drinks. 'Sitting here, with you, drinking hot chocolate enveloped in this atmosphere. I don't even care that I can't feel my bum.'

'I could always feel it for you.'

I shot him a look but he was entirely unrepentant. Finn made me laugh more than anyone I had ever known, but he also made me feel more wanted too. And frankly it was a heady combination that I was still getting used to but happily so.

'Thanks for suggesting this.'

'You're welcome. I'm having a wonderful time.'

I leant my head against his shoulder, sipped the drink and sat watching the scenes around us, absorbing the atmosphere, and storing it away on a shelf in my mind labelled favourite memories. Strangely enough, since I'd met Finn, the shelf was filling far quicker than it ever had in the past.

* * *

'This used to be Finn's old bedroom,' his mum said as she showed me up to the room shortly after we'd arrived. 'Heartbroken he was when we told him we'd ripped down all the Baywatch posters.'

'Oh, I didn't have you pegged as a Pamela Anderson fan?'

'Oh, no love,' his mum said, straightening the curtains in the warm and welcoming room. 'Not Pammy. David Hasselhoff.'

Finn put a hand to his side. 'Oh no, I think I cracked a rib.'

'Well, it wouldn't be the first time,' she said. 'I heard you had the sense to leave him to it on that rugby field.'

'I'm afraid so. Reading in the car was far less stressful.'

'Not to mention warmer, I expect! Good girl.' She turned back to Finn. 'You said she was clever. I think that says it all. The hours we spent on Sunday mornings freezing our backsides off while he ran up and down and got knocked black and blue as a kid. You wouldn't think to look at him now, but he was quite a puny little thing once.' Her eyes were dancing with mischief and I knew now where Finn got it from.

'Mum!'

She leant closer, conspiratorially. 'He's a bit tetchy about it.'

'I'm not tetchy.'

'See what I mean?'

I glanced up at Finn. His face was serious but it was becoming obvious that this was a family who laughed, and teased, together and were all the closer for doing so. He dropped his gaze to me and rolled his eyes in mock irritation.

I turned back to his mum. 'Please tell me you have pictures,' I said, laughing.

'Traitor.' Finn's voice was gruff but I could hear the warmth beneath the words.

* * *

The rest of the evening had been full of good food, laughter and the sense of warmth I'd felt the first time I'd met this family back on Alice's birthday. But this time I hadn't drunk much as I didn't want to be dealing with a hangover on Christmas Day.

'You're looking a bit shell-shocked,' Finn said as he closed the door to the guest room we'd been assigned at his parents' home.

'Am I?'

'Yeah,' Finn said, sitting down on the edge of the bed I'd just flopped onto. 'You OK?'

I pushed myself back up. 'Perfect. Yes, it's a lot but a lot in a good way. I love it. The way you all laugh together, the chatter, the stories of all your childhoods.'

'Some of those I could have done without!' Finn said, laughing as he lay back.

'But I couldn't.' I turned and leant on his chest, looking into those beautifully blue eyes. 'I loved hearing them. I loved hearing about you. Learning about you.'

Finn watched me for a few moments then wrapped his arms around me. 'Come here,' he said and cuddled me close.

'Hey?' Moments later the deep voice burrowed into the comfy, cosy space I was making in my brain for sleep.

'Hmm?'

'Go and get ready for bed.'

I grumbled as Finn unceremoniously tipped me off him. I sat up, rubbing my sleepy eyes.

'That wasn't very nice.'

He gave me one of those sexy smiles that he didn't even know he did and I forgave him. 'You'll thank me in the morning.'

I shuffled my bum to the edge of the bed and padded into the en suite his parents had installed. 'We'll see.'

The next morning Finn, me and his parents left at an absurdly early hour and drove the relatively short distance to

Alice's house. She'd already alerted her parents to the fact the children were awake and raring to go.

'She's calling in back up,' Finn had said, laughing as he'd led the way down the stairs, me following in a rather bleary eyed manner behind. However, within a short time, I had discovered that Christmas with Finn's family truly was as loud, exuberant and 'extra' as he had promised and then some. And I relished every moment.

'Just keep stirring,' Finn's dad had said as he showed me how to make gravy in the roasting pan as the turkey rested. 'That's it. Perfect! You're a natural.'

'I'm not sure about that,' I said.

'Here.' He handed me a spoon. 'Try that and tell me if you notice a difference to the instant stuff. Mind, it's piping hot.'

I tested the gravy as he suggested. 'Oh my God.'

His dad smiled. 'My work here is done.'

'What's going on?' Finn appeared at the door, his face relaxed, one shoulder leaning against the door jamb. 'I can't believe you've got Elizabeth working in here, Dad.'

'I wanted to!' I said, throwing him a smile. 'Come and taste this. I just made my first proper gravy! Seriously,' I said as he took the spoon and dipped it in. 'How did I not know this was a thing?'

'Yum. You're a natural.'

'That's what I said,' his dad called over as he turned from the oven, his glasses completely steamed up. 'Where did everybody go?'

'I love it!' Alice signed as she placed the small box in her lap. 'You shouldn't have.' She leant across from where both of us were sat on the floor with the children and hugged me.

'I wanted to,' I signed back at the same time as speaking the words.

I'd been determined to learn as much BSL as I could before

the big day and although I'd made a few mistakes, I was coming along. I'd accidentally called Finn's brother a potato instead of asking him to pass the potatoes but everyone, including myself, had laughed, but kindly, and helped me correct it. That was also a new experience. I didn't know if it was the relaxed atmosphere of this family home with close and extended members all crammed in together, or the result of my parents' visit and change in attitude to life. Either way, not getting everything right first time was no longer a failing in my eyes. It was part of the learning process. I'd always been on the ball about instilling this into the interns we had at the museum but somehow I'd omitted to take the same lesson into my own heart. But things were changing now. I was changing now. And, so far as I was concerned, it was all for the better.

'Are you coming into the treehouse?' Finn's niece, Lucy, asked once we were all as thoroughly stuffed as the delicious turkey had been.

'You have a treehouse?' I replied, my voice full of wonder as I crouched down to her level.

'Uncle Finn built it for us.' Her twin brother, Luke, joined in the conversation, taking my hand and leading me towards the back door.

'Luke, Lucy. Elizabeth hasn't got any shoes or coat on. And neither have you.'

They looked back to where their uncle, somehow still totally lust-inducing despite wearing a novelty Christmas jumper, was standing with his hands on his hips. Alice had now joined our little group.

'You built them a treehouse?'

'He's done loads for us in this house,' she signed as she spoke. 'Saved us a fortune. Mark's brilliant at lots of stuff but not practical at all. He's the first to admit it.'

'I know the feeling.'

'Finn can create anything. He's always been good with his hands.'

I was rather proud of myself for keeping a straight face and didn't dare look at Finn.

'Come on!' Luke tugged at my hand.

'Elizabeth might not want to see it. Did you actually ask?'

Lucy chewed the inside of her cheek. Luke shrugged.

Finn nodded at him and Luke, with a dramatic sigh, turned to look up at me. I did my best to keep a straight face. From the corner of my eye I could see Finn had a hand across his jaw and I knew he was also doing his best to smother his laughter.

'Elizabeth, would you like to see our treehouse?' The little boy looked back at his uncle.

Finn merely gave a brief raise of his eyebrows.

'I would, thank you.'

A few minutes later, the four of us were bundled up and looking up at the most magnificent treehouse.

'You built this?' I stared at it in awe. It was like something out of a fairytale.

'Yeah. Alice and Mark wanted one for the kids and the prices were extortionate. I knew I could do something for a lot less. And I enjoy making stuff like this.'

'You didn't fancy doing it as a career,' I asked, walking around to see it from all angles.

'Nah,' Finn said, following me as we listened to the children laughing above us. 'I love my job. This is my hobby and I'm happy to keep it that way.'

'You're so clever.'

He gave a laugh. 'Look who's talking! You can learn and, most importantly, retain anything. You read hieroglyphs, read, write and speak Latin. I can't even remember what I need from the shop unless I write it down.'

'That's book learning. This is different. I don't create anything. I wouldn't even know how, or where, to begin. Did you have a plan, or a kit?'

'Nope,' he replied. 'Just asked the kids what they wanted. Brought it back within the realms of reality, drew a design and did some numbers. Then we went off, got some wood, visited a salvage yard and...' He nodded towards his creation.

'Amazing.'

Two small faces appeared at the door to the treehouse and looked down at us.

'Are you coming up?' Lucy asked. 'We have a Christmas tree up here too. Uncle Finn got it for us.'

'Of course you did.' I turned to him, grinning.

'You going up or what?' he said, giving my bum a pat as I put a foot on the bottom rung.

'You bet!' I said, and began climbing the thick-stepped ladder.

16

'Happy New Year!'

My parents' bungalow, in a prime position overlooking the coastal cliffs, had been unrecognisable when Finn and I had pulled up outside.

'Is this it?' he'd asked.

'I think so.'

'Think?' he'd replied, a ripple of laughter lacing his words.

'It looks a bit different from the last time I saw it.'

A second later, the door had opened and Mum had bustled out to greet us, her feet adorned in bright orange Crocs over thick, pink knitted socks.

'Happy New Year!' she said, waving excitedly as she opened the gate to the garden. A space which, once overgrown and neglected, was now tidy with a neat lawn, a large palm tree and various shrubs. Around the lawn, five wire reindeer grazed contentedly.

'Do you like it?' Mum asked, following the direction of my eye line once she'd given me a tight hug and then reached up on tiptoes to do the same to Finn.

'Umm... yes. It's great! I'm assuming they light up.'

'They do!' she said, clearly excited by this fact. 'There are a few more in the back garden. We got rather carried away. But they're such fun, don't you think?'

'I do,' I replied, taking her hand and squeezing it gently. 'I really do.'

Mum turned and reached to take my other one, holding them out in front of her. 'Why didn't you tell us the place looked a state?'

'Oh, Mum! It didn't!'

'We know it did, darling. No wonder you didn't want to come here. It was hardly welcoming.'

'Mum, please don't think that. I was just caught up in my own world but we've all learned some lessons. Let's just focus on that.'

Mum nodded, but neither Finn nor I missed the tears behind the glasses. 'Yes, darling. You're absolutely right. Now, let's get you both inside. It's bitter out here. Oh leave that, Finn, dear. William can come and get those.'

'No need,' Finn said, loading himself up with our bags easily. My parents would soon learn that this man was naturally gallant. The thought that he would let his host, an older man than he, heave our luggage about wouldn't have crossed his mind.

Mum, sharp as always, realised immediately that there was no point in arguing so instead wrapped her arm around my waist and we all walked into the house, past the reindeer which had now lit up as Dad joined us at the door.

'Aren't they wonderful?' he enthused, hugging me close.

'They're great, Dad,' I said, laughing and loving his joy over their latest purchase. 'How are you?'

'I'm fine,' he said, widening his eyes at me with meaning. 'You need to stop worrying. It's not good for you.'

'You're my parents. I'm never not going to worry.'

Dad shook his head. 'Darling, Button,' he said, pulling me in for a hug again. 'We wasted so much time.'

'Come on, none of that,' Mum said, tapping him on the arm. 'I've already gone down that route and got told off so let's just enjoy Lizzie and Finn's company whilst they're here.'

Dad drew in a deep breath, gave a decisive nod and held out his hand. 'Good to see you, Finn,' he said, closing his other hand over their joined ones. 'So glad you could come. How was the journey down?'

* * *

'This is a stunning setting,' Finn said as we walked along the clifftops a couple of days later. Yesterday the skies had teemed with rain on a biblical scale for the entire day but we'd relaxed with my parents, eaten good food, played some new board games (which Finn, as the expert, had explained the rules of as none of us had ever attempted such a thing before) and got slowly and happily squiffy in the now cosy, and uncluttered living room. Outside, the rain had lashed against the new bifold doors Mum and Dad had put in to make the most of the view they'd been less appreciative of before but inside, Dad had chucked another log on the open fire and we'd toasted crumpets and marshmallows and Finn had made us all replicas of the heavenly hot chocolate we'd had in Bath.

This morning, in the ethereally pale sunshine we had woken to, the grass looked a rich emerald green, contrasting with the grey cliff faces and sapphire sea. White horses danced on the waves, chased by the brisk breeze. I wrapped my scarf a little tighter as we trod on along the path and looked out over the ocean, watching as a gull got knocked off course by a sudden gust.

'It really is. I love that my parents have put those big doors in so you can see it from the house properly now.'

'I get the impression there's been quite a lot of changes recently.'

I laughed. 'You can say that again.'

'For the good?'

I thought about how much closer we'd grown. 'Definitely. And of course they love you.'

'Well, they don't know me all that well. Things could change.'

'Unless you have a Mr Hyde side I've yet to discover, somehow I doubt it. Plus you make me happy which as far as they're concerned is more than enough.'

'And what about you?'

'What about me?'

'Is that more than enough for you?'

I slowed my steps and turned my face towards the wind, and Finn. 'What do you mean?'

Finn turned as his arm was pulled backwards where my hand held his. 'Nothing deep and philosophical. I'm just asking.'

'But why are you asking? Does it not feel enough?' I released his hand and shoved my own protectively in my pockets.

'You're reading too much into what was a flippant comment, Elizabeth. Come on.' He held out his hand again. 'What do you think about taking your parents out for a meal tonight? A friend of mine has a restaurant not that far from here. She's just got her first Michelin star.'

'Do you think we'd be able to get in at this late notice? Those sort of restaurants normally have a waiting list.'

'Not when you have someone on the inside.'

'Sounds great, if they can fit us in.'

Finn turned his back to the wind, released my hand and pulled his phone from his coat pocket and made a call. A few minutes later, we had a table for four booked at, what Google informed me later, was one of the most sought-after restaurants in the south-west. Images of celebrities entering and exiting the exclusive establishment filled my screen. I was most definitely not the person to list as your phone a friend when it came to these matters but even I knew who Tom Hanks, Cara Delavigne and Ryan Reynolds were, and apparently all these and more were huge fans of Finn's friend's cooking.

* * *

'This looks swanky,' Dad said as Finn assisted Mum from the car.

'I was just thinking the same thing.'

'Don't worry,' Finn said, beeping the locks closed. 'It's got a really relaxed vibe to it. Mel was keen on that from the start.'

'Until you get the bill,' I said, only half joking.

Finn gave me a look I couldn't quite decipher. I shrugged back. 'It was just a joke.'

'I'm paying anyway.'

'Oh no, Finn. We can't allow that.'

Finn turned towards Dad, his smile slipping back into place. 'Really, I insist. And don't worry,' he glanced back in my direction, 'I get mates' rates so it's not as impressive a gesture as it seems.' He gave Mum a conspiratorial wink. 'Come on, let's get in out of the cold.' Finn strode to the door, opened it and ushered us all in, following in last behind me.

'I'm afraid we're fully booked tonight,' the maître d' said after giving us a cursory scan and apparently found us wanting of both money and status.

'We have a reservation,' Finn said, stepping out of the shadows in the tiny entranceway. The man tilted his head up to take in this new addition to our party and obviously found him rather more to both his own taste and the establishment's. Clearly Finn fit the 'beautiful people only' purview this sentinel held. Whether that was his own interpretation or had indeed come from the owner was unknown. What was known was that three out of the four of us were definitely not experiencing that 'relaxed vibe' Finn had spoken about – and we'd barely got in the door.

'Oh?' the maître d' asked with what appeared to be the shadow of a genuine smile, apparently torn between exercising his power of rebuffing mere mortals and granting hallowed access to those who fit the agenda, like Finn.

'Yep. Name of Finn.'

The man turned back to the screen. 'Ah, my apologies, Mr Finn.'

'No Mr. Just Finn.'

The man gave an accepting nod. Apparently Finn was now on a par with Kylie, Drake and Madonna in that he only needed one name to unlock the magical door. After all this condescension, I was rather wishing we'd gone to McDonalds. And bearing in mind I'd generally prefer to stay hungry rather than eat junk food, that was saying something.

With an understated flourish, he pulled back a heavy, damson-coloured velvet curtain and led us through into the hallowed dining area.

It was small, intimate and appropriately luxe. The velvet theme continued with upholstered chairs and, for those requiring yet another level of privacy than that afforded by the gatekeeper of the establishment, also on the banquettes in the few booths dotted around. Mum and Dad were unusually silent and I guessed they were feeling as overwhelmed as I was. Only Finn seemed at ease. The fun and relaxed dinner I'd hoped for on our last day with my parents was not turning out as planned. But perhaps it would get better when we were sat down.

It didn't get better. The tension I saw in my parents' body language was mirrored by my own. Conversation was stilted and a blend of annoyance and upset staved off any hunger pangs I might otherwise have felt. Here were two people who had spent their years studying and lecturing in some of the keystones of education. They'd given speeches in front of large audiences all over the world and now this piddly little restaurant with its ideas of grandeur had reduced them almost to silence. Had I known this was Finn's friend's idea of 'relaxed', I never would have agreed to coming. A bottle of Dom Perignon champagne had arrived at the table 'courtesy of the chef' a few minutes after we had sat down and I'd necked a glass and a half already.

'Have you got any plans for this year, Mum?'

'Oh, erm, well,' she said, becoming more animated than she'd been since we'd stepped inside. 'We were thinking of taking a trip to—'

'Necker Island, of course, darling!' The woman's alcohol-infused voice speared into our conversation as she passed beside us, her gaze hovering a moment or two longer than required on Finn as she continued her dialogue. 'You know everyone's going for the party and then a few weeks skiing in St Moritz. Where else would anyone be in January?' Her laugh drifted behind her as they were seated a few tables away.

'Shrewsbury,' Mum finished quietly, all excitement and enthusiasm now absent from her voice. 'Not very glamorous compared to private islands and St Moritz, I'm afraid.' She gave a small smile but I saw the discomfort behind it. Dad reached and took her hand in his, a gesture of silent support.

The anger bubbled inside me.

'I know where I'd rather go,' I said, pointedly. 'What are you hoping to see? I've always wanted to go to the library. I hear it's fascinating but have somehow never managed to visit yet.'

'Oh.' Mum perked up a little. 'Yes, that was certainly on our list. Although I doubt it's to everyone's taste.' She gave an apologetic glance at Finn. 'I'm sure it sounds positively dull to a lot of people.'

'Not at all,' Finn replied.

'Have you been?' I asked, turning to him.

'St Moritz?'

I took a deep breath, let it out slowly as I attempted to count to ten, made it to five and hoped for the best. 'The library. In Shrewsbury. Where Mum was just talking about.'

'Oh! Sorry, no.'

'Have you heard of it?'

Finn looked up from the menu. 'Shrewsbury? Of course.' His mouth was set in a line.

'The library,' I replied.

He straightened his back and put down the menu. 'No, I haven't.'

'That's a shame. Charles Darwin was educated there and it's renowned for being well worth a visit.'

'Then I shall have to put it on my list. Sorry.' He gave a small head tilt. 'My secondary school education didn't extend to offering such knowledge.' His eyes flashed at me in annoyance. My intention had been to bring his mind back to less exotic destinations, to point out that Shrewsbury was just as valid a destination as the glamorous ones we'd overhead and that he, apparently had focused on, but instead he'd taken it as a dig that his education was somehow less than ours. I hadn't, and would never imply such a thing. The fact that he thought I would added to my irritation.

'Are you ready to order?' A waiter appeared beside us, preventing the conversation from escalating, at least for the moment.

Yep. One taxi to go please.

Sadly that wasn't on the menu so we all chose something from the exclusive choices available made up of unusually named foods. I'm not sure any of us had the faintest idea of what to expect on our plates, perhaps with the exception of Finn who appeared if not familiar, then at least more confident with the menu choices than the rest of us. Although the food – the small amount of it that arrived on the plate – was delicious, the evening had not been an unmitigated success and I hated that this was not the joyful experience I'd hoped for before leaving my parents and returning to London the following morning. Now that Mum and Dad had discovered a new, wider, lease on life, it was harder to think about leaving. And then Finn had chosen to bring us here where we felt, and were made to feel, out of place and uncomfortable.

'Have you been here before, Finn?' I asked as he finished his pudding. None of us had the appetite for one but Mum and Dad had insisted he have one.

'Yeah, a few times,' he said, placing the fork carefully on the side of the plate before it was quickly whisked away by an efficient server.

'Oh.'

The tension of before still rippled between us. 'What does that mean?'

'Nothing especially.' I lowered my voice. 'It's just that you said your friend ensured it wasn't a snobby atmosphere and clearly it is. I assumed you hadn't been here so didn't realise but I guess not.'

His intense gaze fixed on me. 'It's only you making yourself uncomfortable, Elizabeth.' His voice was low but distinct.

Mum and Dad suddenly found great interest in the textural weave of the fine Irish linen tablecloth.

'No, Finn. It's not,' I replied, my voice equally quiet but equally steady. 'The only one comfortable here is you and that's because you've been fawned over since we walked in. If that chap out there had had his way, the rest of us would have been thrown out on our ears for not fitting the bold and the beautiful theme Melanie has cultivated here.' I turned to my parents. 'No offence. Personally I think you're both fabulously bold and beautiful but you know what I mean.'

'I'm sure it's just us, darling, like Finn said.' Dad made a concerted effort to dispel the gathering storm.

'No, Dad. It's not.'

From the corner of my eye, I saw Finn give a small headshake.

'Oh, are you joining in the general atmosphere of condescension to mere mortals like us that they nurture here?'

'You're being ridiculous, Elizabeth. What's up with you?'

'Nothing is *up* with me!' I whispered angrily. 'I'm just furious that you brought us to such an up-itself place, and if you can't see it for what it is, I'm afraid you're the one being ridiculous.'

He opened his mouth to reply but was interrupted by a woman striding across the restaurant, glad-handing various people until she got to our table whereupon Finn stood and wrapped her in an enormous hug which she returned. Pulling back a little, she cupped his face. 'Oh, it's so lovely to see you again. How are you? Did you enjoy the meal?'

'It was great, as always, Mel. It's good to see you too. Looks like things are going well here.'

She put her hands to her own face this time. 'I can't believe it. I mean it was going well before but since I got the star, it's just gone whoosh!' She illustrated this by soaring her hand up in an angle akin to a ski slope.

'Richly deserved,' Finn said, catching her hand. 'You worked for it.'

'I'm not sure any of it would have happened if it hadn't been for you rescuing the build project initially.' She turned to face us. 'Finn was truly my knight in shining armour.'

'I'm not sure about that.' He dismissed the accolade but Mel was having none of it.

'Don't believe a word. If it hadn't been for Finn, this restaurant wouldn't exist.'

From our experience tonight, I couldn't join Mel in the tragic air she gave to that statement.

'The food was very nice, thank you,' Dad offered up which seemed to kick Finn into gear.

'Sorry. Mel, this is my friend, Elizabeth, and her parents, William and Mary.'

Friend?

They shook hands and Mum gave a nervous chuckle. 'Not the royal ones though, obviously.'

Dad and I giggled, Finn gave a small smile and Mel looked blank. I practically saw the comment soar over her head.

'Sorry?'

Mum waved her hands, colour creeping up her neck and face. I swallowed hard, wanting to make it better for her.

'Just me being silly. Ignore me.' She chuckled again.

Not once in my life had I ever witnessed my mother feel that she, or anything she said, should be so dismissed. She wasn't pushy but she wasn't the type to be walked over either. And here she was, in this stuffy little den of indulgence, telling this woman to ignore her. The storm erupted.

'William and Mary were king and queen in the seventeenth century,' I said. 'Mum and Dad often get teased about their names being the same when they introduce themselves.'

'Oh.' Mel smiled back. 'Sorry. That one went right over my head.'

Finn threw me a dark glance and turned back to his friend.

Mum and Dad returned Mel's smile, Mum giving a small shake of her head. 'No, really. I say the silliest things sometimes.'

'No, Mum, you don't.' I leant over and kissed her cheek to back up the statement.

'The food really was delicious. You're very clever. I can barely boil an egg.'

That much *was* true. Thankfully Dad was a dab hand in the kitchen which had saved us any number of culinary horrors.

'Thanks.' Mel gave a wide, white smile. 'I've got a great team here. Although new opportunities are always exciting. You never stop learning.'

'That's so true!' Mum and Dad brightened at the hint of a subject they could relate to.

Mel briefly grabbed Finn's arm. 'Oh my God. It's going to be so much fun working together again if you-know-what comes off.' Finn shifted his weight, discomfort creasing his face for a second before he smoothed it away. Meanwhile Mel was practically vibrating with excitement.

'Let's see, eh?' Finn said.

'Yep. Anyway I'd better get back to the kitchen.' She reached out and gave him another massive hug. 'So glad you could come.'

'It was a pleasure.'

That was a matter of opinion.

'And thanks for the champagne. You shouldn't have.'

Bloody good job she did. I'm not sure I would have made it through this evening without.

We filed out, collecting our coats on the way, bundling up against the bone-chilling wind and walked hurriedly back to the car. There were rumours of snow for tomorrow and from the temperature, I could quite believe it. Silence reigned and the atmosphere was thick with unspoken questions. I'd always been quite good at controlling my emotions but the best part of a bottle of pop to myself had loosened my tongue.

'I didn't realise you'd actually worked with Mel before.'

Finn gave a casual shrug. 'I thought I told you.'

'No.'

'Oh,' he replied, just as casually. 'I must have forgotten. Why? Does it matter?'

'No. I just thought you might have said.'

His hands gripped the wheel tighter before he stretched out the long fingers and reset his hold. 'Like I said, I thought I had.'

Mum and Dad remained silent in the back of the car.

'What did she mean, about you two working together again?'

'It's just one of a few possibilities I'm looking into for my next job.'

'Right. Is that local too?'

'It's all still very much up in the air at the moment.'

I turned in my seat to face him more, or at least the side of his face, a silhouette in the darkness of the windy country roads, his features illuminated only by the lights of the dashboard. 'But you must know where it would be.'

Finn cleared his throat. 'Yes.'

I waited. Nothing else was forthcoming.

'So?'

'It's in Dubai.' He spoke the words quietly. I only just caught them and I was pretty sure Mum and Dad hadn't heard at all. I soon rectified that situation.

'Dubai?' I replied, somewhat – a lot – louder.

'See?' Finn flashed me a very brief look. 'This is why I didn't mention it. I knew you'd over react.'

'I'm not over reacting! I'm just... surprised.'

'My job has always taken me all over the world, Elizabeth.' There was a defensiveness to his tone that I didn't appreciate.

'I understand that. And I would never want to stop you. I'm just surprised that you hadn't mentioned it at all.'

'It's not even a definite thing yet. I didn't see the point.'

'It's obviously definite enough for Mel to know about it.'

He let out a breath between his teeth. 'Please don't tell me you're going to get jealous about her now.'

'What the hell's up with you?' I asked, carrying on before he had a chance to answer. 'No, I'm not jealous. Don't flatter yourself! I just thought we were at the stage where we discussed things.'

'There's nothing to discuss.'

'Mel obviously thinks there is,' I sniped back.

Finn did another throat clear. 'Do you think we might be able to talk about this later?' He shot me a meaningful look.

I twisted back to face forward, crossed my arms and sat in the thick silence until we pulled up at my parents' house.

'Thank you for the lovely meal,' Mum said, as Finn held out a hand to assist her from the car.

His smile was back in place as he replied. 'You're very welcome. I'm glad you enjoyed it.'

I rolled my eyes in the shadows. *The only one that enjoyed it was you, Finn.*

'Night, darling,' Dad said, giving me a hug. 'You going to be OK?' he whispered as he did so.

I tightened the hug in answer before we parted, his eyes on mine. He gave a small nod and let go.

'Night, Mum.' I gave her a hug too and they quickly made their way out of the cold into the snug warmth of the house leaving Finn and I alone.

The icy wind whipped in off the inky black sea, breakers smashing loud and angry against the cliffs below. It was a moonless night and everything felt bleak, dark and tense. And not just in the landscape. Finn shoved his hands deeper into the pockets of his knee-length, tailored wool coat.

'I'm assuming we're having a conversation about something. Or are we just out here freezing our arses off for fun?' His tone was almost as cold as the weather.

'What the hell is up with you tonight?'

'I could ask the same about you?'

'I was fine until you took us to a restaurant where you're apparently treated like a God and everyone else just feels uncomfortable.'

'Nobody made you feel like that. That's all on you, Elizabeth.'

'Maybe so, but I'd have thought – I did think – you were thoughtful enough to take me and my parents to somewhere that wasn't as stuck up as that place. For God's sake, you said your "friend"' – I held up my fingers in exaggerated bunny ears. I blamed the champagne. Champagne had a lot to answer for this year – 'cultivated a friendly, relaxed atmosphere!'

'She does! And what's that' – he imitated the shapes back at me – 'supposed to mean?'

'Yeah, if you're one of her mates or have a ruddy great yacht parked in the local marina. For mere mortals like my parents and I, it was as snobby as hell! I don't think you could have picked somewhere that we felt more out of place.'

Finn gave a short bark of laughter, all humour removed.

'That's rich coming from you.'

'What's that supposed to mean?'

'You and your parents live in a completely different world!'

'What on earth are you talking about?'

'Academia! It's not the real world. You think tonight was snobby? You should know! Did you ever think how awkward I might feel plonked into your world where everyone swans about being highly educated and looking down on those who haven't got seventeen degrees to their name?'

'I've never, ever treated you like that.'

'You might not have but others have.'

'Have my parents?'

'No, of course not,' he snapped back. 'Yes, they're more airy fairy and distracted than some other girlfriends' parents but not in a bad way. I like them.'

'Oh yes. I forgot you had a plethora of comparisons to make.'

'I didn't mean it like that.'

'Didn't you?'

'No!'

'I'm sorry if you've ever felt that you were somehow less at places we've been. But, according to your reasoning, if you felt that way, it was of your own making.'

'That's not the same thing.'

'Isn't it?'

'No! Nobody turned their nose up and walked away to find someone more worthy of their hifalutin conversation at the restaurant.'

I remained silent for a moment, processing what he'd said.

'When did that happen?'

'It doesn't matter now.'

'It does to me,' I pressed.

'Well, it doesn't to me. I've moved on.'

'Apparently not.'

'Enough. I'm bloody good at what I do and I live in the real world unlike some people.'

I straightened my back. 'Am I included in that particular sweeping statement?'

'No, of course not. I just meant...' The sentence drifted off and we were left in the silence of the night, broken only by the sound of the ocean and the occasional haunting call of an owl.

I heard Finn shift his weight. 'Look. I'm sorry if you or your parents felt uncomfortable tonight. That wasn't my intention.'

'Thank you. I appreciate that you didn't do it on purpose. I do think Mel needs to work on the welcome there though.'

Finn's tone took on a tenseness once more. 'I didn't say there was anything wrong with the restaurant or its atmosphere. I'm just saying I'm sorry that none of you enjoyed it as much I had anticipated.'

'That's because everyone acted like we weren't good enough to eat their tiny bloody portions or squat on those ridiculously uncomfortable chairs!'

'Anything else you'd like to add while you're ripping apart my friend's restaurant, which, for your information, I helped her design!'

'Yes, actually.' Finn had pushed all my buttons tonight. I don't know why or how it had come to this but he'd asked and I was going to tell him. 'The maître d' is a dick. Did she audition applicants on the basis of just how small they could make people feel who didn't fit their particular idea of who should eat in such a hallowed place?'

'Now you're just being spiteful.'

'No, Finn. I'm not. I didn't appreciate the attitude and I certainly didn't appreciate my parents being subjected to it. I'd have thought you might have made more of an effort to choose somewhere where we could all feel comfortable but then I guess you wouldn't have got to show off your Michelin star friend and bask in how much they fawned over you.'

'Oh, for God's sake.'

'Yes, the design of the place is great and very aesthetically pleasing but I wouldn't expect anything less if you were involved in it. It's just the people in it that need work.'

'And that includes Mel, I suppose?'

'I didn't get time to form enough of an opinion to comment. She was too busy being excited about your new project together in Dubai.'

'A project I'm thinking more and more that I might just take!'

'You know what, Finn?' My voice was raised against the now howling wind and crashing seas. A storm had been forecast for the morning and all signs were that it had been right. 'Why don't you do that?'

'Great! Decision made. I thought it might be difficult to choose, which is why I hadn't mentioned it yet but you've made it really easy. Thanks, Elizabeth. I may as well get a head start on familiarising myself with the project so I'll grab my stuff now and head back to London tonight.'

We stood there, the storm building, the atmosphere between us thicker than the clouds smothering the moon above us.

'Right,' I replied quietly and turned towards the path.

'I'll arrange a train ticket for you, of course.'

I was at the front door now, the step lit in a puddle of soft, pale yellow light from the outside lamp. 'That won't be necessary, thank you. I'm quite capable of taking care of that myself.'

'I know you are. But this isn't your choice so—'

'Let's call it a joint decision,' I said, my voice now under control, emotions back to being contained as was normal, now that I was well and truly sober.

Finn's dark features were serious as he met my eyes. 'Elizabeth...'

'Would you like anything for the road? A drink, some fruit?' I made my way into the kitchen.

There was a pause before he answered. 'No. Thank you.'

'I'll let you go and get your things together then.' With that, I turned my back to him and began pulling a mug out of the cupboard to make myself a hot chocolate. I didn't want it but it was something to do with my hands, with my mind, rather than thinking about how things had turned from sunshine to storm so quickly. One minute there were signs of a future together, our similarities and differences combining to make the perfect balance. But in the end it had turned out those differences ran deeper than I had ever suspected and that there was no way to seal the fissures they caused in our relationship.

I took a sip of the warming milk. I couldn't face the thought of chocolate after all now that my stomach was churning and my head hurt with the effort of keeping all the spinning thoughts inside.

'I'll be off then.'

'OK.' I made no effort to move from the built-in padded bench in the breakfast nook. In daylight it looked out over the sea and the cliffs but right now, it was a view of nothingness. Something akin to the emptiness I felt as Finn stood on the threshold of my parents' house. Of my life. 'Drive carefully.'

'Right. Yes. Thanks.'

I heard his exhale.

'Goodbye, Elizabeth.'

'Bye, Finn.' I took another sip of my drink. I wasn't going to let him see me cry. I wasn't going to show anything. His career was all about building things that would last but he obviously wasn't as invested in building this relationship and keeping it on track as I'd thought. As I'd let myself become. Inside everything was crumbling to dust but I was determined to keep the façade in place for as long as possible.

The door closed. The engine started and tyres crunched on gravel. A minute later silence returned. I pushed myself up from the nook, walked to the door and turned the key, shooting the bolt afterwards. Then I sat back down, pulling the thick knitted throw nearby over me and lay down, resting my head on one of the cushions and tucking my knees up to my chest. It was only then I let the tears flow until I fell asleep, exhausted and spent.

17

'Oh, Lizzie! Have you been here all night?' Mum's concerned tones broke into my fitful sleep.

I opened my eyes, knowing without the need for a mirror that they were puffy, red and swollen.

'Oh, Lizzie.' Mum repeated, her words softer this time. 'Is Finn still here?' she asked as I pushed myself upright and shook my head. 'I'm sure it's just a little spat. Everything will work out. We all have those from time to time.'

I repeated the head shake, knowing in my heart that it had been so much more than that.

'He's gone, Mum. And he's taking a job in Dubai.'

'But he's got to finish the museum one first, hasn't he?'

'Yes. I suppose so.' With all the emotions of last night swimming around, I hadn't thought about that. A flicker of cautious hope flamed into life. Everything about our relationship had been impulsive. Perhaps it was time we actually sat down and discussed things properly instead of acting hastily.

'I'm sure once you talk over whatever it is that's bothering you, you'll be able to come to a sensible decision. Sometimes these things blow up and in reality, it turns out they're nothing. You're clearly very fond of each other. That's not always easy to find. Finn seems the sensible, grounded type. I can't imagine he'd throw something as wonderful as a relationship with my beautiful, bright daughter away on a whim.'

It made sense now that I thought about it in the light of day. The storm had passed through in the early hours. I'd woken briefly to the hammering of rain on the windowpanes as the wind whipped the roaring sea into a frenzy close by. But I'd merely closed my eyes and fallen back into an exhausted, fitful sleep. But now the sky was clear, washed clean by the storm. Outside the grass was a bright green, raindrops sparkling on the blades in the watery, winter sunshine. The much-hyped snow storm hadn't arrived. Everything was clearer. Mum was right. I knew that I meant something to Finn and he meant more than he knew to me. Suddenly I was eager to get back to London.

'So he just left you here?' Dad's face was grave. 'I mean not that we mind. The longer you're here the better as far as we're concerned but it's hardly very chivalrous!'

I gave a dry laugh. 'Sadly, chivalry has been dead as long as most of the mummies in our collection, Dad.'

'It shouldn't be and from what I saw, I thought Finn was one of those holding out against the barrage of poor manners. Now I'm beginning to wonder.'

'I think him leaving was the best thing for that moment in time, Dad. Neither of us wanted to put you two in the middle of any more tension.'

'Oh, don't worry about us. God knows we've seen enough arguments and sniping in our careers as to be almost immune to it all now.' Mum gave me a smile as she took my hand. 'We just don't like seeing you upset. Especially as you seemed so happy when we saw you in London and when you both got here.'

'I know. And I'm sure it will all be sorted out. Just one of those spats, like you said.' Mum was right. Nothing could be perfect all the time. We were all individuals, with different views and opinions and feelings. No matter how close you were, no one could agree about everything, all of the time. I'd always doubted those couples who said they'd never had a cross word in decades. If that was truly the case, I was willing to bet there'd been a whole lot of sulking and simmering resentment in place of it.

'I need to book a train ticket.'

Mum and Dad exchanged a look.

'What?' I asked.

'There's a train strike for the next couple of days.'

'What?' My voice pitched to a not entirely attractive level. 'Finn aside, I need to get back for work.'

Dad gave a shrug. 'Maybe he should have thought about that when he left you here.' Finn had most certainly plummeted in Dad's opinion. Should we manage to patch things up, he had some serious character repair work to do.

I picked up my phone and entered a search. 'OK there's a hire car place about twenty minutes away that can do a one-way service. Would you mind dropping me off?'

'If that's what you want.'

'I do, Dad.'

Dad studied me for a beat or two and then picked up his keys. 'Then I'm ready when you are.'

'Aren't you going to have some breakfast before you go?' Mum asked in a tone of concern. There was a time when a day could easily pass with neither of them particularly noticing that meal times had come and gone whilst they'd been engrossed in their studies. From home, I'd gone to university where, as was the norm with many students, I hadn't been especially observant to meal times either. Since working I'd attempted to build in a better routine but it was easy to fall back into the pattern of no pattern. Mum and Dad, however, had obviously embraced all aspects of their new life and Mum was now fussing around me. 'I can make you something quickly.'

'No, I'm OK, really. But thanks anyway.'

She didn't seem happy about this.

'I promise I'll stop on the way to stretch my legs and I'll have something then.'

'Hmm. OK then. But make sure you do.'

'I will, honest.'

* * *

A short time later, Dad was dropping me off at the car rental company, insisting on waiting until he was quite sure I'd got a car and knew where I was going. It had been odd at first having such attentive parents after so long but I'd got used to it quickly and truth be told, I was revelling in it.

The drive back to London was long but the traffic was thankfully kind to me and gave me time to think and plan what I'd say to Finn. I didn't want to do this over the phone. This was something that needed to be done face to face. And tomorrow I'd do just that.

* * *

I stared at the spare desk in my office, then around the room. The decorations had gone, not one trace of tinsel to even hint they had ever been there. It looked barren and bare. And there was one more thing that looked bare. Finn's desk. I placed my bag slowly beside my own desk, turned and walked back out of the room.

'Morning.' I pasted on a smile as Mike began walking towards me.

'Happy New Year.' He beamed. 'How's you?'

'Fine, thanks. I hope you had a good one.' That wasn't what I'd come down to ask but I liked him and ordinarily I'd have been truly interested. Today, however, I was merely going through the motions.

'Yep, we did. From what I can remember.' He let out a booming laugh which echoed in the space. 'So, what can we do for you today, or did you just come for a nice natter and a cuppa?'

'That would be lovely, but I've got a report to write unfortunately. I know which I'd rather be doing though.'

He gave a nod of understanding.

'I, um, I was just wondering if Finn was down here?'

A puzzled look replaced his smile. 'Finn? No, love. I assumed you knew?'

Chills ran through my body and I used every ounce of willpower I had not to let it manifest into a physical shiver.

'He handed in his notice. Immediate effect. Got a better offer apparently.' He gave a shrug. 'Bit of a surprise, I have to say. I've worked with him on a few jobs now and he's always been incredibly reliable. I guess the offer was too good to turn down.'

Unbidden, the image of Mel wrapping her arms around Finn and gazing up at him fluttered into my mind. I swatted it away.

'But doesn't he have a contract? This is an incredibly important addition for the museum. Plans are already in place for the exhibition it's going to house!'

A swathe of emotions rushed through me and top of the list this moment was fury. Finn knew how hard I'd been working on this exhibition. He knew how many tiny parts of the jigsaw from all over the world had to be brought together to make this work and that all of that relied on the space for it being finished. And now he'd just waltzed off? The fact that he'd done so without even giving us the chance to talk things over was something I'd deal with later. Right now I was focused on work.

'He does but seems like this other company wanted him so much that they were prepared to buy him out of the contract.'

'I see.'

'We've got a new chap starting today though and it seems like he's pretty up to speed on everything so I don't think you need to worry.'

'Oh. Right.'

There was a momentary lull in the conversation. The foreman glanced over his shoulder then spoke again, his voice lower this time. 'You alright, love?'

I dredged up a smile and plastered it on. 'Yes, I'm fine. Thanks. Just a little concerned about this being finished.'

'Don't worry. I promise we'll get it done.' His gaze shifted to somewhere past my right shoulder. 'Ah, here's the new project manager now. Rory!' He waved him over. 'This is Elizabeth Rose. She's the curator of collections here, and is the one keeping an eye on us all.' He gave a cheeky wink as he finished his introduction.

'I was told Inis Jones, the head of the museum, was the one in charge?'

I held out my hand. 'We're sharing the task at the moment.'

Rory shook my hand but without much enthusiasm. 'Right. That's a little confusing. Normally there's just one person to liaise with.'

I held on to my smile for dear life. 'We've managed to make it work so far.'

Rory remained unimpressed.

'Right, well, the previous bloke seems to have kept things on track before swanning off so I don't foresee any problems.'

'Good to hear it. I'll leave you to get on then.'

'Yep.'

'Have you been shown your desk?'

'No, not yet. I was familiarising myself with the job first. I'm sure I can find it though.'

I didn't care for the barely veiled condescension in his tone so I nodded and left him to it. He could now spend his afternoon wandering the corridors for all I cared. I gave the foreman a wave, turned on my heel and headed back to my office.

* * *

'So you haven't heard from him at all?' Colette asked as she poured yet more wine. Both of us were perched at her tiny breakfast bar in the kitchen, looking out over the garden. Skeletal shapes danced in the stiff breeze as March gave way to April. Winter was refusing to relinquish its grip, the days cold, the nights ever colder. I longed to feel the spring sunshine warming my skin, for the trees to be swathed in their downy blossoms of pink and white. But it seemed nature had other ideas and whatever the season, my friend still managed to make her garden beautiful in its own way.

I noticed she'd tactically waited until we were on the second bottle of wine before broaching the subject of Finn.

'Nope.' I took a swig. 'Not a sausage.'

Colette and Greg, whose relationship was thankfully still intact and getting stronger with each day that passed, had sadly been caught in the crossfire of ours falling apart but I wasn't about to lose my friendship with Colette over a man, and neither was she. However, I had no wish to talk about Finn so we made a pact not to, and this also avoided putting Greg slap bang in the middle as he was obviously still in contact with his friend.

I knew from gossip on the project that Finn had taken the Dubai job and that the creation of the 'hotel complex to beat all hotel complexes' was being filmed as a documentary series, with Finn being one of the key figures, tasked with keeping the build on time and within budget. Mel apparently was also going to be featured on a regular basis. The same workplace gossip mill tactfully advised me that apparently the producers liked the whole 'simmering sexual tension' between the two. They had then remembered who they were talking to, and hurriedly added that 'TV people always make this stuff up for ratings and clickbait'. I appreciated the attempt at backtracking and, let's face it, it wasn't like my mind hadn't already gone there without being shown the way. But I'd done my best to swerve whenever it wanted to go down that road and took it day by day. I'd never expected to meet Finn and I certainly hadn't expected to fall for him as hard and as fast as I had. It had taken me a while to admit I'd been in love with him. I'd thought I'd been in love with Friedrich but I knew now that had merely been a pale imitation of emotions. That relationship had been comfortable, easy to slip into and easy to maintain. But real love wasn't like that. Real love took time and effort and gave all the more reward for it. I hadn't realised that until the moment I knew Finn had walked out of my life forever. It was also the moment I realised that he hadn't loved me in the same way. He hadn't loved me enough.

'I thought we agreed not to talk about this.' I topped up my wine, having downed a good proportion in the last swig.

'I know, but...'

'What?'

Colette's porcelain skin flushed a dusky rose.

'What?' I asked again, more intent this time.

My friend knocked back the best part of her wine and placed the glass back down in front of her.

'I thought he might have contacted you as he's back in the country for a few days.'

When there was no possibility of seeing him, I'd found the fact Finn was no longer in my life easier to deal with. Knowing he was back in London sent a fresh raft of raw emotion through my body.

'Oh. No. I'm surprised he hasn't been back already. He always said being close to his family was important to him so...' I gave a waft of my hand to finish the sentence, hoping that the disinterested air I'd affected sounded sincere.

Colette gave a Gallic shrug. 'Apparently not. This is the first time he's been home since he left just after New Year.'

'Well, perhaps he's found something – or someone – over there that's keeping him busy and worth staying for.' The words came out sharper than I intended, the spikiness protecting my soft underbelly of emotions like a hedgehog. My hand reached out to Colette's and covered it. 'I'm sorry. I didn't mean to snap at you.'

'It's OK. I shouldn't have mentioned it. Like you said, we'd agreed not to talk about him. I just thought that maybe...'

I shook my head. 'He's made his thoughts on what he felt about our relationship, and how important it was, pretty clear. Can we just leave it at that?'

'Of course,' Colette replied, pulling me into a tight hug beside her. 'He didn't realise what an amazing person you are. Definitely his loss.' She kissed me on the cheek and poured us both another large glass. As I picked it up and took a sip, I wasn't sure that I agreed. It definitely felt like I'd suffered the biggest loss and that Finn had merely moved on. I hoped that time really would offer the healing that the old adage promised.

* * *

Friedrich stood as I approached the table at the restaurant he'd booked for dinner.

'Lizzie, thank you for coming.'

I gave a brief nod as I sat in the chair the waiter pulled out for me. A napkin was then placed delicately in my lap before he silently moved away. Friedrich's tastes in restaurants had improved since we'd been together. He'd taken Bella to the one I'd always wanted to go to. I bit back that thought, shoving it back in the box in my mind marked 'Memories of Finn – Do Not Open'. Now there was this place. Demure, elegant and sophisticated. Before, he'd dismissed such qualities and insisted that restaurants were 'merely a place to provide sustenance'. Not the most romantic. Perhaps that wasn't the only thing that had changed.

'You look very beautiful.'

My head snapped up from where I'd been perusing the drinks menu, partly as something to do. I'd been in two minds whether to come tonight and my nerves were still jittery.

'Oh. Umm, thanks.'

'You seem surprised to receive the compliment.'

I swallowed, trying to regain my mental footing. 'No. It's just... I wasn't expecting it.'

'You should always expect it, Lizzie.'

I put the menu down, placed my hands on the table and met Friedrich's gaze.

'OK, who are you and what have you done with Friedrich?'

His laugh was smooth as he covered my hands with his own.

'Oh Lizzie, I'd forgotten how much you used to make me laugh.'

I did a quick cast back and couldn't remember a whole lot of laughter in our joint past. Not like with Finn... I slammed that box shut again and sat a mental elephant on it to keep it closed, instructing it not to move!

'Can I get you anything to drink?' With perfect timing, the waiter appeared once more beside us, giving me a chance to free my hands in a dignified manner. I made a point of picking up the menu and was about to make my decision when Friedrich chose for us.

'A bottle of the Tattinger, and one of still water.'

The waiter nodded. 'Very good, Sir.'

'Thank you,' I added as I handed the wine menu to the server as I got a glimpse of the Friedrich I had been used to, feeling himself above such pleasantries.

'I hope you like Tattinger?'

'I didn't realise you were celebrating.'

He gave a self-deprecating shrug which sat awkwardly on his features before he replied. 'I was hoping that we'd both have something to celebrate by the end of the evening.'

'I see. And what would that be?'

He gave another smooth laugh but I'd tucked my hands safely on my lap this time. 'So impatient.'

'I'm an archaeologist, Friedrich. Patience is not something I lack.'

He chuckled again. I hadn't meant it to be funny, merely a fact but Friedrich appeared determined to prove his earlier statement of my wittiness correct.

'So?' I pressed.

'I have a question to ask although I think, I hope, that I already know the answer.'

'I see. Then you'd better ask it.'

I had to wait until the server had arrived with, and opened, the bottle in a low key manner, none of that unnecessary flourishment here. After he'd poured and retreated, Friedrich advising that we'd order shortly, I was put out of my misery. Temporarily.

'I'd like you to be part of the dig.'

I snorted the champagne, sending bubbles down my throat, up my nose and, if the result was anything to go by, into my tear ducts. I grabbed at the napkin and did my best to mop up the aftermath, but not before I caught a glimpse of my dinner companion's hint of disapproval. Not obvious to the untrained eye but mine had been honed over several years and some lessons are hard to forget. Unlike other people who would remain nameless, he was less forgiving of accidents and, by the hasty scan of the restaurant he made under his lashes, was far more bothered about what others thought than he pretended to be.

'Are you alright?'

'Yes. Sorry. Went down the wrong way.'

'I took you by surprise. Perhaps I should have waited until you put the glass down.' He flashed a brief smile but I knew exactly what he was thinking and why.

'Yes, you did rather.'

Friedrich laid a hand on his chest. 'My apologies. But you were so eager to hear.'

I bit back the smile. Good old Friedrich. Things were never his fault. I hadn't seen it at the time, even though Colette had delicately tried to explain when she had been blamed yet again for any awkward evenings together. Now the picture was crystal clear I ignored the jibe and sipped my drink. If he was expecting me to agree, he had a long wait.

'So, what do you think?'

'About what?'

His smile was a little too tight but I guessed he was trying. 'Joining me on the dig.'

'I'm not sure I can really leave the museum for that amount of time, especially now that you've accepted Bella's application. She'll be a real asset to the team.'

'Yes, I hope so.'

'She will,' I repeated, unwavering in my support for her.

'Well, it was really your recommendation that swung that decision.'

I stayed silent. Friedrich was clearly unaware that Bella had confessed all to me. But we all made mistakes and I knew for certain she'd learned from it. I admired her for being able to put that experience behind her and not let it hold her back. I'm not sure I'd have been able to at her age. I wasn't sure I'd be able to at this age if I was honest, but that was a question for another day.

'I'm sure Inis will be able to find someone to take your place for the summer.'

I levelled my gaze at him and slowly raised one eyebrow. Friedrich could be obtuse at times but it appeared this was not one of those times.

'Not that I mean you're easy to replace!' The words rushed out. 'What I meant is that I don't think Inis would want to stand in the path of your career.'

'No, I know she wouldn't, but, and I don't mean to be blunt, Friedrich...' I did actually, but I wanted at least the appearance of politeness. 'But at this stage, taking part in another dig, although interesting, won't especially further my career. And we both know that I was up for the leadership of that particular dig which, obviously, would have been a different case.'

'What if we split it?'

'I don't understand.'

'If we were joint leaders? Would that make a difference?'

'I... I don't know. I hadn't thought about it.'

'Would you think about it now?' His voice was low, his gaze fixed on mine.

'Why would you want that?'

'Honestly?'

'Of course.'

'I miss working with you, talking with you.' There was a beat. A pause. 'Being with you.'

'Friedrich, we both know that's not a good reason to make a career decision.'

'I've thought it through,' he said, his eyes now bright with excitement. That I didn't doubt. Friedrich was nothing if not logical and thorough. 'Pooling our respective knowledge and instincts makes a lot of sense. And now you can have the lead you wanted.' Tact had never been one of my ex's strong suits. 'We both can.'

'I don't understand.'

'What?'

So many things...

'Firstly, why you would want to share the position. You've always been so...' How best to say this with more delicacy than he would? 'Focused. I know you've been looking to lead a dig for ages too, and now you have that opportunity.'

'True. But wouldn't it be so much better together?'

'But surely there's only enough funding for one lead?'

Friedrich waved away the query. 'All sorted.'

'How?'

He let out a sigh. 'Does it matter?'

'Yes, Friedrich, it does. As much as I'd like it to, my house doesn't run on fairy dust. I need to know I'd have enough money to pay my bills and put food on my table.'

'I spoke to the main backer. He's happy to put up a bit more in order to have two experts running it. The likelihood is that with both of us running the dig, we'll be more successful anyway which is good for the sponsors and the board.'

'Out of interest, who is funding the expedition?'

Friedrich waved his hand in a dismissive manner. 'Nobody you'd know. Loaded but not terribly bright. I've got him wound around my little finger. Hence being able to get you on board.'

I tried not to let Friedrich's natural tone of condescension rankle. 'There's a reason most teams, in any field, only have one leader. Have you ever heard of the phrase "too many cooks"?'

'Of course, but that's not us. We work well together. We are of the same mind. Symbiotic.'

I was beginning to think that the champagne had gone to my companion's head. If a straw poll had been held as to whether or not Friedrich was a fan of speaking in such purple prose, the result would have been a resounding no. This was a side of him I'd not seen and I couldn't help but smile. Friedrich, however, took this as a sign of agreement.

'I knew you'd see the brilliance of it! Shall we order?'

Truthfully, I was not at all convinced but I was bloody hungry. I'd consider the proposal later without Friedrich interrupting my thoughts.

* * *

'Are you taking the Tube or a taxi?' Friedrich asked as we exited the warmth of the restaurant into the clear, cold night.

'Tube, I guess. Unless you want to share a taxi?'

'Are you still at Primrose Hill?'

'Yes.'

'Then we're in different directions. But we could walk to the Tube station together?'

Thoughts of a cosy cab ride rather than the bright, rattling Tube disintegrated into dust and I fell into step beside Friedrich as we made our way towards the brightly lit entranceway and descended down the escalators deep into the bowels of London.

'Goodbye then, Lizzie.'

I turned to return the goodbye and the kiss that Friedrich had been aiming at my cheek landed squarely on my lips. Surprised, I stepped back.

And then I saw him. Waiting on the platform, his body half angled towards us. Our eyes connected. It felt like a lifetime and a fraction of a second all at the same time. Then he turned away, and stepped onto the train that had just rattled into the station, brakes squealing. And once again, Finn was gone. Pain and anger bubbled through me. Pain that I thought I was finally putting to rest.

'What the hell are you doing?'

The smile slid from Friedrich's face. 'I was going to peck you on the cheek.' He gave a shrug. 'You moved.'

'You shouldn't have been trying to peck anything!'

Friedrich shook his head. 'We're old friends, Lizzie. More than old friends. Old lovers.'

'Less of the old, thank you! And *none* of the lovers! All of that is well in the past where it will stay. Even if I agree to lead this dig with you, all *that* stuff is forgotten. We would be colleagues, nothing more.'

He gave a shrug. 'OK, if that's what you want.'

'It is what I want, Friedrich.'

'I just thought that tonight... and you asked if I wanted to share a cab?'

'To share the fare, Friedrich. Nothing else!'

'Oh.' He seemed genuinely surprised.

'Look, send me over your proposal and in the meantime I'll think it over. I'm not saying yes yet.'

The confidence was back now. 'But you will.'

The whoosh of hot air and a deep rumbling sound announced the presence of the next train.

'I need to get home. I'll let you know when I've decided.'

'OK.'

'I'll need to talk to Inis first too.'

He shrugged.

'Night, Friedrich.' I turned and hurried to the train, found a seat and stared out of the window opposite me. As the train pulled away, the lights of the station disappeared and darkness replaced the view. My reflection looked back at me as my mind bubbled with the thought that had circumstances been just a fraction different, I might have been sat opposite Finn now. We might finally have had a chance to talk. But one stupid move from my ex had ruined the moment. And, by the cold look on Finn's face as he turned away, it was not a moment I would ever have again.

18

'Is that really what you want?' I'd dropped round to chat Friedrich's offer over with Colette having spent the last few days tumbling the option over in my mind. After the third message from Friedrich asking if I'd made a decision, apologising for the misunderstanding as we'd parted and requesting another chance to get things right, I'd politely asked him to give me some space to think.

Colette looked positively horrified.

'It's not such a bad proposition.'

My friend's eyebrows shot up so high, I was pretty sure the only thing actually keeping them on her face was her hairline.

'It's a terrible proposition! *Terrible!*' She reverted back to her native language for added emphasis.

'OK, it's not quite the same as leading a dig on my own but he promised that all the papers and any credits would be joint and decisions made together after calm, logical discussion. Logic is kind of his superpower so I'm not worried about that aspect.'

Colette shook her head. 'I need a drink.'

'It's ten o'clock in the morning!'

'*Exactement!*' She threw her arms in the air. 'That is how bad an idea I think this is.' She rummaged in the fridge, pulled out a half empty bottle of wine and took a large slug, bypassing the need for a glass. Wow. She *really* did not approve of this.

'I think you're over reacting a bit, Col.'

She slammed the bottle down. 'And I think you're under reacting! Getting back together with Friedrich is quite possibly the worst idea you've had, second only to dating him the first time around. In fact, probably worse as you already know that he didn't make you happy before.'

'Who said anything about getting back together with him?'

'You did!'

'No I didn't.'

'You did!'

'No,' I repeated, slowly. 'I didn't. This would be purely a work thing.'

'Really?'

'Yes.'

'Oh.' Her energy dropped about five levels. 'OK. That's a little different.'

She took another slug of the wine, placed the novelty stopper in the shape of the Eiffel Tower back in the top and put the bottle back in the fridge.

'Although,' she said, turning back from the baby-pink fridge to face me. 'I still think it's a terrible idea.'

I let out a sigh. 'Maybe I shouldn't have come to you to discuss this. You're a little biased against him.'

'I am not biased at all. Yes, I think he is a condescending toad with a superiority complex but I can still be objective.'

'Clearly.'

Colette gave a shrug then let out a sigh. 'OK. So, no, I don't think it's a good idea. You can get leadership of your own dig.'

'Apparently not.'

'Well, not this one but there will be others. I don't trust him.'

I opened my mouth to reply but she held up a hand. 'And I know what he's said. But what Friedrich says and what he does are two different things. Even you know that.'

There had been evidence in the past to corroborate this but his general behaviour the other night, excluding the unexpected goodbye kiss, had suggested that perhaps the changes he'd talked about had truly been put into practice.

'I know, but I do think he's changed. It's been a few years since we were together.'

'But only a short time since he had a fling with Bella, promising her a place on the dig before turning around and insisting it went through the proper channels after all.'

'These things have to be done properly.'

'And there you go.' Colette flung up her hands.

'There I go what?'

'Defending him. Finding ways to explain his behaviour, just like you used to before.'

'I'm not defending him!' I said, defensive now of myself.

'You are! Yes, I'm sure these things do have to go through the proper channels as you say, something Friedrich would have known too! And yet he still chose to romance Bella and lead her down the golden path.'

'Garden.'

'What?'

'Garden path.'

'Really?'

'Yes.'

'Oh. Neither of them make sense to me but...' She waved her hands. 'Whatever path it was, he led her down it, knowing that he didn't have the authority to grant her a place on the team there and then anyway.'

'He's got a fairly large say.'

Colette let out a string of words in rapid fire, some of which I guessed were expletives but although I'd got fairly fluent, when she spoke at the same speed as a machine gun, I was lost.

'*Tu peux répéter plus lentement, s'il te plait?*'

Colette looked at me. I looked back at her. Tension vibrated in the air until it was burst like a balloon with the pin of her laughter. She stepped towards me and hugged me tight and I returned the embrace. Pulling back a little she took my face between her hands.

'I just don't want you being used, *ma chérie*. You've worked too hard in your career to be a stepping stone for someone else.'

'I really don't think that's what this is about.'

Colette tipped her head one way then the other. 'Only he knows that for sure. Just be careful. You've too much to offer to get caught up with him again.'

'I told you, that's definitely not my plan.'

'Plans change.'

My friend clearly wasn't convinced but, reluctant to reignite the tension, wisely let it go.

'Just be sure to check the small print. Don't take what he says at face value.'

'I promise.'

She smiled, kissed me on both cheeks and released me. I wandered over to the window that looked over the garden. I knew that the greenhouse was currently full of seedlings and cuttings, and by the looks of the pile of seed catalogues on the side, she wasn't done yet. I really needed to take a leaf out of her book – no pun intended – and do something with my own garden. My grandmother had been an avid, enthusiastic and bold gardener. I felt a wash of guilt as I thought of how it now looked.

'She wouldn't mind.'

I turned to find Colette standing beside me.

'Your grandmother. That's what you're thinking, isn't it? That your garden isn't as manicured as it once was.'

'I've let it get into a state. It was so beautiful when she had it.'

'And it will be again, if you want it to be.'

'I've literally no idea where to start.'

'Nobody does at the beginning. Perhaps I can come round some time and we can do a bit together?'

I reached for her hand. 'I'd love that, thank you.'

She squeezed my hand. '*Moi aussi.*'

We stood looking out of the window in contented silence for a few moments until I spoke, my eyes still fixed on the garden, the hints of the renewing season of spring poking through.

'I saw Finn.'

Colette turned so fast I was a little surprised there wasn't a sonic boom in her wake. 'What? When?'

'At the station the other night, after I'd had dinner with Friedrich.'

'Did he see you too? Did you speak to him?'

'Yes, he saw me. No, we didn't speak.' I let out a sigh. 'That was the moment Friedrich, unbeknownst to me, thought it would be a good idea to kiss me goodnight. As I wasn't expecting it, I turned to say goodbye and ended up getting kissed on the lips. It was only then I saw Finn. He was standing at the same platform I was about to go to.'

'And?'

'And nothing.' I shrugged. 'He saw me, I saw him and he turned away and got on the train.'

I could practically hear my friend's blood beginning to boil once again. 'So, let me get this right? You had the chance to speak to the love of your life and, once again, your ex managed to ruin things.'

'It obviously wasn't intentional and I think you're being a little overdramatic calling Finn the love of my life.'

'Am I?'

'It doesn't really matter now, does it? I suspect he's back in Dubai now being a TV star.'

'He flew out a couple of days ago apparently.'

'Just after I saw him then. So there were clearly no plans to stay.'

'From his perspective, I suppose it looked like there wasn't any point. Friedrich has the ability to ruin everything, even when he's not trying. Too bad for him I wasn't so easily pushed about.'

'What?' I turned to face her.

She waved her hand. 'Oh, you know he didn't think I was worthy company for you.'

'That was just his way with everyone.'

'Quite.' She looked away.

'Colette. What is it?'

'I already told you. It's nothing you didn't know already.'

'And yet I'm getting the feeling I don't know everything that I should do.'

Colette chewed her lip and studied a print of Paris in the rain that hung on her wall.

'Right,' I said, marching over to the kettle. 'I'm going to make us some tea and you're going to tell me exactly what you've been hiding all these years.'

She let out a laugh, half nerves, half relief. 'What is it with you English and tea?'

'It's the rules. Just go with it for now, OK?'

She nodded and took a seat at the table before looking back at me. 'OK.'

Three cups of tea later, I sat back.

'Why did you never tell me any of this? That he'd spoken to you like that, or made you feel that way? I'd have gone mad.'

'Because I know you'd have done just that. You seemed...' She waited, considering her words. 'I'm not going to say happy because I've never truly believed that, but at least contented. And Friedrich is clever in all manner of ways. I didn't want to risk him twisting things and ruining our friendship for good. So I kept things to myself but I refused to step back entirely.'

'Colette,' I said, as I grabbed her hand. 'I never would have believed him over you. Don't you know that?'

Her big brown eyes filled with tears. 'I couldn't risk it. You're my best friend and I was scared I'd lose you.'

I shook my head. 'Not a chance. You, my friend, are well and truly lumbered with me.'

A little while later, we'd stacked the used tea things in the slimline dishwasher and I was preparing to head home.

'I'd better be getting on. What are you up to for the rest of the day?'

'Greg's coming round shortly, ostensibly for lunch but I've decided I need a pond in the garden.'

I screwed up my face. 'What's that got to do with lunch?'

'Nothing. It has to do with free muscle.'

'It's a good job he loves you.'

Colette gave that dreamy smile that manifested whenever she spoke about Greg. At least something worthwhile had come out of that first evening other than a broken heart. I'd dismissed her description of Finn as the love of my life, but the truth was, as she knew, she was 100 per cent correct.

* * *

'If you're sure that's what you want.' Inis's reply echoed Colette's when I asked to talk to her, off the record, about Friedrich's proposal. 'Why are you smiling?'

'Because I have a feeling you and my best friend are in cahoots!'

Inis spread elegant hands on the desk in front of her. 'Perhaps we both just care about you and have your best interests at heart.'

'And you don't believe Friedrich does?'

There was just enough of a pause to answer the question without her needing to actually form the words.

'Your silence speaks volumes.'

Inis didn't deny it.

'I just think you can get your own dig.'

'OK, now I definitely know you and Colette have been talking.'

My boss grinned before glancing down and noticing a bit of baby dribble on the front of her silk blouse. 'I think I need to put all of my nice clothes away until Jakob is at least eighteen.'

'At least. Don't worry. It doesn't show.'

Thankfully, Inis's pregnancy had progressed well and she'd delivered a healthy baby boy on New Year's Eve. She was now back at work part-time while her husband had taken on the role of full-time carer for their child.

'Thank goodness for patterned fabric.' She gave an eye roll but it still wasn't enough to hide the joy that radiated out from her whenever she spoke about her family. It made me think about Finn's family and how his niece and nephew were getting on without him. I knew he'd be missing them. They grew so quickly and I recognised the same joy on his face when we'd spent time with his family as that which Inis showed now. He may not be their father but I knew that he'd still do anything for those children.

'If you want to go for it, Lizzie, then I will back you 100 per cent.' My boss jolted me from my wandering thoughts. 'Of course, you'd leave a huge gap here during the time you're away but I'll sort something out.' She looked down at the desk.

'But?'

'Sorry?'

I tilted my head to the side. 'There's definitely a but.'

She flashed a brief smile. 'But.'

'I knew it.'

'Be careful, Lizzie. Some people will do anything, use anyone, to get to where they want to be.'

'I know. I've been in this business long enough to know it's as cut-throat as any commercial endeavour, but I know what I'm doing.'

'OK then.'

'I'll let you know when I decide.'

'Thanks. In the meantime, everything seems on track for the exhibition.'

'Yes. Just the finishing touches to the space now and the first loan piece is due to arrive next Monday.'

'How's it been with the new project manager?'

'It's OK. He's been getting the job done.'

'Doesn't seem such a relaxed atmosphere down there now when I've popped in.'

'No, but maybe that's just because the deadline is looming. Deadlines can make people tense.'

'Yes, that's true. Or perhaps it's just that Rory has a stick up his bum and people don't appreciate his attitude.'

'There's that too.'

We exchanged a conspiratorial giggle and I pushed the chair back and made to leave.

'Are you happy, Lizzie?'

'Oh God, yes. I'm not trying to get away from the job here!'

Inis waved her hands. 'No, no, no. I know that. I just... don't take this the wrong way.'

'Why do people say that? It always means they're about to say something you're not going to like.'

She flashed a grin. 'It was lovely seeing you come out of yourself... before. It was as though you were discovering who you really were.'

'Or maybe it was just a silly flash in the pan. I'm thirty-seven years old, Inis. If I don't know who I am now, it's probably a bit late, don't you think?'

Her face was serious. 'No. Not at all. It's never too late. Look at your parents? They thought the world was nothing but academia but they've discovered that while that's important, there's so much more to enjoy alongside it.'

I thought of my parents and the photo Dad had sent me yesterday after Mum had tried her first open water swim. The day might have been sunny but she'd been as blue as a Smurf. From her expression I'd have guessed she was going for Grumpy Smurf. I got the feeling it wasn't something she was planning to do on a regular basis. But Inis was right. A short time ago, they'd barely noticed that the sea was there, let alone taken a dip in it.

'I'm OK, Inis, I promise.'

She gave a nod that still had a hint of apprehension about it and I walked out of the office.

* * *

'He's just in a meeting.' The intern that greeted me had pale blue, wide-set blinking eyes behind wire-rimmed spectacles. His skin was almost unnaturally pale and I began to wonder if Friedrich kept him in the dark until he was needed. 'It's due to finish shortly if you don't mind waiting?'

'Thanks. That'd be great.' We engaged in small talk as the young man showed me to Friedrich's office before he excused himself and headed back to work. I had no doubt that my ex ran a tight ship. Anyone studying under him would learn a lot but there would be no slacking. Our interns were expected to do the work but we also endeavoured to make it a welcoming and relaxed environment, reasoning that this would bring out the best in them. That was just one of the things I wanted to discuss with Friedrich today.

I'd lain awake last night turning things over in my mind and I knew I needed to give him an answer. Despite everyone's reservations, I'd pretty much decided that I'd take up the offer. There was no sign of any other leadership gigs coming my way any time soon so a joint one was at least one step closer. I was ready to commit but there were a couple of points I wanted to go over first before signing on the dotted line. Not that I had a dotted line to sign on as Friedrich was still yet to send me the final paperwork.

I got up from the hard seat opposite his desk. There was certainly no chance of any visitors getting comfortable in that chair. I glanced around, checking the coast was clear and gave my numb bum a quick massage and began a mosey around the room, tilting my head to the side as I reached the bookcases, reading the spines. The shelves spanned the length of the room, Friedrich's desk sitting in front of them. I made my way along, feeling that sense of calm that always came over me when I looked at books nestled in their rightful place.

'Oof!' My attention was rudely redirected as I whacked my

hip bone on the desk chair. Rubbing the area to prevent a bruise (did that actually work?), I gave the chair a small shove further under the desk so that I could view the books directly behind it. As I did so, something caught my eye – the contract I'd been asking Friedrich to send me. A lover of books and the tactile feel of paper, my ex had never fully embraced the digital age and was still prone to printing out forms, emails and other things that could easily have been filed digitally. I picked up the document, reasoning that I may as well make use of the time and read through it while I waited.

19

'Lizzie! What a lovely sur—' Friedrich's welcoming smile slid off his face as he saw my own thunderous expression. His eyes darted to the contract still in my hand. He stepped forward to reach for it but I moved quicker. 'It's not what you think.'

'And what exactly is it that I think?'

'It's just the way it's written. You know these lawyers and their legalese.'

'Obviously as someone in the lowly position of "supplementary staff" it's understandable that you would think I might struggle with comprehending such complicated terms and conditions but, hmm, let's see. From what it says here, you are the one and only lead of the team. Absolutely nowhere does it suggest that that role is to be shared.'

'I just haven't had time to get it amended yet, that's all.'

'How strange that it has your signature on it then, with today's date, advising that the team is now all in place with, now what was the exact wording, ah yes, here it is, "we reiterate that the hiring of supplementary staff with the specificity of field knowledge required now being added to the team is done so on the basis of forwarding their own research only, and that there is no extra funding available for these additional persons".' I looked back up at Friedrich. His face was now as pale as the intern's, which was a perfect contrast to my own which from feel alone was chilli red with fury.

'At exactly what point were you going to tell me that I was not only *not* going to be joint lead of the dig, but neither was I actually going to be paid at all.'

'I told you.' Friedrich cleared his throat and drew himself up. 'You're misunderstanding.'

'Really? Then do explain how else one is supposed to interpret this?' I thrust the paper at him and he flinched. A silence so thick you could have cut the air with a wooden spoon hung heavily between us.

'I have answers.' He sniffed. 'I'd just rather discuss them when you're calmer and less hysterical.'

'Hysterical?'

'Yes. It really is quite undignified.'

If he thought this was undignified, he wasn't going to like what was coming next. I made a step towards him.

'Dr Heckler?'

Both of us spun round at the interruption. The intern who had shown me in was now back at the door, his pale eyes darting from one to the other of us.

'What?' Friedrich snapped.

The young man gave an audible gulp. 'I... I'm sorry to interrupt. It's just that you said to let you know when Mr Matthews had arrived.'

'Matthews?' I swivelled my head back to face my ex. 'He's the money man?'

'What? No! Not that Matthews.'

But I was already on my way. 'In the lobby, is he?' I asked as I marched past, the sound of Friedrich's footsteps walking hurriedly to catch me up. He would never demean himself to run.

'There's no need for you to be here now,' Friedrich said as I walked purposefully down the winding mahogany staircase at the centre of the old mansion that housed Friedrich's office. 'Clearly you've decided not to be a part of this project.'

'You lied to my face,' I said, stopping momentarily to glare at him. 'Blatantly. You said the money was all in place.'

'It is all in place!'

'Just none allocated for me. Oh, and also that minor fib about me leading alongside you and being named on any research papers from the dig.'

'Nobody ever looks at things like that.'

'Of course they do, and you know it! Having peer-reviewed articles published is all part of taking part in any expedition. Do stop being so bloody condescending, Friedrich. You know, Colette called you that and I defended you.' I gave a short bark of humourless laughter. 'What an idiot I was.'

'It's hardly like you need the money. Your house is already paid for!'

'Oh my God!' I threw my hands in the air. 'Have you really still got a chip on your shoulder about that? It's been years and quite frankly, I'd far rather have had the chance to have my grandmother around, given the choice.'

Friedrich huffed air out of his nose.

'Everyone was right about you. They said you weren't to be trusted but I gave you the benefit of the doubt. I thought you'd matured but you haven't, have you? The only question I have now is why the hell did I waste so many years of my life with you?'

'Rather have spent it with that gorilla you were seeing, would you?'

I gave myself a mental kick for being unable to prevent the

automatic flinch and hoped Friedrich had been too wrapped up in himself to notice. But of course that would have been too much to ask. He took it and ran with it.

'So perfect, was he?' He looked one way, then the other in an over-exaggerated manner. 'Funny that I don't see him now.'

'Shut up, Friedrich. You know nothing about it.'

'I know he was obviously so besotted with you that he jetted off around the world to be a TV star with his new Michelin-starred chef girlfriend.'

I came to a halt and just stared at him. 'Were you always this petty and nasty and I just didn't see it or is it something you've cultivated in the time since we split up?'

'At least I've cultivated something. I can just imagine the scin-tillating conversations you had with him. Or perhaps you've added some picture books to your library since I was last at your house.'

We were at the lobby desk now, both the receptionist and Jed Matthews, the tech billionaire apparently involved in financing the dig, doing their utmost not to be agog at the scene unfolding in front of them, and failing. I couldn't blame them. Had it been me on the other side, I'd have opened the popcorn by now.

'Hi, Jed.'

'Hey, Lizzie.'

'Do you mind?' I reached past him and grabbed the large iron age axe that stood on display at the edge of the reception desk. As I turned back overwhelmed with fury, hot tears and a whole bunch of emotions I was yet to dissect, a large male hand encir-cled mine. His other one gently removed the weapon from my hand and handed it to the receptionist.

'Put that somewhere safe for the moment, would you?'

Eyes still on stalks, she nodded and did as Jed said.

'Now, why don't we go somewhere quiet and calm down.'

'She's crazy! I could have her arrested!' Friedrich snapped, his voice a whole octave higher than usual as he spouted threats. If I'd had my way, it would have been several octaves higher still by now but perhaps it was just as well Jed had been there. Colette was a wonderful gardener but a poor baker and I imagined it was a lot harder to hide a file in a carrot than a carrot cake.

'True. And I could withdraw all funding for this institution right now.'

Friedrich looked like he was about to both spontaneously combust and vomit at the same time.

'But neither of us are going to do those things, are we, Friedrich?'

He shook his head, mute. I reckoned that was the only reason he hadn't thrown up. I lived in hope for the spontaneous combustion.

'Now,' said Jed in a tone more suited to addressing a couple of small children who'd just been caught fighting in the playground. 'Let's head to the conference room and have a nice, sensible chat, shall we?' The southern drawl of his voice, together with the relaxed vibe he always gave off helped bring me back from the ledge.

Friedrich followed us one step behind. I could practically hear him seething. Jed's hand was still loosely encircling my wrist. Probably just as well. The corridor was lined with myriad potential weapons. Better safe than sorry.

We sat down at the table, a large swathe of polished walnut that had once graced the dining room of the grand London mansion. Jed was careful to place us a little further apart than arm's length from each other.

'It's nice to see you, Lizzie.'

I'd been taking deep, calming breaths all the way here and had now got myself under some semblance of control.

'And you, Jed. I had no idea you were involved in funding the dig.'

The brows on the handsome face drew together and he looked from me to Friedrich, then back to me again. 'Really?'

'Yes.' I flicked Friedrich a dark look. 'Surprising, isn't it?'

The hint of a smile played at the corners of his mouth.

'I had no idea you were involved either. From what I understood, you hadn't been interested in applying.'

I screwed my face up in confusion. 'But I did apply.'

Jed's expression mirrored my own. 'I wasn't involved in the interview process. That was done by someone more knowledgeable about these things.'

We both swung our gaze towards Friedrich who was now studying his nails.

'Someone who was perhaps more pally with you, Friedrich?' I felt my blood boiling again.

Jed pulled out his phone and tapped a few times. 'Chester Reece-Jones. Ring a bell?' He looked towards me.

'Yes, it does. Assuming it's the same Chester Reece-Jones who was Friedrich's mentor at university?'

'That doesn't mean anything. The job went to the person most qualified,' Friedrich snapped, the tips of his ears now tinged with pink.

'Except you're not, are you? Which is why you wanted to add me to the team. The "specialist knowledge" backup.'

Jed gave a small tilt of his head. 'Interestingly, that was what I was here to talk about today.'

'Well! Looks like you came on the right day!' My hands were still clenched on my lap. Jed hadn't made his billions by not being astute.

Friedrich shoved his chair backwards as he stood from the

table. 'You have no need to be here, Lizzie. This is none of your business. As the lead on the dig—'

'Joint lead.'

'What?' his voice was sharp and thin.

'I thought I was to be the joint lead.'

We'd already been through this but I'd now reached pettiness level on the argument scale and I wanted Jed to realise what a snake he was investing in. Assuming he didn't know already. He was hot as hell, and from all accounts and dealings with him in the past, he had a brain as sharp as his cheekbones. Most definitely not how Friedrich had referred to him at the restaurant.

'You know that's not true,' Friedrich snapped.

'But that's what you told her?' Jed interjected.

Friedrich's head spun towards him, panic registering on his face momentarily before he smoothed it away. 'It was merely a misunderstanding.'

'Yes, you know,' I butted in. 'The kind of misunderstanding that happens when someone tells you one thing and then you find out totally by accident that actually, none of it is true. And that not only are you *not* being given the position you were promised, you're not even going to be paid a wage.'

Jed's face lost all expression and he turned back to Friedrich who was now practically purple with barely suppressed rage.

'If you hadn't been snooping on my desk, you wouldn't have known that anyway!'

'That's not really the point, is it, Friedrich? Assuming it's true.' Jed's melodic southern drawl was measured and calm.

I remained silent, although with difficulty and only because I knew Jed believed me.

'She's misunderstood.'

'In what way?' Jed answered, his tone reasonable but with a hint of 'I can guarantee if you mess me about you'll regret it'.

'Well, umm, it's more a matter of Lizzie misunderstanding what I said originally. I never promised her the lead. Obviously that was always going to be me.'

'Yes, *obviously!* Thanks to you being chums with the bloke organising it. Funny that,' I mumbled.

Jed swung me a look. I'd moved from petty to petulant on the scale now.

'Sorry.'

The blue eyes gave the briefest flicker of amusement before he turned his attention back to the other side of the table. I looked up at the clock.

'Look, I need to get back to work. I've got all the answers I need here. I have a pile of stuff to do and I've wasted enough time on this.'

Jed stood. 'Yes, of course.' He gave me a quick hug and saw me to the door. Friedrich stood up.

'Can you hang on there a moment, Friedrich. Lizzie may have her answers but I still have a few questions of my own.' Friedrich's high colour once more paled until he matched the bleached whale bone that served as an art installation in the room. I turned and left. I may have been smiling.

* * *

I began rereading the email once more from the beginning.

It was good to see you a few days ago. Having spoken over the situation with the board, we feel that the dig would indeed benefit from your knowledge and specific expertise.

As such, it would of course be difficult at this late stage to replace the current lead but we would like to formally offer you the position of joint lead. Any papers you write in association with any discovery or research from the expedition would be written in your name only.

The funding has been adjusted to reflect the addition to the team. Details of this, including financial renumeration due to you, can be seen in the enclosed contract.

Should you be willing to proceed, please do take time to read through the attached and ensure you are happy with everything. If there is anything you wish to discuss, we will all be most happy to do our best to accommodate any changes.

Best wishes,

Jed Matthews

I sat back in my chair and wondered what the hell I should do. On the one hand this was an opportunity I had been waiting for. Jed's assurance that any peer-reviewed papers would be mine alone gave me peace of mind. Unlike some people, I knew him to be a man of his word. On the other hand, I would still have to work with Friedrich which did not exactly give me the warm and fuzzies. And there were a lot of sharp tools to hand on a dig. However, even though Friedrich could be astoundingly obtuse at times, I knew even he was bright enough not to push his luck twice.

I pressed 'reply' and began to compose a message.

* * *

The grand opening of the Pharaohs of Egypt exhibition in its brand-new location was about to take place. I stood and took in the sight before me, thinking how this had once, quite literally, been a building site. The remembered panic of how this could ever come together was replaced by the image of Finn, assuring me that it was all in hand and everything would be perfect in the end. He'd been right on one aspect. His replacement, who he'd apparently had a hand in choosing, might not have been the most personable, but I had to give credit where it was due. He'd finished the job on time, and within budget by following the plans his predecessor had set in place.

'Doesn't it look magnificent?' Beside me, Inis's voice was low and wondrous.

'It's incredible. I never thought it would look this good.'

'You did a brilliant job liaising, Lizzie.' She hooked her arm around mine, both of us looking out at the two colossus that framed the entryway to the main exhibition. 'Even though I know that wasn't always easy.'

'Don't worry about it. I'm a big girl. I can look after myself. It's all character-building anyway, isn't that what they say?' I turned towards her.

'That's what they say.'

'There we are then.'

'But forget character-building.' Inis took a step back from me. 'Can we talk about wardrobe building? You look stunning!'

I gave an unnecessary smooth of the black sheath dress I wore, accessorised with gold jewellery. Between us, Colette and I had decided that the full-length Grecian style dress was a fitting tribute to the location without being at all costumey.

'Thanks.'

'I love the new look in general. It seems like you're a lot more comfortable in your skin these days.'

I turned back towards the exhibition, my eyes roaming over the space. 'I think I am. A lot's happened over the past year, not just with the whole Finn thing, but Mum and Dad, and Friedrich and all sorts. It made me take a hard look at myself and decide whether I was actually happy with what I saw. I was so bothered about other people's opinions and felt the only way

I would be taken seriously was if I looked like their image of what they thought a woman in my position should look like. Now I've realised that I can, that I need, to be myself. I'm damn good at my job and how I dress has absolutely no relevance to it.'

'Yes, it can be tricky to navigate, can't it? Certainly in the more stuffy departments.'

'Quite.'

Inis threw a glance over her shoulder, checking for earwiggers. Determining we were still out of others' earshot, she took a small step back towards me. 'I am sorry things didn't work out with you and Finn, though. I have to say I was surprised. When he took me home that time, all he did was rave about you.'

I gave a low chuckle. 'That must have made for a very boring journey.'

'Not at all. In fact I was agreeing with him. I know you had several other choices when we offered you the position here and some were more money than we could table. But I'm forever thankful that you chose us.'

I touched her arm. 'So am I. Money is definitely nice. No one is going to argue with that. But you have to love what you do too otherwise what's the point?'

Inis gave me a long look. 'You really do.'

'What was that about?'

'What?'

'That look.'

Her expression was all innocence. 'I don't know what you mean.'

'And I don't believe a word of it.'

'Come on,' she said, that twinkle of mischief still in her eye. 'I think we both deserve a glass of something fizzy and expensive before the peace is shattered. Our wonderful sponsor, Jed

Matthews, sent over a single bottle of Cristal to my office – I can't think of a better time or a better person to open it with.'

'You won't get any argument from me.'

Inis took the bottle from where it was cooling in a separate ice bucket and wrangled out the cork as we did our best to muffle the sound so as not to draw attention, giggling like a couple of kids. The tension of the build, and the coming together of the exhibition was finally at an end. Tickets were already sold out for months in advance and hopefully tonight's reviews would help boost further sales. We weren't worried about those being anything but good – we knew the show was spectacular with many never-before-seen items on display. Of course, there were certain parts of the project that I wished had gone differently but not once had I ever wished that I hadn't met Finn, or had that time together. He'd opened my eyes to a new way of being, of believing in myself and not caring what others thought I should or shouldn't be, or do, or wear. He'd led me through a door to a new sense of freedom and that had not only enabled me to connect more strongly with my parents and their own new take on life, but also with my closest friend.

Colette and I spent more time together now doing things that before I would have avoided because I'd thought I should have been doing something more serious, more studious. And the fact that she got to help me choose a whole new wardrobe had been the icing on the cake. Although I was the one getting new clothes and loving it, Colette was in seventh heaven in her role as stylist and I was more than happy to let her take the lead while I learnt.

'Cheers!' Inis and I clinked our flutes and toasted all the hard work and long hours we'd put in to bring this endeavour to tonight's pinnacle. Inis poured us both another glass before we took a deep breath and went to join our guests and the TV historian who would be cutting the opening ribbon.

* * *

'Lizzie! There you are! I've been trying to get to talk to you all evening. The exhibition is a roaring success, don't you agree? Absolutely exquisite. I shall be coming to view it several times once it's open officially. And don't you look stunning?' I'd known Professor Kareski for many years and had long since learned to navigate her tendency towards stream of consciousness speech. She was sharp, witty and fiercely intelligent. I liked her a lot.

'Thank you,' I replied, sensing a pause. 'And thank you for coming tonight. I'm so glad you're enjoying the exhibition.'

'Oh I am! I am! And may I congratulate you on your champagne too. Proper stuff, this. None of that cheap stuff that sticks your teeth together. The museum must be doing extremely well with sponsorship!' She chinked her glass against my almost empty one and laughed before sipping her own.

'We're lucky to have Jed Matthews as one of our patrons. The Veuve Cliquot was courtesy of him.'

She gave an appreciative waggle of her eyebrows. 'Gosh, it must be such a drag when you have to have meetings with him. Fancy having to stare at that face for hours.'

The professor had a voice that was used to carrying across lecture theatres and symposiums and on occasions, especially with the help of alcohol, she forgot to adjust the volume. I looked over her shoulder to where Jed was in earnest conversation with a board member. His wife, Milly, was standing beside him and caught my glance, grinning. I grinned back.

'Who are you smiling at?' Professor Kareski asked, craning around. 'Oh, hello!' She raised her glass to Milly. 'Just talking about your lovely husband.'

Jed's eyes darted towards us. He gave Professor Kareski an

amused nod, and then returned to his conversation, his arm moving to rest casually around his wife's waist.

A while ago, I would have been a teensy bit mortified as, from the look on his face now, Friedrich's pal, Chester, currently was. But I'd changed and most certainly for the better. Professor Kareski said what she thought, made no attempt to be someone she wasn't and from what I saw, was doing her best to have a ball as she went through life. Who wouldn't want that? I knew now that I did.

She turned her attention back to me. 'Lovely couple. Adore the pants off each other.'

Chester gave a sputter and stalked off, his metal Blakeys clack, clack, clacking on the wooden floors. Professor Kareski watched him go before looking back at me.

'Good. Now that we've despatched the spies in the camp, there's something I want to ask you.'

* * *

'And before you give me your answer, although I suspect you'll want time to think about it, annoyingly,' she teased, 'I've spoken to your boss already. In fact, Inis was the one who told me to go ahead and ask you when we had dinner the other week. You know we studied together?'

'Yes, yes I did.' I thought back to my boss's cryptic words and that strange look earlier this evening. Things now slotted perfectly into place.

'Good. So you don't need to worry about that aspect. Of course she'd rather keep you but she also knows that sometimes people have to move on, and she's one of the good ones. Inis would never hold someone back to benefit herself.' She gave me a brief, purposeful look before continuing. 'As she thinks the sun shines out of your proverbial, you can see how strongly she believes this is the right step for you too. But,' Professor Kareski held up a finger, 'the most important thing is that you think it's right for you. We're prepared to wait for you to—'

'Yes!'

For once, the good professor was lost for words. Her eyes widened and a smile began to grow, tipping the scarlet painted lips upwards.

'Definitely, yes!'

She found her voice. 'Are you sure? I mean, you can have all the time you need to think it over. It's a big step.'

'I don't need the time.'

Professor Kareski threw her arms around me, hugging me tightly to her tall, bony frame. 'That's fantastic! Alongside the papers you've written, and the role that you've played in the education programme here at the museum, you've really been a leader in the field and a great example for other educational institutions to follow. You're a natural teacher.'

'I hope so.' My confidence wavered as visions of students snoozing in my classes filled my mind.

'I know so!' she said, taking my arm. 'And don't worry if the odd one falls asleep. They do that from time to time. Don't take it personally.'

'You must have read my mind.'

'I read your face,' she replied, laughing. 'Anyway, I'd better stop hogging you and let you mingle and revel in the success of all this.' Professor Kareski spread her arm to encompass the exhibition as she spoke, her colourful Bakelite bangles clacking together. She gave me another hug then turned and disappeared into the throng of chatter and laughter, the sounds echoing in the crisp, new space that was everything and more we had hoped it would be. Finn had promised that the build would go to plan, and he'd been as good as his word.

My thoughts drifted across the ocean to where he was now furthering his career. Had that move led to a new relationship too? I knew it would only take one question to Greg to find out... No! If it had, then what did it matter? We were no longer together. Our relationship had been a flash in the pan. The result of too much champagne and pure lust. There was no way that it could have lasted. Even though, in private moments, I still wished so hard that it had.

'There you are!' Colette jolted me from my thoughts and swept me up into a huge hug. 'This looks amazing! I've no idea what most of the exhibits signify, but it all looks brilliant!'

'Thanks,' I replied, laughing. 'I can do you a private tour sometime, if you like?'

'Really?' Greg's eyes lit up as he hugged me too. 'That'd be amazing, wouldn't it, Col.'

'Yes, we'd love it.'

I smiled at the familiar shortening of my friend's name, a privilege that, in all the time I'd known her, only I had been given. It would be so easy to wish I'd never gone out that night, never met Finn. But the biggest and best reason I didn't regret that night was that it had brought these two people together. Colette had never been as happy as she was with Greg and, as far as Finn had been concerned, Greg felt the same. The love they had for each other practically radiated from them. It was really quite nauseating – but only when I was in a bad mood. Most of the time it was absolutely wonderful.

'I just need to pop to the loo. Can you look after him for a moment?' Colette asked me.

'I'll try not to lose him.'

My friend grinned then strode off across the hall on her sky-high ultra-thin stilettos, garnering admiring glances as she did so. I looked up to see Greg's eyes following her, a smile on his lips.

'You've got that dopey look on your face again.'

He let out a laugh. 'I know. I can't help it. Which brings me to something else. Can I ask you a favour?'

* * *

'So thank you all for being here tonight.' Inis finished her speech. 'And enjoy the exhibition!' A round of applause echoed in the hall as I walked up to meet Inis coming off the small dais that had been put in place for her presentation.

'Was that OK?' she whispered.

'Perfect. Can I borrow the mic for a minute?'

I looked out at the sea of faces that had begun to turn towards me, some of them a little irritated that their soiree and unlimited champagne was being interfered with yet again.

'Good evening. I apologise for interrupting your evening but this won't take long. Tonight there is a very special guest here.'

The crowd began looking a little more interested now, casting glances left and right trying to spy who it might be. Colette gave me a silent 'Ooh' and peered at the gathered throng.

'Colette? Would you mind joining me up here?' Her head swivelled forward and her eyes locked on to mine, confusion writ large on her face. She didn't move. 'Hurry up, woman!' I laughed, jolting her out of her shock. The crowd made a clear path and I held out a hand to assist her and her mad shoes onto the tiny stage.

'What are you doing?' she whispered, forgetting in her daze that the mic was on. A ripple of amusement drifted over the guests.

'I have someone here who wants to ask you something.' With

that, I kissed her cheek, gave her a massive hug and stepped back. Greg held out his hand to help me step down and I handed him the mic. Behind me, Colette already had her hand to her mouth, tears glinting in her eyes.

'I'll go and get a box of tissues,' I said.

He nodded his thanks, gave me a quick hug and took to the stage. It was cramped but to his credit, he made it work, getting down on one knee and taking her hand. I glanced around as everyone watched and listened. It wasn't only Colette who needed tissues now.

'*Oui!*' Colette cried, sobbing now. 'I mean, yes! Yes, yes, yes!'

A huge cheer went up as the applause broke out, accompanied by whoops and more cheers.

'Shame they weren't that enthusiastic about my presentation,' Inis said, catching my elbow and laughing as she dabbed at her eyes.

'Thanks for letting this happen.'

'Why wouldn't I?'

'Some people wouldn't like to take the focus away from the actual exhibition, I guess.'

'Well, I'm not *some people*.' The pointed look she gave me as she said it made me smile. She may as well have said I'm not Friedrich. It was what she'd meant and perhaps what I'd meant but I knew he wasn't the only one who might think like that. I'd not really noticed the snobbery in the world I operated in before, not until Finn brought it to my attention. Thank God I hadn't had that at this job. Inis was a brilliant boss and for a moment, I began to second guess my earlier, perhaps rash decision to move on.

'So I saw Professor Kareski having a very in-depth conversation with you earlier.'

I felt the colour whoosh up from my chest to my face. Inis laid her hand on my arm. 'Don't worry. She spoke to me first.'

'Yes, she said she had but still...'

'But still what? This is what you wanted, isn't it? I know how much you enjoyed getting involved in the educational side here, on top of your other duties. Selfishly, I asked her not to say anything until the exhibition was completed.' This time it was my boss's turn to flush. 'Was that horribly self-serving?'

'No,' I laughed. 'Not at all. It makes sense and I would have wanted to see this through anyway.'

'Good.' She made a 'phew' gesture, mock-wiping her brow, a wide smile breaking on the elfin face. 'So, what did you say?'

'Umm, I sort of said yes.'

'Sort of?' Inis laughed.

'Definitively.'

'Good.'

I shook my head. 'I'm not so sure. Perhaps I should think about it some more.'

'That's fine. I don't think she was really expecting an answer tonight, especially since there's champagne involved.'

I pulled a face. 'Yeah, not all my impulsive decisions made after quantities of champagne have worked out that well.'

Inis's expression softened. 'I'm sorry about that, Lizzie. I really am. Are you OK?'

'Yeah.' I nodded. 'I am. If nothing else, this came out of it.' I tilted my head towards where Greg and Colette were being congratulated by a bunch of people they didn't know and absolutely loving it. 'I can never wish it hadn't happened if this was a result.'

'That's a very magnanimous view.'

'Is it?' I asked. 'I'm not so sure. Colette has been there for me through a lot. And she's put up with a lot, some of which I had no idea about. It's about time she found someone who truly appreciates the wonderful woman, and friend, she is.'

'And what about you?'

'What about me?'

'What about someone to appreciate the wonderful woman you are?'

I let out a sigh. 'Who knows? Besides, if I take this job, I'm going to have plenty to occupy me for while.'

'If you take this job?'

'Yes.'

Inis drew herself up to her entire five foot two inches then looked down at her feet. 'This is when I wish I'd worn heels.'

'Would it help if I sat down?'

'No. But let's pretend you are.'

'Fair enough. Go ahead.'

'You're taking that job, even if I have to fire you to make you.'

'I thought you liked me!' I replied, laughing.

'I do. I love you. You're one of the main reasons I was able to keep mostly sane during my pregnancy and I can never repay you for that.'

'Except by firing me.'

Inis grinned.

'There's nothing to repay. I didn't do anything that anyone else wouldn't have.'

'You know you did.' With that, she gave me a squeeze and headed off to do more professional mingling.

I stole a glance at Colette and Greg, basking in happiness. If I took the lecturing position, which it seemed that both Inis and I knew I would, it would keep me busy. Perhaps it would also be a way to keep my thoughts from drifting to what might have been.

Unexpected tears prickled at the back of my eyes. I told myself they were tears of happiness for my friend and made my way towards the small courtyard that had been part of the new addition. A thoughtful haven incorporated so that staff had somewhere to come and enjoy their lunch or just a little nature in the midst of the city. Fairy lights wound around the slim trunk of the central feature tree and the area was bathed in a soft light from artfully hidden uplighters. A recycling water feature provided subtle noise distraction from the city outside the walls as well as providing water for the birds that were being encouraged by a couple of feeders hung from the walls. Insect houses and lush, almost tropical, planting completed the scene. It was perfect. I'd watched it coming together and been excited about one day sharing a quiet, celebratory drink with Finn here. But some things just weren't meant to be.

'Do you like it?'

I spun round so fast, I was in danger of leaving my eyeballs behind.

We stood there for a moment, staring at each other until I gave myself a crash refresher course on how to form words.

'Finn... what are you doing here?'

20

'I could ask you the same question.'

My brow wrinkled. 'I think all that sun must have gone to your head. I work here, remember?'

His mouth tipped briefly into a half smile. 'Not something I'm ever likely to forget. But from what I understood, shouldn't you be somewhere in the deepest, darkest depths of Egypt about now?'

'And shouldn't you be in the deepest, darkest depths of Dubai?'

The other side of his mouth joined in and I saw the smile I'd loved from the first moment I'd met him.

'Touché. How about you go first?'

I paused, then turned away from him, swallowing hard as my hand reached to touch the furry leaves of a plant that felt like puppy-dog ears. I'd thought I was getting over Finn. Yes, it still hurt, yes, I still missed him but I'd convinced myself it had been a little less every day. His appearance tonight had well and truly blown apart the myth I'd been telling myself. I hadn't got over him at all and I couldn't decide if seeing him tonight made me happy or mad as hell.

'I didn't go,' I said, my back towards him.

'I kind of guessed that.' His voice was soft and closer than it had been. I kept my back towards him.

'Then you have your answer.'

'OK,' he said, closer still. 'Perhaps I didn't ask the right question?'

'Which is?'

'Why didn't you go?'

I closed my eyes, trying not to remember how good being this close to Finn felt. How soothing his voice could be one moment, and how downright sexy the next. My chest tightened as anger, hurt, love and want collided, tears burning in my eyes.

'What do you want, Finn?' I asked, spinning to face him. He was so close now that I could have reached up and kissed him. And part of me really, really wanted to. I gave that part a hefty mental shove and glared at Finn.

I saw his Adam's apple bob. 'I want to apologise.'

'For what? Walking out on our relationship without giving it a chance? Buggering off to Dubai without even saying goodbye? Leaving this job without notice because you want to be a reality TV star? Or perhaps,' I said, giving him a solid poke in the shoulder with my finger, 'you might like to apologise for letting me fall in love with you when you had absolutely no intention of us ever going anywhere!'

Finn hadn't moved. Although he had flinched when I'd poked him, which gave me some satisfaction.

'Here.' He passed me a beautifully pressed Egyptian cotton handkerchief. I snatched it from his hand with far less grace than I should have done and tried to mop my tears as delicately as I could.

'Thank you,' I said, with as much gratitude as if he'd just

handed me a full doggy poo bag. 'It took Colette ages to make me look like this and you turning up has ruined it.'

'Sorry.'

I flicked a glance up. At least he had the sense to look remorseful.

'But it's not ruined and you still look beautiful if that helps?'

'No! It doesn't bloody help! Not in the slightest. And you don't get to say that to me any more.'

'Sorry. You do though.'

I glared up at him, my vision less blurry now the tears had stopped. 'Thank you.' This time my words were a little more dignified. 'But you still haven't told me what you're doing here.'

'I came to see you.'

I gave a head tilt.

'Greg told me he was going to propose tonight and I'm afraid I shamefully used that as an excuse to be here.'

'You didn't need an excuse. I sent the invites myself so I know you were on the guest list. Inis insisted on it although I never expected you to accept.'

'It was an opportunity to see you.'

'Well.' I cleared my throat and took a step back. 'You've seen me now so I'd better get back to—'

'I'm sorry,' he said, reaching for my hand and folding it within both of his own as he once more closed the gap between us. 'For everything you said. For all that and more. I've never ever walked out on a job before—'

I snatched my hand away. 'That's the bit you're most sorry about?' I yelled at him, all pretension of composure now gone. 'The bloody job? You know what, Finn? Never mind any of what I said because you've well and truly shown your true colours now. What the hell was I thinking falling in love with you? But you can rest assured that *that* will never happen again so next time we meet, which unfortunately we will due to the fact that our respective best friends just got engaged, it will be purely as acquaintances. You've no need to worry that there will be any repeat of the ridiculous behaviour I showed tonight. Enjoy the exhibition.'

Head held high, I turned away from him, every fibre of my being engaged in trying to hold it together until I could get home, which was the only place I wanted to be right now.

Finn's long stride covered the ground quicker than I could in the heels Colette had talked me into buying and his bulk was now in front of the doorway. Bloody shoes!

'Would you mind moving please?'

'Yes. I would. Very much so.'

'OK. I was being polite. I don't actually give a shit if you mind or not. Bloody well move.'

'Not until you listen to me.'

I huffed out a humourless laugh. 'I think I've heard all I need to hear from you to last me a lifetime.'

'Tough,' he fired back, 'because I have something else to say.' I opened my mouth to parry with a smart-arse remark but he beat me to it. 'You're right. I made a bloody hash of that apology.'

I folded my arms, my expression still firmly set to 'annoyed'.

'And of course the job isn't the main thing I'm sorry about! Are you nuts?'

'Wow, thanks. Compliments too.'

He tipped his head back and looked up at the sky that, had it not been smothered with the city's light pollution would have twinkled with a million stars. After a small headshake, he focused his gaze back on me.

'None of this is going how I planned it.'

'Life's like that it seems.'

'Do you mind if I start again?'

I shrugged as though I couldn't care less while my insides flip-flopped about like they were practising to compete in the Olympics' gymnastics.

'Can we sit down?'

'If you want.'

A resigned smile teased his lips. 'You're not going to make this easy, are you?'

'I wouldn't want to put you to any trouble.' I made to push past him. Yes, it was about as effective as me trying to shift one of the colossus in the museum by myself but this was more about making a point.

'No, wait.'

I looked up at him with the most pissed-off face I could manage. Funnily enough, it came pretty easily. His eyes dropped momentarily to my lips which Colette had painted earlier in a fiery scarlet with all the skill of an Old Master. I saw him swallow before his gaze drifted back to mine.

'God, I want to kiss you but I'm guessing if I tried I'd get a knee in the nuts.'

'You guess right,' I said with a lightness that I most certainly didn't feel. My heart wanted nothing more than for him to do just that but, luckily, my brain had the upper hand just now.

'Right,' he said, dipping his head briefly before looking back at me, squaring his shoulders and taking my hand. I let him lead me to the bench tucked in the corner of the courtyard in the only part that wasn't overlooked by the rest of the building. He took a seat and, after a brief moment, I followed. My hand was still in his and my brain was telling me to take it back but this time my heart won the wrestling match and my brain returned to the corner to sulk.

'Elizabeth, as you've seen, I'm not always the best with words when it comes to things like this.'

'Have a lot of experience, do you?' I snapped childishly.

He let out a sigh and dropped his head for a moment. My heart marched over, punched my brain and knocked it out cold.

'Sorry.'

Finn looked up and I shrugged. 'Defensiveness.'

He gave a couple of nods. 'I know. I get that and I don't blame you. If it had been the other way around, I'm not sure I'd be even sat here now. So.' His voice cracked a little and he cleared his throat. 'What I wanted to say, and what went so much better in my head, is that I am so, so sorry I left that day like I did. You didn't deserve that and you certainly didn't deserve to come into work and find that I'd walked out on that too.'

'So why did you?' I asked, quieter this time. I was exhausted from it all now. From the months of heartbreak, from pretending I was fine when I was anything but and from wondering what the hell had gone wrong.

'I... think I panicked.'

'Panicked?'

'Yes.'

'I wasn't about to demand marriage, Finn!' I felt all the muscles that had finally begun to relax tighten once more.

His eyes widened. 'No! no, no, no. That wasn't what I meant. Actually I'd have been pretty damn happy if you had.'

'Really?' The word came out on a surprised laugh.

'Definitely!' That smile I knew, and loved, so well flashed briefly before his face settled back into a serious expression once more.

I let out a sigh. 'Finn. I'm so confused.'

'I know.' His hand tightened around mine. 'I know you are and I'm so, so sorry. I love you, Elizabeth. I knew that the moment I met you. I know people say that love at first sight doesn't exist and maybe it doesn't but love at first few sentences definitely does. You're funny, you're so bloody intelligent and you're the most beautiful woman I've ever known, inside and out.'

'I think you've been on Jed's champagne.'

'No,' he said. 'I haven't. I haven't had anything because I wanted to do this stone cold sober. Although the more I think about it, maybe a drink would have been better. I couldn't have made more of an arse of it than I already have.'

'That's true.'

There was the whisper of a smile around his mouth but those stunning blue eyes remained serious.

'Where was I?'

'Saying I was beautiful,' I reminded him, desperate to see the smile spread. It did, for a brief moment.

'So beautiful. And all the other stuff I mentioned just makes you more so to me.'

I felt the tears threaten again and heard them in my voice when I spoke. 'You can see why I'm confused.'

He nodded, swallowing audibly.

'Firstly, can I just say that I never, ever intended to make you or your parents feel out of place when we went to dinner. They're great and I'm really sorry if they did.' He shook his head. 'There's no if. I know that. I know they, and you did and I let it happen. I have no idea why. I guess I just got caught up in the fact that, for once, I was the one that felt comfortable.'

'So you made us uncomfortable to make up for it?'

'No! Not intentionally but what I didn't do was call out that arsehole of a maître d' when he spoke to you like that. I've been to Mel's restaurants so many times that it's like going to Pizza Hut to me. It didn't occur to me to pay attention and realise that not everyone else was as comfortable as I was.'

'I see.'

'And for that I can only apologise to you all. When I finally picked apart what the hell I was doing and what had gone wrong, I told Mel that actually, the atmosphere at the restaurant is pretty intimidating.'

'Oh!'

'Yeah. She was pretty upset. It's kind of her baby.'

'You didn't need to do that, Finn.' In all the emotion, I'd forgotten about Mel.

'I did. I don't want other people to feel like that. I like to get involved in projects where everyone can benefit. That's why I was so excited about the job here at the museum.'

'I can see how a seven-star Dubai resort would slot nicely into that mission statement.'

He ran his free hand across the back of his neck.

'Yeah, I know. I kind of lost my way there for a bit. But I've found it again now. Because of you. At least I hope so.'

'So how's life in the heady world of reality TV?'

He gave a sharp shake of his head. 'Ridiculous and awful. I don't know what I was thinking. Actually, I do. I wasn't thinking at all. I was being an idiot. I should have talked to you about things rather than just take Friedrich's word for—'

'What? What's Friedrich got to do with any of this?'

Finn's brows drew together. 'I heard his message, Elizabeth. I know he wanted you back and that you're a good match, operating in similar worlds and both being scarily intelligent.'

'Finn, what message are you talking about?'

'The one he left on your parents' answering machine when we were down for New Year. You were out watching the lifeboat in the bay and I'd nipped in to get my camera. The phone was ringing and eventually switched to answerphone. I know I shouldn't have listened to it, that I should have gone and got you but... stupidly I just stood there.' He paused. 'And for some reason what he said about you two being a perfect match made sense. I felt like I stuck out like a sore thumb at that book launch we went to together so when he mentioned that—'

I shot up from my seat. 'I am going to kill him!' I looked down at Finn, who'd remained seated, his brows still raised in mild shock. 'My parents never, ever use their answerphone. It just came as part of the phone and they haven't worked out how to switch it off. Their view is that if something is that important, the person will ring back. The fact that my phone was off would have given most people the hint that I didn't want to be disturbed but, of course, that wouldn't apply to Friedrich! And then the opportunity to give a brief, uninterrupted lecture on his view of things? Well, that was a chance not to be missed, clearly!'

Finn gave a shrug. 'It wasn't all that brief, actually. And then I saw you at the station...'

I could practically hear my blood boiling in my veins and guessed that my face now probably matched my lipstick. 'I'm going to bloody mummify him. Alive!'

Finn winced. 'Remind me not to get on the wrong side of you.'

'You.' I pointed a long, red, entirely fake nail at him. 'Are most definitely not off the hook so don't get too cocky over there.'

'No. No, of course not.'

'I mean it!'

'I know!'

'Stop smiling!'

'I'm not!' he said, the corners of his mouth tilting. 'Not intentionally anyway. You're making me smile!'

'How on earth am I doing that?'

'Because you always did. And probably because you're currently more mad at someone other than me.'

'Yes. Well. Like I said, I'll come back to you.'

The words, spoken without thought, hung between us in the still, warm air of the evening. Finn's eyes locked onto mine and we both stood there. I wanted to say so much, say that I would do just that, that I wanted that. But the words stuck in my throat. His expression clouded and the smile of before returned but this time it was draped in sadness.

'Please don't look at me like that,' I asked, my voice barely a whisper.

'Like what?' His own voice was low and cracked.

'Like I just broke your heart.'

'You did.'

'You broke mine first.' My throat was so tight and raw, I could barely get the words out.

'I know. And it was, without doubt the stupidest, most idiotic, most unforgiveable thing I've ever done and, by the looks of things, I'm going to spend the rest of my life regretting it.'

'Finn...'

He closed the distance between us in a flash, his hands taking mine, lifting them to his lips to kiss before holding them tight against his chest. 'It's true. I've known it for months. Pretty much since I made the senseless decision to believe Friedrich's claim that you were just using me to make him jealous, which by the way, he said had worked.'

'I really am going to kill him!'

'I'll help you move the body.'

The laugh bubbled treacherously in my throat – I'd strictly forbidden any lowering of defences.

'I couldn't ask you to do that.'

He huffed out a dry laugh. 'Believe me. It would give me great pleasure.' The expression on his face turned serious. 'I would do anything for you, Elizabeth. Give anything to turn back time, tell you about that call. Discuss things with you. Ask you if you felt the same.'

'Of course I didn't feel the same!' I snatched back my hands and gave Finn a hefty thump on the chest at which he let out a satisfying 'oof'. So satisfying that I did it again.

'You idiot.'

'Believe me. There's no name that you could call me that I haven't already called myself but,' he wrapped his hands gently back around mine, 'I'm going to hold on to these for now. You're leaving bruises.'

'I wouldn't want to spoil the shirt-off shots that programme no doubt has you doing. You'll be quite the pin up when it comes out.'

For the first time since we'd met again, I heard the low, melodic rumble of his laughter.

'It's not funny!' I snapped, pulling at my hands to which Finn held tight.

'Oh, I beg to differ. It's hilarious.'

'No, it's not! Do you ever watch television? Most celebrities these days are either from soaps or one of a myriad of reality shows.'

'I can guarantee that's not going to be me.'

'And how's that?'

'Because I turned it down.'

'What?'

'The TV show. I turned it down.'

'No you didn't. I *know* you're working out in Dubai, Finn. Don't lie to me.' The anger bubbled again.

'I'm not!' he said, his eyes intense, willing me to believe him. 'Yes, I'm working in Dubai. The project is interesting and they were keen for me to manage it. But I refused to be a part of the filming.'

'But I thought...'

'Thought what?' His voice was soft again now, wrapping itself around me like silk.

I looked up. 'I...' *God, I wanted to kiss him.*

Stop it, Lizzie. You do not want to kiss him. He broke your heart, remember?

Yes, I know. I most definitely do not want to kiss him. How could I possibly? I mean look at him.

Oh God, I so want to kiss him.

'I thought you... and Mel...'

He shook his head. 'No. Never. Yes. We flirted when I was working on the restaurant before but she was with someone at the time so nothing ever happened.'

'And out there? I thought one of the highlights of the programme was the sexual tension with you and her. The whole will they, won't they?' As Finn's hands were still wrapped around mine and resting on his chest I wobbled my head from side to side for emphasis.

'Even if I'd taken part, it would have been most definitely they won't.'

I dropped my head down, staring at his hands. 'Maybe you should have.'

'No. I shouldn't.' He paused. 'Look at me, Elizabeth.'

I followed his request. Clearly my brain was still out for the count.

'She's not you. No one else is you. And you are the one I want.' His chest expanded and slowly retracted. 'You're the one I love.'

'Finn...'

'Wait! Before you say anything, I know I cocked up massively. Monumentally! And I am so, so sorry. I am not a man who's begged for anything in life and frankly I never thought anything would ever be important enough to do so but that was before I met you. So I'm begging you now. Please, Elizabeth. I know I hurt you. I know I acted like a dick and if I could turn back time I would. But if you could see your way to forgiving me for all of that, I would spend the rest of the time we have together ensuring you don't regret it.'

'That's quite a claim.'

'You're quite a woman.'

'Wait... the rest of the time we have together?' I asked. The words drifted around my head until they bumped squarely into a very loud alarm bell. 'Oh my God! You're ill, aren't you? That's why you've come back.' I felt all the emotions burst inside me. Suddenly Finn's hands were cupping my face, his lips kissing mine before pulling back.

'No! No, sweetheart. I'm fine. I promise!'

Emotions collided. Seeing Finn again, hearing his loving words and the momentary panic at his phrasing rushed through me, and tears began to dampen my cheeks. 'But you said,' *hitch*. 'it like,' *hitch*. 'you weren't going to be around...' *Huge hitch*.

'That's not what I meant.' He kissed me again. 'Please, please don't cry. I can't bear it. I promise you, I'm fine. Elizabeth, look at me.' The large hands warmed my face but my gaze was focused firmly on the third button of his shirt. I couldn't look up. I couldn't.

'Look at me.' There was a soft command in his voice that I couldn't ignore. The blue eyes fixed on mine. 'I am perfectly healthy. I had a full, in depth medical before I left for Dubai.' I felt my eyes widen. 'Only because it was part of the deal,' he filled in hurriedly. 'Not because there was anything to worry about. I got a clean bill of health.'

'Are you sure?' My hands were balled into tight fists now, the nails digging deep into my palms.

Finn reached for them, one hand in each of his own and brought them to his lips.

'I'm sure.'

'You know what? People need to stop frightening the shit out of me. First my parents, and now you.'

'Does that reaction mean you still kind of like me?'

'No,' I said, tears still tracing down my cheeks and ruining my once-perfect make-up. 'I can't stand the sight of you!'

The smile that made my insides turn to liquid flashed at me. 'That's good. Because I can't stand the sight of you either.'

'Good. Now that's clear, there are two things I need you to do.'

'Pay a hitman?'

'No, but thank you. Friedrich is certainly not worth all the fuss of going to prison for. Besides, from what I hear, karma has got its eye on him.'

'That sounds interesting.'

'Not interesting enough to talk about now.'

'OK. So what is it you want me to do?'

So many ideas crammed themselves into my mind at that moment – not one of them appropriate for the setting.

'Go and get Colette and tell her to bring her make-up. Hopefully she'll be able to affect some sort of repair to this.' I made a circle shape around my face with the palm of my hand towards me. 'Is it that bad?'

Finn paused a moment too long before answering. 'No... not really.'

'Wow. That bad. OK. Tell her it's code red.'

Finn made to move then halted. 'What's the second thing?'

I grabbed the front of his shirt. 'Bloody well kiss me.'

His hand wrapped around my waist, pulling me hard against him as his voice, rough with emotion, breathed close to my ear. 'I thought you'd never ask.'

EPILOGUE

LATE SUMMER, THE FOLLOWING YEAR

Friedrich's refusal to listen to anyone else on the dig, and his tyrannical leadership had not gone down well with his fellow archaeologists, or the sponsors.

Word of his behaviour had also got back to the museum he worked for and, perhaps sensing a long-awaited opportunity, they had 'suggested' that his position there be amended to be less public-facing. Friedrich, who had always enjoyed the sound of his own voice had vehemently disagreed and instead flounced off back to Germany, but his reputation preceded him and, surprised that institutions were not falling over themselves to employ him there either, he had apparently begun writing his memoirs. I could hardly wait.

The dig I led earlier this year went better than I had ever imagined. An educated hunch I'd talked over with Bella had paid off, the proof of which was now with the Egyptian Museum of Antiquities. I'd even been involved first-hand at unearthing it – thanks to Finn's leaflet for the hypnotherapist all those months ago, claustrophobia was no longer a problem. It would, of course, take time to discover who this unknown tomb belonged to as the cartouches had been damaged long ago but patience in this job really was a virtue.

Home life was also vastly improved now that Finn had moved in. He helped me keep things more organised and tidy and I'd also taken Colette up on her offer to help me tackle the garden. Thanks to the free muscle I had on tap, it was back to looking just as beautiful as it had when my grandmother had owned the house. Actually, dare I say, even more beautiful. Spurred on by Colette's idea of a pond, we'd now installed one in our garden too and had giggled at night in the spring when the croak of frogs drifted in through the open window. Every day with Finn made new and precious memories, the shelf in my brain I'd reserved for them was overflowing and I loved it.

And today more wonderful memories were about to be made. Despite the media whipping themselves into a fury over the possibilities of a dramatic summer storm, a graceful dawn developed into the most perfect weather for the wedding. An azure blue sky played host to the odd puffy white splodge of cloud, and the gentlest of breezes rippled the leaves, taking just enough edge off the heat at Colette's parents' summer retreat.

The picturesque cottage is surrounded by a vast, rambling garden in a small village a little way outside Paris. Today the garden is host to a large marquee, shining brilliant white in the sunshine. The poles holding it up are garlanded with fresh flowers from the garden and the inside is lit with as many fairy lights as we could get our hands on. I'm standing behind Colette, waiting for her musical cue, her arm tucked within her dad's. He's already had a blub, bless him, but both of us told him he had to stop because he'd set us off and there wasn't time to fix our make-up.

I took a peek a few minutes ago, just to check that Greg was there. Not that I had any doubt. He's been head over heels for Colette since he laid eyes on her. Finn is, of course, his best man. And my God, he looks gorgeous. The deep grey of the suits Colette (obviously) chose do amazing things for his eyes.

Colette has been the most amazing bride. Not a hint of Bridezilla to be seen although I knew she was, quite naturally, nervous because yesterday she announced we were going shopping. Colette always shops when she's nervous. So yesterday we went shopping. For my wedding dress. In Paris. I know. I couldn't believe it either. Finn is dying to see it but he has to wait. As befits him, he's chief Project Manager of Operation Wedding so I know it will be perfect. He is, of course, aware that if he walks out on this particular project I will end him, and Colette has promised to help me move the body. He's sworn that that will not happen. Ever.

As the music begins, we walk slowly down the aisle, Colette giving little waves here and there as she passes people. And then we're at the front. Her dad gives her a hug and two kisses and then she turns to me, large brown eyes shining with happy tears, and passes me her bouquet, pauses and gives me a hug and a kiss on each cheek too. That night we'd gone out to get plastered I'd felt like everything was over. That all I'd done, worked for, spent my life on, was wasted. And I'd been completely wrong. That night turned out to be just the start, not only for me and Finn but also for Greg and Colette. From me losing what I had thought was the most important thing in my life, we both ended up finding what really mattered.

I step back and Finn catches my eye and smiles that smile – the one he reserves only for me. This was just the beginning.

ACKNOWLEDGEMENTS

As always, thanks to the entire team at Boldwood Books for being such an amazing, supportive and utterly brilliant group of people. I will always be grateful for you choosing me to be one of your authors. #bestpublisherever

Special thanks, of course, goes to my fabulous editor, Sarah Ritherdon, for her support, knowledge, and just being there. Thank you so much, my lovely!

Also thanks to everyone else involved in making this book the best it can be including the wonderful copy editors and proof readers aligned with Boldwood Books. No matter how many times I read through a manuscript, I still manage to miss things so knowing that their eagle eyes will be scanning each page is such a relief.

A big shout out to fantastic human and brilliant writer, Rachel Dove. Thanks for the videos and the laughs, mate.

And, of course, thanks to James, who has always been my biggest cheerleader, believing in me even when I don't myself. Also for being happily on board for research trips. For this book it was a request to drive to Wales in order to visit the Egyptian Museum at Swansea. Thank you. LY LM xx

(Ps: If you're in the area, the museum is a great place to pass some time. The demonstration of mummification is hilarious, and something to behold!)

ABOUT THE AUTHOR

Maxine Morrey is a bestselling romantic comedy author with twelve books to her name including *#NoFilter* and *Things Are Looking Up*. She lives in Dorset.

Sign up to Maxine Morrey's mailing list for news, competitions and updates on future books.

You can contact Maxine here: hello@scribblermaxi.co.uk

Follow Maxine on social media:

facebook.com/MaxineMorreyAuthor
instagram.com/scribbler_maxi
pinterest.com/ScribblerMaxi

ALSO BY MAXINE MORREY

#No Filter

My Year of Saying No

Winter at Wishington Bay

Things Are Looking Up

Living Your Best Life

You Only Live Once

Just Say Yes

You've Got This

Just Do It

LOVE NOTES

LOVE IN EVERY CHAPTER

WHERE ALL YOUR ROMANCE
DREAMS COME TRUE!

THE HOME OF BESTSELLING
ROMANCE AND WOMEN'S
FICTION

WARNING:
MAY CONTAIN SPICE

SIGN UP TO OUR
NEWSLETTER

https://bit.ly/Lovenotesnews

Boldwood

Boldwood Books is an award-winning fiction publishing company seeking out the best stories from around the world.

Find out more at www.boldwoodbooks.com

Join our reader community for brilliant books, competitions and offers!

Follow us
@BoldwoodBooks
@TheBoldBookClub

Sign up to our weekly deals newsletter

https://bit.ly/BoldwoodBNewsletter